W9-BQT-036

The Good
Know Nothing

A Tom Hickey Novel

Ken Kuhlken

Poisoned Pen Press

Copyright © 2014 by Ken Kuhlken

First Edition 2014

10 9 8 7 6 5 4 3 2 1

Library of Congress Catalog Card Number: 2014931729

ISBN: 9781464202865   Hardcover
       9781464202889   Trade Paperback

The Good Know Nothing is a work of fiction. Names, characters, places, and events either are products of the author's imagination or are used fictitiously. The author's use of names of actual persons, places, and events are not intended to change the entirely fictional nature of work.

All rights reserved. No part of this publication may be reproduced, stored in, or introduced into a retrieval system, or transmitted in any form, or by any means (electronic, mechanical, photocopying, recording, or otherwise) without the prior written permission of both the copyright owner and the publisher of this book.

Poisoned Pen Press
6962 E. First Ave., Ste. 103
Scottsdale, AZ 85251
www.poisonedpenpress.com
info@poisonedpenpress.com

Printed in the United States of America

For my earthly treasure:
Darcy, Cody, Zoe, and Nicholas

Acknowledgments

Thanks to all who've offered wisdom, some of which I've learned to apply; to my Grandma Mary Garfield, for giving me the secret of art; to the storytellers from Homer to Hillerman who've helped me glimpse beyond; and to Twist Phelan, for the P.V. story.

Chapter One

The abomination we call World War I cost about nine million lives. Then, before the survivors could dry their tears, an influenza epidemic wasted another twenty million of us.

Next came Prohibition. How the temperance peddlers swindled Congress into enacting such a law at that most ill-advised time, sensible folks found beyond comprehension. They knew full well booze was proven to lighten grief for a few hours.

Even preacher Aimee Semple McPherson, darling of puritans and future employer of Tom Hickey's sister, quoted King Lemuel's proverb, "Let them drink wine and remember their sorrows no more."

Prohibition, a blunder of unfathomable magnitude, launched an era of violence beyond what even wild-west Los Angeles could abide. During the first six months of its reign, seventeen LAPD officers, two percent of the force, got shot down.

The police department, under Chief James Davis, turned its guns on renegades: bootleggers who failed to pay up, Communists, and "Wobblies," agents of the Industrial Workers of the World. Whoever failed to abide the big shots' rules.

Under Chief Davis, cops either played the big shots' game or got the boot. During one shake-up, dozens found themselves dismissed on spurious misconduct charges.

One dismissal would've been Detective Tom Hickey, if not for the intercession of Port Commissioner Kent Parrot, the city's kingpin political fixer.

Chapter Two

Kent Kane Parrot, once a USC lineman, played both quarterback and referee in the big shots' game.

Los Angeles, a famously wide-open town, attracted the ambitious, the ruthless, and the simply mean. Politicos, racketeers, cops, judges, prosecutors, juries—most of them on the take. Parrot knew which to connect to whom, to what end, and for how much.

Crime boss Charlie Crawford called the plays from the sidelines, in concert with oil baron Edward Doheny, land tycoons such as *Times* publisher Harry Chandler, who owned more acreage than any other human being, and William Randolph Hearst.

Hearst was royalty. Detective Leo Weiss, Tom Hickey's oldest pal and mentor, argued that Hearst and his news empire ruled the nation.

Chapter Three

When the police chief ordered Detective Tom Hickey to kill a guy, Tom didn't bother to argue.

Chief James "Two Gun" Davis had only last month publically renewed his familiar promise that the LAPD would hold court on outlaws in the city streets. "I want them brought in dead, not alive," he informed a crowd of newshounds, "and I will reprimand any officer who shows the least mercy to a criminal."

From the Davis perspective, a criminal was anybody who broke the rules. Donny Katoulis, the subject of Tom's assignment, broke more than one. The chief alleged that Al Capone had sent the gunman to hit bookie Buster Sykes. Capone had paid L.A. a visit, assessed the risks and benefits of establishing a subsidiary of his Chicago enterprise, and rewarded Sykes in advance for assistance. The bookie stiffed him.

On a blustery spring Friday around twilight, Donny Katoulis tailed Buster Sykes to a parking lot off Sunset Boulevard.

Sykes was the lover of Mayor Frank Shaw's favorite niece. The mayor was an ambitious fellow, who had spent the months since his inauguration earnestly collaborating with crime boss Charlie Crawford. Their efforts had raised corruption in the city to new depths.

Four .32 caliber slugs eliminated the bookie and cost the mayor a generous associate.

The way Tom figured, Mayor Shaw was out for more than revenge. Cops, crooks, tycoons, publishers, and politicos worked "the system" to such profitable effect, they roused the envy of smart guys out east. So, Tom surmised, the mayor suggested to Davis that Capone ought to get sent a message.

Davis advised Tom that Katoulis would board the Union Pacific Los Angeles Limited for a departure at 6:20 p.m. He assigned Tom to assure the gunman didn't reach Chicago.

Tom imagined Davis called on him because the chief figured whoever got done in, the cop or the gunman, good riddance.

Chapter Four

The Limited was an all-Pullman, all-sleeper, first-class-only operation. Tom boarded, lugging the overnight case Davis had issued him. Inside he'd found the key to Pullman compartment C-14, a photo of the target, a Maxim silencer, and a Browning .32 caliber semi-automatic. Not an LAPD weapon.

As Davis handed over the case, he had said, with the darkest of his variety of smirks, "You're a college boy, Hickey. I'll let you in on some irony. The gun is registered to Benny Katoulis, brother to the Katoulis of your assignment."

Tom went directly to the dining car, which his target would need to pass through en route from boarding to C-14. He perched on a stool at the brass-railed bar, ordered a Dewar's on the rocks, and waited.

The conductor shouted "All aboard." Then Katoulis appeared.

While the gunman ambled with a mild swagger through the dining car, he appeared to notice nothing except a certain leggy redhead whose left hand and earlobes sparkled with diamonds. From his double take, Tom suspected Katoulis would've invited himself to join her, if not for the palooka whose right hand she was holding.

Because Tom had the key to the gunman's compartment, he supposed the chief's preferred method would be for him to wait until the wee hours. As the train approached some jump-off stop in the Nevada desert, he could attach the silencer to the

Browning, silently enter, creep to the bunk-side, and fire the shot or two, further muffled by a handy pillow.

Mission accomplished, he could wipe down and drop the gun someplace even the dimmest Union Pacific dick couldn't miss. Thereby framing the weapon's previous possessor, brother to the deceased and another of Capone's hired guns. Newshounds would delight in such a story of betrayal.

A problem with that strategy was that Tom wasn't wedded to anybody's rules except his own. So when the gunman returned to the dining car and seated himself at a vantage for eyeing the redhead, Tom picked up his Scotch and overnight bag and moved. He joined Katoulis, sitting across the narrow ebony table with its doily and crystal salt and pepper shakers. He made a wry smile and nodded.

He and the gunman stared eye-to-eye. Katoulis lifted and lowered his thick eyebrows as though aping Groucho Marx. His voice was both nasal and gravelly. "Seat's taken."

"Uh huh," Tom said. Under the table, he slipped the Browning out of the carry-on beside him and onto his lap.

He made Katoulis for the sort of handsome Greek he met on the job and at the Wilshire Boulevard barbershop. The sort who sat in the barber chair daily, purchased his wardrobe only from tailors, and kept one comb for his wavy hair and another for his eyebrows. The sort who made the slickest Italians appear rustic.

"We got business?" the gunman asked.

"Buster Sykes."

"You his pal?"

"Never mind the small talk. Care to know why I'm here?"

The gunman shrugged, and didn't show the least tic or wince.

"I'm here to guarantee you don't get to Chicago," Tom said.

Katoulis reached into a breast pocket, brought out a pack of French smokes, and lit one with a lighter that had magically appeared in his other hand. "That's your problem, Jasper."

"Yep," Tom said. "Here's my solution. San Berdoo's coming up. You're going to jump off and make tracks. Find a new town."

"That so?"

"Athens is jake, I hear."

Katoulis drew smoke up his nose. "Say I tell you to go poke your sister."

Tom's trigger finger slid inside the guard. He pulled a deep breath through his nose. "I'll have to kill you."

"You that tough?"

Tom shrugged. "Thing is, you're one guy. I've got thirteen hundred boys in the backfield, everyone of them licensed to kill. So I could drop you right now. Boom. Self-defense. You've got eyes and ears. You know how the system works."

That Katoulis would disappear, Tom held not even a hope. But he did suspect the man might catch a different ride to Chicago and advise Capone that the cops in L.A. belonged to their own mighty formidable mob. Meaning outside interests would be wise to steer clear.

Tom found a table of his own, ordered another Dewar's. An hour later, he tailed Katoulis to a cab stop out front of the San Bernadino depot. Then he bought a ticket home.

Chapter Five

Tom was hardly alone in adapting the system's rules to a version of his own. Leo Weiss, who had coached and served as Tom's consultant since before Tom joined the force, contended that every L.A. cop, lawyer, business owner, and crook modified the system to meet his own standards and justifications.

More than once, Leo had waived his scruples for Tom's sake. No sooner had Tom gotten his uniform, almost eleven years ago, than Leo visited the Hall of Records archives and requested the closed file on the two-decades-past murder of the heir to an outlandish number of oil wells.

The records clerk was Madeline, a bright and gifted redhead of the flapper variety. The whole package, in Leo's assessment. A married fellow like himself who caught a glimpse and whiff of her spent weeks plagued by treacherous daydreams.

Madeline shoved the fat bundle across the counter and handed him a pen and sign-out sheet. In place of signing, he returned the sheet and pen along with a green-tinted picture of Andrew Jackson.

She passed it back. "You and Tom go out for Scotch and tamales. Tell him it's on me."

The voice of a Lorelei, Leo thought. "Now, how about you erase this transaction from your splendid mind, and I forget how you got the dough to treat us?"

Madeline reached out her graceful hand. And for a dozen years, neither of them mentioned the exchange to Tom or anybody.

Chapter Six

As a rule, Tom tried to avoid thinking about rats. Ergo, he spent copious time and energy casting aside thoughts about the police chief.

He and Davis had first tangled more than ten years ago, even before he joined the force. Only Tom's alliance with Kent Kane Parrot had landed him the job as a beat cop and later as detective. Not that Tom had asked for favors. He didn't need to. He and Kent Parrot had both starred in football at USC. The man had sensed in Tom a kindred spirit. Tough and clever. Back then, all through the '20s, nobody crossed Parrot.

Times change. Parrot, pulled for mysterious reasons from his position as the game's fixer, moved up the coast to Santa Barbara not long after Tom dropped the ball on the Donny Katoulis assignment. Why Davis hadn't then dumped Tom was another mystery. No matter, Tom held on to the job and supported Madeline and Elizabeth by gritting his teeth and usually gutting out whatever lousy play Davis called him to run.

Last month, the chief had ordered Tom to Yuma, on the Arizona-California border. The detail amounted to busting the heads of Okies who wanted into the promised land. Tom might've obeyed, or might've quit the force. He hadn't yet decided when the police commission issued a sudden ruling: uniforms only, no detectives on the Yuma detail.

The ruling granted Tom such relief that on his way home he stopped at the market on Oxford Avenue and Wilshire

Boulevard, picked up a fifth of Dewar's, a chocolate cake, and a tub of strawberry ice cream.

The Hickeys celebrated. Madeline, whom Tom had married and delivered from her day job in the Hall of Records archives, joined him for a double on the rocks. With some minutes to spare before her ride to work came honking, she sang "You Ought to Be in Pictures" for Elizabeth, their only child, a five-year-old, emerald-eyed, auburn-haired ringer for her mom.

After a suitable call for her encore, she crooned "Moon Glow" for her husband, using the whole catalog of her effervescent, hourglass-figure charms.

With Madeline gone, Tom played his clarinet while Elizabeth danced around the parlor. She danced with such vigor, when they strolled the half mile to Wilshire Center and back, Tom needed to carry her most of the way.

All was well.

Then came morning, and Bud Gallagher.

Chapter Seven

Bud was Tom's sole remaining connection to Charlie Hickey, the father who had vanished twenty-five years ago. Back then, Charlie and Bud worked as butchers at Alamo Meat, a wholesaler. Used to be, Bud could lift a side of beef. The way he looked now, a hamburger patty might take him down.

Tom hadn't seen him for a month or so. Bud must have lost thirty pounds since the old days. His eyes, once shiny brown or black, depending on the light, had gone as speckled gray as what remained of his hair. He wore a constant grimace and a stoop, no matter if he walked, stood, or sat. A disc in his lower back had worn down to a nub, and the booze that eased the pain was rotting his liver. Last time they met, Bud smelled of whiskey. This time it was something sweeter. Gin or rubbing alcohol.

When Tom let him into the cottage, Bud made for the sofa. "Madeline around?"

"Still asleep, late night."

"Where's she playing?"

"Did her last night at the Bohemia. Next, who knows? She and the boys auditioned for a booking on Catalina."

"The Casino, you say?"

"Yes, sir. It's a long shot, though."

Elizabeth came toddling from the bathroom and latched onto Tom's leg. She peeked around it. "Are you Mister Bud?"

"That I am, baby."

The girl made an anguished face. "You look pretty bad."

"Indeed I do. Say, Tom, we need to talk in private a minute. How about it?"

Tom pried his daughter loose, kissed her hand, and sent her to play with Chewy, or Chuey, however one spelled the name she had given the rag doll her dad had paid a hungry Okie family man top dollar for. He said "If you need a grownup while I'm gone, you wake up Mommy. Promise?"

"Otay." She chuckled. Last Saturday at the Egyptian Theater they had watched a couple of *Our Gang* movies. Buckwheat was her favorite.

Tom followed Bud, who plodded to his Buick, opened the passenger door, and lifted a bulky package off the seat. The package, which he handed to Tom, was long and wide as a theme tablet, about two inches thick, and wrapped in slick butcher paper.

"What's this?"

"Hold on." Bud turned and hobbled up the sidewalk of Hobart Place past two bungalows to a vacant lot Tom had helped neighbors clear and rake. Elizabeth named the place Popeye's Park, for no reason Tom could detect. A tire swing hung from a live oak. Cats plotted strategy while circling a goldfish pond. Bud lowered himself onto the only bench. Tom sat beside him.

After Bud caught some breath and composure, he said, "I've got a confession."

"You make me for a priest?"

"This one ain't like that. See, there's things I could've told you about your old man. Only, you know how it goes, the time never felt quite right."

"I get you." Tom stood. His fingers, on their own volition, made hard fists. Charlie Hickey and his disappearance formed the puzzle and the baggage of Tom's life. From the deepest recesses of what churchgoers like his sister, Florence, called his soul, he believed that discovering the truth about Charlie would somehow set him, and Florence, free.

A thousand times, Tom had asked himself what could make a good man run off and leave his two kids with a savage woman.

"Sit down," Bud said.

"Not on your life."

Chapter Eight

"Might be I told you some of it before." Bud shot a glance at Tom's face then turned, leaned a bit forward and peered down the street as though hoping for reinforcements. "You want the whole story?"

"Right from the start."

"Well then, here goes."

He turned back toward Tom but kept his head slumped down. "Suppose you've got a crazy woman that bore you two kids, and now she's making like Lady Macbeth, threatening to sling them both in the tar pits with the mastodons and all. You get me?"

"Sure I do. Suppose you're Charlie, married to Milly." Tom's brain flashed a picture from his childhood. His mother with her teeth bared, hands clawed, screaming curses at baby Florence. He slapped a hand to his temple. The picture only dimmed.

"Okay then," Bud said, "suppose you are Charlie, married to Milly. What do you do?"

"How about get her locked up?"

"Charlie had been a lawyer, he'd of done so. He was damn sure smart enough to be whatever he chose, had the money been there to front him." Bud's voice came higher, closer to shrill, and when he looked up, a spark like new life appeared. "Maybe you didn't see Charlie's smarts right off the bat, but get him telling a story, you might as well be listening to Mister Dickens." Bud's hand let go of his knee and landed on the package at his side.

"Like I said, Charlie's saddled with this loco woman and her two swell kids. What's he going to do?"

Tom caught himself biting his upper lip. "Beats me. What *did* he do. Besides run off."

"Well, first, before he had any notion of running off on his own, he gave Milly an ultimatum. Shape up, quit the beatings and the threats, or else she'll come home and find them gone. Him *and* the kids. Now, you might guess what that ultimatum did to her. Only you'd be wrong. She didn't say a word. Milly acted like he'd shocked some sense into her.

"Only not many weeks passed before—" Bud choked on a breath. He shut his eyes and wiped a hand over his face. "A young fella gets stabbed in the back not six or eight blocks from your place. You recall?"

Tom gave his head a quick shake that felt more like a tremor. "I didn't read the news when I was five."

"Sure. Well, Terence Poole was the fella's name. Son of Talbot Poole. Big oil."

"Okay," Tom said. "Go on."

"Probably don't remember when the police came after your old man."

Though Tom could've painted an image of Charlie Hickey down to the part near the center of his dust-brown hair, blue eyes that readily twinkled, rolled up shirtsleeves and squarish, deep cleft chin, he only recalled snippets of scenes from before Charlie vanished. Nothing about the police. He shook his head.

"The police was Milly's doing," Bud said. "She meant to pin that murder on Charlie. Her being a seamstress to those movie idols, you know how it works when you've got friends in high places, you can make things happen."

Bud allowed a long pause, no doubt to assess how Tom would react to such a hideous claim. But Tom gave no sign except his jaw had locked.

"The way Charlie figured," Bud said, "what with Milly's connections and his own damned wife turning him in, he'd be good as hanged if he stuck around.

"Now, I didn't know the whole story back then. See, Charlie only wrote me now and then, asking for news about you and Florence."

Tom knelt in front of the man, grabbed hold of both the bench to the right of Bud's legs and the package to the left. He leaned in close and demanded, "He wrote you, and you didn't tell me?"

The old Bud didn't take guff from anybody, no matter what for. Even last year, he might have risen and dared Tom to sock him, so he wouldn't need to throw the first punch. This Bud leaned back on the bench. "You want to finish me off, be my guest. Just, in the ruckus that follows, don't forget to take this." He patted the package.

Tom backed away and dropped into a catcher's squat.

"You were a kid," Bud said. "Think about how it feels now, and you're what, thirty? Back then, you didn't need to know. And for God's sake it's sure Florence didn't need to."

Nothing Bud said could have softened Tom's anger like the notion of protecting the sister he had mostly raised on his own. "That so? Then why tell me now?"

With a glance at the package, Bud said, "Tear it open."

Chapter Nine

Tom's hand quivered as he peeled butcher paper away from the top of the package. Then he stood staring at dense black-ink handwriting on paper like newsprint, going brownish and brittle. He turned to Bud. "What is it?"

"Tommy, your old man never meant to forsake you kids. What he did was go looking for a home. Someplace Milly wasn't, and wasn't liable to find."

"Says who?"

"The letters I got, long before this came." He laid a big, age-blighted hand on the package. "Soon as he found a place, got himself a livelihood, he meant to come steal you away."

"And if, in the meantime, Milly bumped us off?"

"I had my eye on you two. Charlie's first letter warned me I had better. Said if I judged Milly was about to do you or Florence real harm, I had damn well better snatch you myself. I would of done just that, only hell, you grew so big and tough so fast, I judged you could stand on your own and protect your sister. That's exactly what I wrote him."

"Where is he?"

"Damned if I know. Used to be here and there. Down south, Mexico. Out at sea. I wrote him care of general delivery, New Orleans, but looks to me like he got all around the world."

Tom stood and paced a few steps, confounded by a throbbing that commenced above his eyes and petered out around his knees.

Without intending to sit, he found himself on the bench. He nodded toward the package between them. "Charlie send this?"

He sat up taller and his voice rose, as if for a proud announcement. "Yes, sir, he did. All four hundred fourteen sheets, both sides, in his own handwriting. "

"When?"

"November nineteen and twenty-three. A day or two later, I hadn't yet figured what I should do with it, I brought the wife to a Trojan game. Watched you charging like *el toro* through the Oregon line, and said to myself, 'Leave it lie, Bud. The kid's on his way to glory, doesn't need to get blindsided. Anyway, Charlie wants you to give Tom his story, he'll say so.' Thing is, he never gave a word of instructions."

Bud again became a slumping penitent. "Another something held me back. See, Charlie made a trip through hell and came out the other side with a head full of wild ideas, the kind can torment a young fella with principles and high spirits. A fella like you Tom. Ideas that, in times like ours, can send a good man straight down to the grave."

The two locked eyes, and Bud said, "Communist, anarchist, Wobbly ideas. Maybe I wouldn't give it to you now except, well, here's why.

"As you know, I do a lot of reading. Down at the library, a couple old gals are sweet on me, and they lead me to the sort of books I like best, which is stories about real folks having big adventures, the kind that'll make your blood boil.

"Day before yesterday, this old gal is so keen on a book she gives me, I find a bench on the patio and begin to read then and there." He looked up at Tom, rolled his dull, cloudy eyes, and shook his head. "I don't get all the way through page one before I stop to think 'What the blazes?'

"The young fellow telling the story, says he's from Ohio, signs on a merchant ship bound for Europe. Over there, on account of woman trouble, don't you know, he loses all his papers. Well, anymore, since the war and all, a guy can't hardly scratch his nose without having papers, and he sure can't sign on a ship or cross any of the world's countless borders without papers, save on the sly. What this storyteller, name of Gerard Gales in the book, what he does is, gets himself deported and kicked from jail to jail, Belgium to Germany, France to Spain. At last, all he can figure to do is ship out on a vessel no man with papers, or with a dash of concern for his life, would give a thought to boarding. The tub is what they call a death ship, good for nothing but to be scuttled for the insurance money."

Tom was only half listening while most of his mind played defense, ripping out against bitter thoughts toward his father.

Bud gave a look of distemper over Tom's inattention. "Title's *The Death Ship*. The book writer calls himself B. Traven. No front name. Just the letter B.

"Thing is, Tommy, hardly a line in that book you won't find in this one." He patted the wrapped stack of paper between them.

Chapter Ten

On the way home, carrying the package, Tom banged his shin into a stack of bricks and tumbled off the sidewalk. He also tripped in a rut and got his ankle wrapped in an ice plant runner.

While untangling himself, he noticed a silver Plymouth parked just around the corner on Second Street, in the same spot he had seen it day before yesterday. And the same fellow, a young man either short or slouching, sat behind the wheel. Before, he had imagined the fellow was waiting for Jack Beauregard, a neighbor several doors father down Second, to drive off so he could pay a call on Priscilla, Jack's winsome daughter. This time, Tom began to wonder, and might've gone to the Plymouth for a talk, except his mind was on other business.

He found Elizabeth playing teacher, drilling Chewy the rag doll on his ABCs. Madeline was still asleep and might be for hours. She hadn't come in until after four. She and Paul the bandleader often lingered after hours, working out arrangements. Singing with the Paul Perkins swing orchestra was more than a job. Tom preferred not to imagine what would befall them if Madeline were called to choose between family and career.

He phoned his sister, caught her on the way out the door to the nine a.m. service at Sister McPherson's Angelus Temple, and got her okay for him and Elizabeth to stop by around noon.

After some minutes on the floor beside Chewy, during which Elizabeth complained that the rag doll just wouldn't talk with a grownup around, Tom helped his girl into a gingham dress and patent-leather shoes.

He jotted a note. "Back about 3." Which was as complicated a statement as he could express. If Madeline had awakened and quizzed him, he likely couldn't have told her the news except in single words like, "Bud," "my dad," "a book," "Florence's."

Still he remembered to bring a sack of stale bread for the ducks. From the Hobart Place court where, to Madeline's displeasure, she and Tom had lived the eight years since their marriage, he drove the few shady blocks past bungalows and Craftsman cottages to Wilshire Boulevard, the speedway from downtown to the Pacific. He turned west and soon found a parking spot in front of Miracle Mile Bookshop. Though Elizabeth was only a week out of kindergarten, she already loved books like *The Velveteen Rabbit* and *Now We Are Six*. She tried to steer her daddy to the kids' corner, but today Tom resisted. To keep her from protesting, he claimed the ducks in Echo Park needed breadcrumbs in a hurry.

A college girl with bottle-thick glasses and a sashay walk led them straight to the only copy of *The Death Ship*. She lowered the specs on her nose and raised her pinstriped eyebrows. "Been selling like gangbusters. Swell story, if you like grim and you don't hold a beef against the Wobblies."

"I'm a cop," Tom said. "Grim's a way of life."

"What do you think of Wobblies?"

"Them, I can take or leave."

She passed him the book then raised her hands and cocked her head and hips, as though daring him to pat her down. "You caught me red-handed, officer."

"Doing what?"

"Not a thing, but what I was thinking could sure land a girl in hot water."

Having not yet recovered from the shock of Bud's news, Tom couldn't feign enough interest in the girl to avoid wounding her feelings.

Sunday traffic was slow, on account of cruising sightseers on Wilshire Boulevard and a picket line outside City Hall. Even the typists and clerks had gotten bit by the union fervor. Gals who suffered their steno jobs while waiting to be discovered by a film scout or producer were posing in willowy skirts or bare-legged playsuits and waving to passing motorists as if they topped a float in the Rose Parade.

Tom hoped they didn't find themselves canned, replaced by scabs, so he wouldn't have to meet some of them while working vice.

Beyond downtown, on Glendale Boulevard, the flock was already converging upon Angelus Temple, a place Tom admired more for its architecture, which recalled Roman coliseums, than for its message.

Echo Park bordered the temple. On this hot and breezy August day, scores of the faithful released after the nine a.m. service picnicked or lounged in the shade of oaks and elms or rowed on the park's centerpiece lake. The scene was worthy of a bachelor's dream. Three or four women to each man. Sister Aimee Semple McPherson's bold and vibrant style lured females by the thousands, even a few almost as young, lovely, vivacious, and clever as Florence.

Tom's little sister had graduated from Hollywood High and earned a teaching certificate from UCLA. She lasted in that racket three years, longer than Tom had predicted. Then a girlfriend, probably a rival, snitched to the principal about the cigarette or two Florence puffed each night and about her occasional outings to nightclubs. With her teaching career up in smoke, and Mr. Right apparently in the wind, she turned for advice to Sister Aimee, a sometime friend of the family, since their mother had once been a devotee and the preacher's favorite seamstress. That move landed Florence a position as a housekeeper, cook, companion, and chaperone to the girls residing in the dormitory of Angelus Temple Bible School.

Florence lived alone in the studio side of a duplex on Portia Street, a short and shady walk from the temple, the Bible school, and Echo Park. She grew potted strawberries in her tiny concrete backyard. This time of year they were most plentiful, and big as apples. Elizabeth ran and picked a handful even before rushing to the aunt she favored over everybody.

As a wild high school and college girl and as a grammar school teacher, Florence had aged like humans generally do. But in her new churchgoing life, she had discovered a fountain of youth. At twenty-six, she looked eighteen again. Today she wore a sleeveless dress in a flower print on a background of yellow that complemented her honey-blond curls. Mr. Rockwell should paint her, Tom thought, and title the painting *The Spirit of Springtime*.

Her smile showed her dimples, a family trait from Charlie's side. She kissed Tom's chin. By the time she turned and opened her arms to Elizabeth, the girl's puffy cheeks were inflated with strawberries. She leaped into Florence's arms.

"Baby," Florence said. "How about you tell me what's got your daddy looking so serious."

Elizabeth crooked around and studied Tom's expression. "Bud Gallibur."

"Hmmm. Used to be, Bud was a joker. What's up, Tommy?"

He was hardly ready to give Florence the news Bud had dropped on him. Almost ten years back, when they learned just how demonic their mother was, they took a mutual vow to dismiss the past and to consider their parentage an excuse for nothing.

Since then, Florence had gone from stormy to sensible. For all Tom knew, Bud's story might shanghai and carry her back to treacherous places.

Besides, so far, Tom hadn't even begun to accept the truth of Bud's story. He had no record or memory of Charlie's handwriting, or of Bud's. That Gallagher had gone senile and conjured a wild tale and copied *The Death Ship* word-for-word onto aged paper was of course possible, though unlikely. But no less unlikely was that Charlie Hickey, a butcher of little education, had gone seafaring and written a story the bookstore clerk, a USC literature major, called a modern classic.

Supposing he came to believe Bud's story, he couldn't yet imagine into what kind of darkness the news would send him. Or what on earth he, or he and Florence, ought to do about it.

So he reached for his billfold, peeled off a five-dollar bill, and handed it to his sister. "You girls have some fun. Give me a few hours."

On his way to the door, he patted Elizabeth's wavy hair and stroked her soft and bulging cheek.

Chapter Eleven

Tom walked past the lake to the far end of Echo Park and used the trunk of an oak for a backrest. He set the manuscript on the grass to his right, the book on his lap. He read back-and-forth between the two, at first line-by-line, then sentence-by-sentence. Though the book left out some words and added some, he hadn't finished a page before he felt convinced the one had become the other.

The book used chapters. The manuscript didn't. Tom read both to the end of the book's chapter one. Then he laid his hat on the manuscript. It was hard enough attending to an account of what might be the subsequent life of the father who deserted them. Reading what could be his dad's own hand felt brutal.

Even while he read the book on its own, without glancing at the manuscript, Tom heard his father's voice. Though he couldn't recall any phrases Charlie used, or many of his common words, he recognized the whimsy and the feeling that Charlie preferred nobody take him quite seriously.

Over the years of trying to make sense of his father's disappearance, Tom had come to suspect Charlie might've used the joker's attitude as an antidote for the pestilence of living with Milly. She was so stern, humorless, and cross, a child couldn't miss the implication that making one wrong move could turn her into a dragon that would burn him to ashes.

The book writer, like the father Tom imagined and barely remembered, was a fellow of light heart and goodwill. And Tom didn't need many pages before he agreed with Bud that Charlie Hickey was mighty smart if he had written these pages.

An hour or so into the book, he read, "An unanswered question flutters around you for the rest of your life. It does not let you sleep, it does not let you think. You feel that the equilibrium of the universe is at stake if you leave the question pending. A question without an answer is something so incomplete that you simply cannot bear it."

The universal questions, what created all this and to what purpose, some folks, like Tom, managed to hold in abeyance. But two uncommon questions had haunted him these past twenty-five years.

Suppose Bud had answered the one: Why did Charlie leave them?

The other, why he didn't return, still demanded an answer.

Chapter Twelve

Tom no longer harbored a doubt that Charlie Hickey wrote *The Death Ship*.

Still, had Elizabeth's presence given him an excuse for postponing any talk about the subject until the tempest in his mind calmed, he would have waited. But he found his little girl curled up on the love seat, out cold.

"How'd you get her down?" he asked his sister.

"Conked her with a mallet."

Tom nodded and sat beside Elizabeth, where her legs would land when she decided to stretch out.

Florence peered at the book atop the stack of paper on her brother's lap. "You were going to tell me about Bud."

"Was I?"

"You had better, or else."

"Or else what?"

"Now brother, haven't you learned a girl doesn't reveal her methods until she has to?"

He moved the book to his side, lifted the manuscript and held it out for her. "From Bud. Could be the Charlie Hickey story. By Charlie Hickey."

Florence rose from the wicker chair and stood still, only enlarging her round sapphire eyes. She didn't reach for the package. After a minute, she back-stepped and sank into the chair. "Don't make me wait, Tommy. Does it end with him coming home?"

He set down the manuscript, picked up the book and delivered it to her. "Your copy."

She glanced at the cover. "No, no games, Tommy. Just tell me, first of all, is Daddy alive?"

"I'm sure going to find out."

"And then."

"Bring him home." He nodded, turning the assurance into a promise.

Then he returned to the love seat, lifted Elizabeth's outstretched legs and laid them across his own. With the manuscript perched on his knees, he assured her that the manuscript and book were the identical story, in practically the same words. And he recounted what Bud had told him. About the murder in their neighborhood and their mother attempting to pin it on Charlie.

With that revelation, Florence's eyes pinched shut. Glistening specks appeared on her eyelashes.

He told her about their father's promise to find them a home, get settled, then come steal them away from Milly. He laid a hand on the manuscript. "This was the last Bud heard from Charlie, about a dozen years back."

"Christ," Florence mumbled, and because she believed in the virgin birth, resurrection, and the rest, he supposed she meant the expression as a prayer. She buried her face in her pretty white hands. A few little sobs came out of her. When she moved her hands, her cheeks were damp and sparkly. "Where'd it come from?"

"New Orleans," he said just as Elizabeth awoke with groan.

Right away, the little girl sat up and rubbed her eyes. "I dreamed about a big duck."

"Donald?" Tom asked.

"No, silly. A real live duck that quacks but doesn't talk." While Elizabeth stood and ran the few steps to her aunt and bounded onto her lap, Tom went to the wall phone and dialed his home number.

Madeline sounded groggy. He asked if she would like him to stop at the meat market on the way home. "Sure," she said. "I'll do the potatoes. Tom, I've got to rehearse tonight."

He might've objected or at least experienced disappointment, as Sunday was the orchestra's only night off. Instead, he felt a surge of relief. The longer he could postpone telling Madeline about his impending search for Charlie Hickey, the better.

Chapter Thirteen

Tom killed time at the meat market, listening to the butcher gripe. About moochers, good customers losing their jobs and switching from meat to beans, and crooked competitors selling bull meat as ground round.

When Elizabeth gave up hanging on Tom's leg and began tugging on it, he selected a small rump roast.

At home, he busied himself with the roast and volunteered to take over Madeline's tasks of steaming potatoes and carrots. He set the table with plates, napkins, salt and pepper, and a dish of crushed horseradish, poured himself a tumbler of Dewar's, dropped in a single ice cube, and considered going for another bottle. Just in case.

Madeline used the time to play with Elizabeth and Chewy. Now and then she glanced over at Tom with the look that often caused him to spill thoughts he didn't mean to let out. Not only was Tom, even after nine years, a sucker for her beauty, especially the ivory skin that dipped, rose and curved in all the right directions. He also believed she could read his mind, which made every attempt at deceit futile.

Over dinner, she asked, "Florence okay?"

Madeline never seemed to tire of revisiting the puzzle of Florence the vamp becoming Florence the church mouse. Though Tom's sister had played the innocent for two years now, Madeline hadn't given up expecting her to backslide.

"She's swell," Tom said. He was carving the last of his meat when Elizabeth knocked her plate off the table. Her cheeks sucked inward and her eyes brimmed silvery. Tom scooped her up, put her on his lap, and fed her the rest of his meal. And so evaded further questions.

The clock chimed seven and Madeline went to dress and finish her hair and makeup. She came out in a skin-tight red velvet number with bare shoulders. Tom said, "One look at you, Miss America turns green."

As utterly as Tom was a sucker for Madeline's wiles, she was a sucker for praise. They made a complementary pair, he thought, and wondered what kind of hell losing her might put him through. The notion of losing Elizabeth, he refused to entertain.

On her way out, Madeline gave him a look that translated, "You sure owe me some answers as soon as I get home."

Tom couldn't even fool his five-year-old. While they played Chinese checkers, she stared at him and wrinkled her nose. At last she wagged her head and recited a common query of her mother's. "Are you thinking about how to catch the bad guys, Daddy?"

"You found me out, Miss Sherlock."

The girl giggled, puffed her chest, and lifted her chin to signify "mighty proud."

Tom read her to sleep with the antics of Peter Rabbit. After he closed the book, he stayed a minute listening to her tender breaths. He kissed her forehead and tucked her in. Then he rushed out of her room before the sight of her pristine loveliness led to fears about Madeline stealing her away, which she damn well might. Married or not, Madeline's nature was nearly as wild and free as Florence's before her conversion. No telling what would come over Madeline if her husband gave up what little security his job offered to run off chasing Charlie Hickey, or Charlie's ghost.

He phoned Leo Weiss, whom he'd known and admired forever, as long as he'd known Bud Gallagher. Not long after Charlie disappeared, Leo had come to the aid of the Hickey kids. When Tom, at sixteen, snatched his sister and fled from their mother to start a life on their own, they would have gotten pinched and sent back to Milly, if not for Leo. He advised and warned her of consequences, some legal and others outside the law.

Both before and since Tom joined the LAPD, Leo was the only cop he trusted without reservation.

Tonight Leo answered the phone with a yawn.

"You sitting down?" Tom asked.

"What else, at this hour?"

Refilling your tumbler, Tom thought. "Can I impose upon you?"

"Have at it."

In Tom's frame of mind, talking was an arduous chore. Still he set out, with plentiful stops to compose himself, the story Bud had fed him.

After part one, why Charlie disappeared, Leo cut in. "Old Gallagher, you told me he reads day and night?"

"That he does."

"Could be he's popped his cork, too many dime novels."

"Sure. Nevertheless, think back to nineteen-ten. One Terence Poole shot down on Alexandria Boulevard. I suppose you were walking a beat in those days."

"Boyle Heights."

"Murder of the year," Tom said. "Terence Poole, son of Talbot Poole, the oil tycoon."

"Rings no bell," Leo said in the hesitant then off-handed manner of a bad liar.

Tom moved the receiver away from his ear and glowered at it, and wondered if he had misheard. "You say what?"

"I don't recall the incident."

Unless a tumor or a bullet had invaded Leo's brain, he couldn't have forgotten an unsolved celebrity murder. Especially since newshounds resurrected the Terence Poole case only a few years ago when Hugh Plunkett knocked off his pal Ned Doheny, son of L.A.'s first, richest, and likely most crooked oilman.

"Set me straight here," Tom said. "Why is it you and Bud, all these years, think it's fair game to hold to hold back what I ought to know?"

A prolonged exhale preceded, "Hear this, Tom. Anything I held back, if I did, I did for a damned sure good reason which you've got no business questioning. Now you want to go on with the tall tales, or are we done?"

Tom let the receiver hang from its cord. He reached for his pipe and tobacco, filled, tamped, and puffed, hoping the smoke could medicate away the darkest edge of his anger. When he picked the receiver up, he asked, "You still there?"

"I am."

"The thing is, tall tales don't usually come with solid evidence." After an account of the revelations Bud delivered, Tom said, "I read a good chunk of the manuscript and half the book. I heard Charlie's voice jump right off the pages."

"You remember Charlie's voice, do you?"

"He was a kidder. And he called everybody *sir*. Even little me. Yes sir. No sir. It was Charlie's trademark."

"Give me a minute," Leo said.

He was gone long enough to water the tulips and refill his favorite Coconut Grove cut glass tumbler. Then he picked up and demanded, "Say Charlie wrote the book. Now what?"

"You tell me."

"Why should I?"

"Maybe this time I'll take your advice."

"Okay, then. Hire a shamus."

"Let me calculate," Tom said. "At thirty bucks a day plus expenses, we could afford about six hours."

"Borrow."

"From who?"

"Me, if I'm all you've got. Take on the job yourself, you're nuts. Granted, there are occupations more princely than wrangling lowlifes for the LAPD, but you'd pay hell trying to find one these days. Maybe you didn't hear about the chief revising upward, once again, his priority of ridding the department of Tom Hickey, when the Commission wouldn't let him send you to Yuma to knock around the Okies?"

"Sure, I heard."

"Beats me how you rigged the Commission. You suppose Parrot still calls the shots, all the way from Santa Barbara?"

"Could be."

"All the same, miss a day of work for a reason less critical than, say, a bullet in the brain, he pulls your badge. And if you go snooping, on your own, into a case from twenty years back, he could make it stick."

"Twenty-six years," Tom said.

"That makes a whopping difference?"

"Makes it coincide with the Poole murder. Leo, a job's a job. This is family."

"You want to see what becomes of a family without a job, look around. All over town. Bums and hobos I can largely ignore. Kids on the beg, they get my attention. The thieving, trash-picking, sleeping in alleys around town, all that doesn't move you, take a Sunday drive out to Yuma. Talk to the wives, ask what they think about men who can't make a living. Still not convinced, ask their bony kids. When I'm telling you to hire a shamus, I'm thinking about your girls."

Most insults Tom could shrug off, but one coming from Leo stung deep. "My girls, is it? Hey, I'm thinking about Florence, who wants her daddy back. Elizabeth deserves a grandpa, don't you suppose?"

"Phooey," Leo said. "Stand up and take the blame. Florence can live with a mystery. I'd bet the same goes for Elizabeth. You're the one that's got to know the truth about every blessed thing."

Chapter Fourteen

Florence often enjoyed a late walk, just before bedtime. As long as she avoided the park, where boys and girls gathered after dark to get boozed up, chase each other, shout and laugh like banshees, the neighborhood was charming and quiet.

The route she preferred was about a mile, up Logan Street, across Sunset Boulevard and Montana Street, to Grafton and around the block, then back toward home on Lemoyne, which took her past the Bible school and dormitory.

Tonight she had gone an additional half mile into Elysian Heights, reliving scenes from *The Death Ship* and questioning if they could truly be about her father.

On her way home, from a block away, she saw a familiar Plymouth parked across the street from the dormitory. The first two times she had noticed the car were in daylight, while leaving work. Once it appeared unoccupied. The second time, a little man sat behind the wheel. A brown fedora pulled low kept her from getting the view of his face she would've preferred, because tomorrow she would ask the Bible school girls if anyone knew him. She imagined he could be looking out for a girl he was sweet on, one of the several who had fled from a checkered life to seek God with Sister Aimee.

Tonight she crossed the street and softened her steps as she approached the car, which was parked midway between two street lamps but close enough so a peek through the window revealed a small fellow dressed all in brown. He was sprawled across the front seat, apparently sleeping.

She considered hustling home to phone the police, but though her brother was a cop, she considered the LAPD a gang more inclined to brute force than to mercy. For all she knew, they might roust the little man and beat him silly, though he could be innocent of anything but losing his job.

Half the people in L.A. couldn't afford rent. Sure, most of them couldn't afford cars either, but the Plymouth might be all that remained of the little man's assets and dignity. This fellow could be as deserving of mercy as Charlie Hickey, aka Gerard Gales, hero of *The Death Ship*.

Chapter Fifteen

Tom sat in the dark and devoted a few minutes to weighing and countering Leo's arguments. Then he turned on his bedside lamp and lay with the manuscript at his side, wishing he would've thought to locate and buy or borrow another copy of *The Death Ship*. The effort of reading Charlie's own handwriting wrenched his heart and sapped his spirit. Still, he read a couple dozen pages, all the while switching between anger, hope, and acute sadness, until he chose to try for escape in sleep.

With the manuscript set aside and lights off, he thought of Leo's warning and recalled the bleak and puzzled faces of boys and girls in bread lines and on the corners with their hands out or caps shilled with a few pennies on the pavement beside them. And he wondered how long before the Paul Perkins Swing Orchestra would book its last gig. Nine out of ten dance bands, including Ernestine's Boys, the orchestra he used to lead, had given up over these past few sorry years. Or, how long before Perkins opted for a new kid singer. Madeline would smack into the thirty-year mark before summer's end.

When she came in, he was still awake. He listened to the rustling as she peeled off her outfit and hung it. Once she was settled and warm beside him, sleep came. But not for long. He was up at dawn and playing jacks with Elizabeth. Then he fixed hotcakes with strawberries his sister had provided.

Just after seven, the phone rang.

Florence sounded giddy as a schoolgirl meeting Errol Flynn. "Tommy, what you flatfoots need is a Tracy like me. I found our daddy. Well, sort of."

Tom hadn't felt such a jolt since a Stanford football helmet rammed his belly. "How so?"

"Okay, I called this Al Knopf. The publisher, you know. I guess those New Yorkers are no early birds. Nobody picked up until after nine-thirty, their time. Then, after I convinced the switchboard dame I was not some crazy scribbler calling to pester anybody, she gave me over to an editor by the name of Chet.

"A sweet chap, this Chet, except he didn't want to spill the beans on our B. Traven, who, by the way, has a whole routine worked out to explain why the nom de plume and all. His line is that the author doesn't matter, the story ought to get read without any such distraction as knowing about the guy who made it up. Sounds like the humbug a fellow might float if he's living in fear of a dragon-lady. But now that Milly's long gone, we just tell our daddy the coast is clear, and he'll come running. Won't he?"

"Could be," Tom said, though his mind and gut both contended that life was never so simple.

"Okay, I got a little ways off the track. Ol' Chet, remember, he didn't want to spill the beans. So I wheedled a bit, then I got snippy, which is a talent of mine, you'll remember, and finally I yelled at the poor guy. He held his ground. Got to hand it to him. Nice and all, but he just wouldn't even start to break till I fell to blubbering and told him my long-lost daddy wrote the story. Sure, he didn't believe a word, thought I was crazy, till I told him about the manuscript, which I assured him I've got. And which, so I say, my attorney is anxious to read.

"Now he asks me to hold. Begs, actually. Probably ran to consult with big shot Al Knopf himself.

"He comes back armed with the hooey that Mister B. picks up letters at a box in Mexico City. No telephone. They send him wires care of Western Union. Let's send him a wire, Tommy."

Tom knew his brain's best function wasn't making snap decisions. Choosing the right moves required consideration, especially when life called for strange and uncharted plays. "Let me think on it."

"What's to think?"

"Well, suppose Traven isn't Charlie?"

"Tommy, do you make our daddy for a red of some kind, like Gerard Gales in the book?"

"Whoa," Tom said. "Back to supposing this Traven isn't Charlie. If he isn't, he's a book thief. At least."

"You mean he might've killed our daddy, and now that he knows we're onto him, he might skip out?"

"Or worse."

"Sure, he might even try to knock us off. So I shouldn't have called his publisher, or if I did, I shouldn't have given Chet the whole story. Tommy, maybe I'm no Tracy after all."

"You're a better detective than most, Sis. And even the best slip up. Still, next time you've got a plan, how about you run it by me?"

"Then we're a team? Hickey and Hickey?"

"It's got a ring, all right."

"Okay, partner. Well, you better be thinking full steam ahead and get back to me with an assignment. On the double. Say, how about we trade, the book for the manuscript?"

"Sure, I'll swing by." He hung the phone receiver into its cradle, caught a deep breath to fuel his willpower, hoisted Elizabeth onto his shoulders, and ducked the both of them into the bedroom.

Madeline tossed and groaned as if in a vexing dream. He sat on the edge of the bed and moved the little girl to his lap. She leaned over and tickled her mom in the ribs, then hid behind Tom and giggled.

Madeline eased open her still darkened eyelids, rolled her head and stretched her long white neck. A smile parted her lips. Tom smiled back, thankful this appeared to be one of his wife's cheery days. She peeked around Tom's side. "Hey, big guy, what are you doing with a pretty girl on your lap?"

"Mommy, it's me," Elizabeth said.

Tom lifted and dumped her sideways into Madeline's out-stretched arms. As his girls smooched and snuggled, he said, "I've got some news."

"So do I."

Because Tom felt certain his news would deflate her high spirits or more likely kill them outright, he gladly deferred to Madeline.

She asked, "How would you two like to go swimming every day, in the ocean?"

Elizabeth threw her arms high. "Hooray. Hooray."

"You could take up golf, Tom. They've got a nifty little course, or so the boys tell me."

"Who's got a golf course?"

"Mister Wrigley, don't you know."

"Catalina?"

"Yes indeed. Paul got the word."

If Tom hadn't already been sitting on the bed, now he would have flopped into a chair. The word Paul Perkins got could be the one every artist awaits. The big break. Several evenings a week, a broadcast of the Catalina Casino Ballroom orchestra beamed out of radios coast to coast.

"In a month you'll be on top," Tom said. "Making records and all. Maybe you'll be the one brings back the age of the gal vocalist."

"Not so fast, Bub. We're not in the chips just yet. Kay Kaiser has the four broadcast nights booked. We play the downtime, Monday, Tuesday, Wednesday." She landed a flurry of kisses on Elizabeth's soft and beguiling cheek. "Guess where we get to live all summer, Toots?"

"On a beach?" Elizabeth peeped.

"Well, on an island." Her mother made a lopsided grin. "And where on this island are we going to stay?"

"In a tent?"

Madeline laughed so gaily, even Tom's dread concerns couldn't keep him from joining in.

"In a swanky hotel," Madeline proclaimed. "For free."

The girl sang, "Yippee."

Madeline rolled onto her side and sat straight up. "What's your news, Tom?"

"I'm cooking breakfast," he said.

Chapter Sixteen

After breakfast, Elizabeth wandered off toward the parlor. Tom cleared the dishes. Madeline remained seated at the dining nook table. He felt her watching, awaiting either his announcement or his qualms about her plans.

"So," he said, "my job's on the mainland. You're on the island, with Elizabeth, you say?"

Her eyes narrowed to slits. "Sure. Where else would we put her?"

"With Florence, maybe. She's got a troop of Bible school girls to help, and they'll sure fall for Elizabeth. Days off, Florence brings her to Catalina. My days off, I bring her. Your days off, you come home."

"All that back and forth, I don't know."

"Be good for her," Tom said. "She'll get so many boat rides, before you know it, she'll be talking like Popeye."

Tom supposed his wife's frown was on account of delight getting tempered by the mundane details of reality. She said, "How about you start us off with the paid vacation you're supposed to get? What's it been, three years now since you took a day?"

"Close." His vacation, he couldn't honestly address without referencing the Charlie Hickey news. But Madeline was about to go off largely on her own. She didn't expect and likely wouldn't allow Tom to stand in her way. In fairness, she couldn't object to Tom's plans taking a sharp turn. Or so he allowed himself to hope.

"Let's go into the parlor," he said. "Get comfortable."

He found Elizabeth on the parlor floor teaching Chewy to sit up straight. Tom sat in the chair across from the sofa, which Madeline preferred and which he usually avoided as it reminded him of Milly. His mother had re-stuffed and upholstered the relic in a daisy pattern. The sofa, a rosewood desk Florence treasured, and a couple lamps, were the only remains of Milly's home that hadn't gone to the Salvation Army or the landfill.

When Madeline joined them, she went to the sofa, sat with her chin propped on her hands, elbows on her knees, and stared at Tom. "Your turn. Let's hear your big news."

He nodded, feeling as apprehensive as if he were about to announce that he had made a sudden blind leap of faith and volunteered himself and family as missionaries to Tasmania.

He gave the capsule versions of his visit with Bud, the plot of *The Death Ship*, part one, and Florence's phone call to the publisher. All the while, he watched for a sign that Madeline might share at least a morsel of his excitement.

Instead, her eyes gradually rounded while her posture and limbs stiffened into a pose fit for somebody held at gunpoint. Then she began to shake her head, and kept on until he came and sat beside her, brushed her hair aside, and rubbed the back of her neck. He didn't ask what she was thinking. Soon enough, she would tell him.

Elizabeth, carrying her rag doll, came to sit on her mother's lap. Madeline wrapped her arms around the girl's shoulders. And clasped her hands atop her daughter's belly. "I don't like it, Tom."

"How so?"

"I don't like ghosts. I *really* don't like being haunted by them. And I bet I'll hate whatever you've got a mind to do about it all."

At least for now, he wouldn't give the part of Bud's story in which Milly chased her husband away by running to the police to accuse him of murder. What Madeline knew about Milly wasn't much more than what had come from the newspapers. Neither Tom nor Florence cared to remind anybody, especially those they loved, that they had issued from the womb of a monster.

Besides, Madeline steered clear of horror stories, the genre into which most every recollection of her husband's and his sister's childhood best fit. Over the years, Tom had concluded that his wife's heart and mind were far more fragile than she let on. Madeline was tough only because she wore heavy armor.

"Babe," he said, "it's not the end of the world."

She turned just far enough to let him glimpse a look he could read: Maybe it's not the end of the whole world, but it's likely the end of ours. "What are your plans, Tom?"

"I've got to find him."

"No matter what?"

"I've got to try like hell."

"Don't you think being a cop and a dad is enough to keep you jumping?"

"So you'd have me do what?"

"Send Florence after him, for God sake. That crooked preacher of hers can help. McPherson could give her a world of advice. She knows all about folks who run off and leave their kids behind."

Tom knew precisely in what regard his wife held Sister Aimee Semple McPherson, whose disappearance had cornered the headlines throughout most of 1925, the year Tom and Madeline met. Her implication that the preacher and Charlie Hickey were made of the same stuff meant that, whether or not she intended to, she had labeled Tom's father a villain.

His nature called him to retaliate. Instead, he pardoned himself and walked out front for a breather.

Chapter Seventeen

Ten years back, when Tom met Madeline in the Hall of Records archives, Aimee Semple McPherson was under investigation by the Grand Jury.

The evangelist idol of millions had vanished from an outing at Ocean Park beach and been presumed drowned. Her legion of devotees mourned for a month, until she staggered out of the desert into Agua Prieta, across the Mexican border from Douglas, Arizona. A quarter-million blissful souls greeted her arrival by train at Los Angeles Central Station.

For weeks radio and newspapers captivated the world with Sister Aimee's tale of kidnapping and escape. But soon a less heroic story emerged, and evidence accumulated. This version held that she ran off with Kenneth Ormiston, the engineer in charge of her radio station.

The Grand Jury settled nothing, and Sister's integrity became one of those topics most everybody felt qualified to debate. Madeline sided with Sister's rival preacher, Fighting Bob Shuler. Not that she cared a whit about his dogma. She simply appreciated the debunking of a swindler. On the radio, Shuler interviewed folks who claimed to have entered an Angelus Temple service on crutches, left them behind after a "healing," and got rewarded by as much as $10 for the performance.

Tom took exception to Shuler's muckraking, as he wasn't anxious to convict anyone who fed more hungry people than any municipal service or charity, and who took in and found homes for hundreds of orphans and castaway babies. Neither was he likely to convict the woman who provided Florence with a job and some peace of mind.

By the time Tom returned from his breather, Madeline had adjourned to the bathroom. He sat on the floor beside Elizabeth, who besieged him with what-ifs. What if Chewy started talking? What if Chewy was a girl? At his most engaged, Tom found such questions daunting. He couldn't fathom how one might honestly answer a kid's what-ifs without entering a whole unfamiliar vein of philosophical inquiry.

This morning, he could only answer with either a smile or a cryptic nod. He was busy pondering the case for sending Florence to Mexico City. Sister Aimee, whether saint or swindler, was so fond of Florence, vicious rumors had surfaced. And Aimee had known their mother well enough to recognize how desperately Florence and Tom might long for some uplifting resolution to the mystery of their father. She would grant all the time off Florence requested.

Still, Tom was the man. The detective. The big brother who wouldn't think of sending his sister into danger alone.

Madeline returned from her bath with hair straight and damp, and wearing a lacy slip. She took her place on the sofa, leaned back, and made her gaze languid and pensive. After some minutes, she said, "What's it going to be?"

"I'll get a week off, fly to Mexico City. Elizabeth can bunk with Florence. You go on to Catalina and settle in. You'll hardly know I'm gone."

"Don't try to play me for a sucker, Tom. All goes well, you'll come back in a week, but never on this Earth does all go well. What I'm seeing is a wild goose chase."

"A week, then I'm home."

"Says you." Madeline's singing could make a torch song into a lullaby, but the voice she used now was raw. "Says the guy who doesn't know how to give up." After a colossal sigh, she sprang to attention. "Here's what we're going to do." Her eyes sparked with such determination, Tom inferred an addendum: *That is if you're not keen on being single again.*

He looked away and watched his daughter, who gave no sign of noticing her mother's sudden passion. He turned back to Madeline and nodded, since a man's best chance of calming a woman was to shut up and listen.

"What do book writers dream about?" she asked.

"Search me."

"Hollywood. Movies. Tom, you don't have to go anywhere."

Chapter Eighteen

Madeline's admirers were a multitude. More than a few were Hollywood big shots. Among that set, which she evermore viewed as her set, marriage didn't rank as a sacrament. Sure, Madeline loved Tom, or so he believed. But love wasn't her all-in-all.

He would first try playing the game her way.

Milton Hopper worked for Paramount. His gift, according to Madeline, was writing and directing slapstick. He must have clout, Tom supposed, or he couldn't have brought such celebrities as Harold Lloyd and Chico Marx to meet her and watch her perform.

Hopper's excuse for as yet failing to audition her was that she deserved a lead in a dramatic role and Paramount was on the rocks. Antitrust lawsuits followed by bankruptcy had slowed production to a drizzle.

While she slipped into a sleeveless pleated sundress, Madeline told Tom, "If I keep my eyes on Hoppy while I sing 'Night and Day,' he's mush. After he's swilled a cocktail or three, I tell him unless my dear husband can lure this writer up from Mexico, Tom's liable to take a bullet down below the border."

"What's he got against me taking a bullet?"

"He's a husband already. Not in his dreams would he want me available."

"In his dreams, you are what?"

"A side dish."

Though Tom hardly enjoyed the image, he retained the stoic demeanor. "How did you get wise to his dreams?"

"I'm a woman."

"I noticed."

"Women are mighty clever. Not all of us, but as a rule."

"Oh."

"Besides, I'll turn on the tears. He'll pitch this book thief an audience with Zukor himself, lace it with talk about DeMille producing, Gable playing the lead. Wait and see, you'll have your man here in town on the double."

In a truly curious manner, Tom asked, "And Hopper gets what out of the deal?"

"Just dreams, my darling." Madeline perched on the edge of the bed and inspected her manicure. "He's a softy, a romantic. He'd buy me the moon if it came up for sale. And he'd expect nothing more in return than a smile."

"What kind of smile?"

"One that lets him imagine I might not dash his hopes."

Tom paused in buttoning his shirt. "Let me see it."

She only rolled her eyes.

"Suppose you're selling him short?"

"Okay, let's say the little man gets fresh. I haul off and bust him in the nose."

Tom said, "You don't, I do."

Then he agreed to her scheme, though his heart, mind, and body objected. First, the thought of exploiting his wife's allure troubled him. Second, to hold still while waiting for Madeline's pal to summon the writer might prove more than his patience could bear.

Ever since Bud delivered the news, Tom felt ill at ease in his body and mind, now that he'd gotten infected by what psychologists termed a fixed-idea.

The challenge of finding the truth about Charlie Hickey was more than a task, deeper than an obsession. An assignment had morphed into one of those passions darkly related to honor and revenge. The kind that could drive people mad.

Chapter Nineteen

That balmy August evening, around Elizabeth's bedtime, as they returned to the cottage from a playtime in Popeye's Park, Tom once again noticed the silver Plymouth—this time crossing Hobart Place on Second Street, heading toward Wilshire.

Tom watched the car drive out of sight and determined that next time he would catch up with the fellow. He went inside and fetched his girl's nightgown. Then Leo phoned.

On a dozen occasions over the past year, Tom had heard Leo ranting his disgust over Hearst's *Examiner*'s soft-pedaling the collapse of civilization in Germany, the expulsion of Jews from influential professions, the barbarism of the storm troopers, and Aldolf Hitler's climb to absolute power. When Hearst met with Hitler and reported that he judged the man rational and reasonable, Leo phoned Tom but could hardly rant coherently. Still, Tom caught enough.

The Reichstag had authorized the sterilization of individuals suffering physical and mental handicaps. "Being Jewish, for one handicap," Leo said. In Leipzig, a young American by the name of Philip Zuckerman was taking a Sunday stroll with his German wife and her father and sister on a weekend when some 140,000 storm troopers showed for one of their frequent orgies of drilling and drinking. A band of them noticed the Zuckermans, made them as Jews, and attacked in such a fury of kicks and punches that both were hospitalized. The U.S. consulate got involved but took no action, even though Mrs. Zuckerman, several months pregnant, lost her baby. "Not a word in the *Examiner*," Leo said, and repeated twice.

Jewish doctors and dentists got run out of business, as the social insurance system refused to pay them. Jewish dressmakers got barred from a fashion shows. Jews could no longer work as cops. And Jews were banned from the lakeshore beach at Wannsee.

"Not only Jews, Tom. Every German of goodwill is terrified. They've quit vacationing in communal ski lodges for fear they might talk 'treason' in their sleep. They postpone surgeries because the ether might have them speaking their minds."

After each of Leo's reports, Tom prepared himself and Madeline for the day he would enlist, as soon as the U.S. decided for war. Which, according to Leo, would only occur when Hearst, with his government-by-media, gave the okay.

But for now, Hearst reported the progress toward Hitler's upcoming Olympics as if they were set in a sunny, prosperous, and peaceful land.

"And what are the headlines today?" Leo demanded. "Okay, I'll read them. 'German Employment Reaches All Time High.' 'German Mark Stable at Two and Forty-eight.' 'Peace Village Awaits World Athletes.'

"From the *Examiner*. That's Hearst's take on the world, Tom. Hitler's prepared a Peace Village. Good God, the fool goes to Germany, meets with Hitler, and comes home thinking what... that his charm talked the führer into revising *Mein Kampf* so it advocates brotherly love?

"Tom, Hearst bullied Congress and McKinley into invading Cuba. You tell me he couldn't have, with a well-wrought phrase and a fifty-million circulation, put the brakes on these damned Olympics. You tell me that, then you're a liar."

Tom didn't agree or argue, just listened until his friend allowed him to beg off so he could go tuck Elizabeth into bed. Leo's last words were, "Hearst is not only a greedy swine. He's a Nazi."

Chapter Twenty

Milton Hopper gladly obliged Madeline and invited the author known as B. Traven to Los Angeles, all expenses paid. Only the details required settling.

Hopper inhabited a cramped office on the Paramount lot in Burbank. The walls were papered with posters of the studio's films and stars. *Dr. Jekyll and Mr. Hyde.* Fairbanks. Valentino. *A Farewell to Arms. Duck Soup.* Mary Pickford, whose movies Tom avoided. The sight of America's Sweetheart recalled his mother, who not only resembled the star but also had worked as her seamstress.

When Tom met Hopper for the first time, he shook hands with more crush than was his habit. The man winced but maintained an actor's cordial smile. He was tall, soft, and pallid, his head shaped like a football. Tom thought he could double for William Randolph Hearst, except his voice was rather gruff and an octave lower than the tycoon's.

Rather than sit, Tom leaned against a poster of Mae West. After a few terse replies to pleasantries, he said, "Madeline's a good girl."

"Sure, Tom. No question."

"Call me 'Detective.'"

Hopper leaned back and chuckled. "Say…I'm no suspect."

"And I'm no rube, Mr. Hopper. Here's the deal. The writer shows, I owe you one. My wife doesn't owe you a thing."

Hopper raised both hands, palms out. "She's a pal, Detective, and one doozy of an entertainer. I surely do mean to find her the appropriate role."

Tom straightened his hat. He didn't begrudge his wife's career, only some of the duties it called for. Before he turned toward the door, he said, "Wife and mom's a plenty appropriate role."

Chapter Twenty-one

Much of what Tom knew about the system that ran Los Angeles came from Leslie White, whom Tom considered an unimpeachable source.

Les and Tom had worked together when theater impresario Alex Pantages stood accused of raping a seventeen-year-old dancer. In those days, Les was an investigator for the district attorney. Tom got mistakenly assigned to the case during a spell between chiefs of detectives, and shuffled off to a homicide detail as soon as Davis caught on.

In Tom's estimation, Les had rare integrity and a keen eye for humbug. Having served the city in a half dozen roles, he had witnessed and scrutinized plenty enough to draw up a game plan showing how the system worked for the benefit of all the players. He even wised Tom up about the motives behind businesses, rackets, publishers, cops, and lawyers agreeing to team up against the powerless. Because they needed each other. Newspapers needed the businesses' advertising. Businesses sold goods and rented properties to the racketeers and funded the politicos' campaigns. Cops and lawyers got sponsored by the racketeers' payoffs.

Five years ago, Tom and Leo, in consort with Roger Dalrymple, a new and naïve assistant DA, secured the conviction of a Glendale councilman for the rape and murder of his Japanese gardener's daughter. Dalrymple soon landed in Phoenix which, in the eyes of Californians, was next door to Hades. And Tom, ever since, had gotten partnered with one rookie after another, most of them miserable companions. A thug who clearly would prefer to commit—rather than discourage—homicide. A transplant from Dixie who yapped incessantly in a nasal drawl. And lately with Milo Saropian, a small-town kid who'd served a few years in uniform for the Fresno police. A thirst for adventure had lured Milo to the big city. He and Tom got along quite well. Apparently the chief had made a bum call.

Earl Balsac, current chief of detectives, was no pal of Tom's. But Leo Weiss had known the man forever, and some of what Leo knew involved the whereabouts of mislaid evidence. Since Balsac didn't care to go public with his transgressions, upon Leo's request, he approved of Tom using a week of vacation. But to retain a sliver of dignity, he bargained. The leave would only commence the day after Tom and Milo busted a certain upstart prostitution ring.

The ring had welshed on the rules by mocking the request for a charitable donation to the Masons. Besides, the girls in question were younger, fresher, and easier on a John's budget than those chaperoned by Cherry O'Day.

In addition to her vocation, Miz O'Day also hosted a poker game frequented by Grand Poobahs of the Masons and charter members of the California club.

Balsac told Tom, "Don't waste the court's time on the quiffs. Send them packing and bring me the kingpin."

Over the weekend just past, Milo had sacrificed most of his paycheck—and perhaps his virginity, Tom thought—cavorting with a Texas kitten who called herself Muffy. They made friends. And Milo teased the kingpin's name and whereabouts out of her.

On Monday, he'd passed the kingpin's name to Tom, along with assurance that Muffy was a good kid who would testify provided they find her a job as a steno. "Claims she can type like the wind," Milo said, with the endearing trust of a rookie.

Spooking the chippies was no trick. Not a hard case among them. The oldest might've been twenty. They lived and worked a few miles east of downtown Burbank on a single block of a cracker-box tract, each lot featuring a citrus tree and a prickly pear cactus.

Tom and Milo walked door to door. Tom showed his badge. The girls' eyes lit. A few of them squealed, wept, or shuddered. Not one bothered to play the role the kingpin, Louis Wester, assigned them. Muffy had clued Milo that Wester coached his girls to pose as simple housewives. In the event the law encountered more than one together, they were to play the simple housewife and her cousin or cousins.

Meaning to scare them out of the life, Tom used his bulldog demeanor. He took notes, demanded each one's name, age, hometown, next of kin, and learned they had trekked to the promised land mostly out of the dustbowl. From Kansas, Texas, Oklahoma, Tennessee. He gave each of them a flyer describing the services of Traveler's Aid. If bus fare was still a problem, he advised, they should stop by Angelus Temple on Glendale Boulevard and ask for Florence, who could arrange for some of Sister Aimee's Christian charity.

He left each of them with a glance that warned of hell to pay if they failed to heed his advice. He looked so menacing, even Milo gaped with admiration.

A vicious expression came naturally these days. He'd often wondered if his temper developed on account of Milly's genes, or if it resulted from the challenges and disappointments of his life. Whichever the cause, it spooked him. As a cop, he'd always been more afraid of maiming than getting beaten, of killing than of getting murdered.

At a few of the homes, one palooka or another appeared and objected to their presence. Then Tom drew his .38, held it at the ready, and stood overseeing while Milo socked the fellow until he behaved. Tom had learned not to throw any punch he could avoid. Because the guy might fight back, and Tom might explode.

Two of the palookas dictated and signed statements asserting that Louis Wester had employed them as solicitors and chaperones. Another, whom Tom thought he vaguely recognized, refused to speak or sign or show identification. A girl called him Rusty. His left ear sported a notch about the size of a large tooth bite. Tom imagined he earned the feature in some shantytown venue that alternated cock-fights with bare-knuckle boxing. Or else he tried the wrong move on one of the chippies.

Milo would've kept thrashing the palooka into submission or unconsciousness if Tom hadn't given the order to move on. The rookie was no brute, only a kid who still believed the citizenry was by and large law-abiding and good and that the criminal element was rotten but could occasionally be thrashed into mending its ways.

This pimp would only get meaner, Tom felt sure. Something about him gave Tom a shiver of recognition, as though he'd crept out of a nightmare—like one of those creatures lurking in the background waiting for a chance to snatch our souls and carry us into the place they inhabit, beyond redemption.

Louis Wester owned a trucking firm. When Tom and Milo arrived at his Duarte warehouse with a warrant, they found him waiting, flanked by a pair of stocky lawyers whose current chore was to restrain him. He was taller than Tom's six-two and nearly as wide as both detectives standing side-by-side. He yelled threats and accused various police commissioners, state congressmen, and judges with whoring at Cherry O'Day's and committing a wide variety of felonies, misdemeanors, and other abominations. When he collapsed, one of the lawyers attempted to catch him in a rolling chair. The chair's arm goosed him.

Wester's ruddy face darkened from rose to purple. His eyes flicked up and back. His breaths came with gurgling sounds.

Tom made a judgment call of the kind least likely to please Chief Davis, who always preferred to save the city the annoyance of yet another trial. To the lawyers, Tom said, "Get the slob to emergency, County General. Don't let him out till we come visit, first thing tomorrow."

Chapter Twenty-two

Tom, like Bud Gallagher, was a devotee of the city's central library on Flower Street. Back when Florence was in high school and Tom drove a wholesale route for Alamo Meat, he often took his lunch break on a bench near the library entrance. He ate while gazing up at the pyramid tower with suns on either side, and at the severed hand holding the Light of Learning torch. After work, he often returned to the enchanting place for a book that might pique wild Florence's interest. He imagined coming home from work to find her reading. Then he wouldn't need to go out and search the speakeasies.

Today, he hustled through the rotunda with its glossy chessboard floors, passed beneath the solar system chandelier, and rode the elevator to the spacious reference room with its high ceilings and lamp-lit mahogany tables.

He stopped in the doorway and peered around for Helga the librarian. The day before yesterday, he had phoned Bud and asked him to cajole one of his librarian admirers to research B. Traven.

Almost as much as he admired the library, Tom esteemed librarians. He enjoyed bibliographic research on his own, but he was a novice in the field compared to the pros, whose knowledge he considered nearly magical.

Bud had sent him to Helga, whom Tom found at her post behind the reference counter. She was a rosy-cheeked gal of middle age, wholesome as a milkmaid, whose eyes sparkled as brightly as did her rhinestone-rimmed specs. Tom introduced himself.

"Yes," she said. "Mister Bud is my dear friend." She handed him a typed document, three stapled pages. "I took the liberty to translate. Quite well written. How well translated, as the translator, I shall not judge."

He accepted the document and thanked her. He would've dashed off to a reading nook, except she asked about Bud's health.

"I'm no doc," Tom said, "but my guess is he's not got long."

She nodded in dour agreement and added that day-by-day he acted more feeble. "Only prayer may save him."

He smiled and escaped. Outside, in the shade of a flowering jacaranda, he sat on a bench and read.

The article concerned *The Death Ship* and a second B. Traven novel, *The Treasure of the Sierra Madre*, both published to high acclaim in Germany. The writer contended that B. Traven was most assuredly one Ret Marut, who first gained recognition as an actor and playwright. During the war, this Marut had published an antimilitary, anarchist magazine called *The Brickburner*. He continued in politics after the armistice as propagandist for the short-lived Bavarian Free State. Such audacity earned him a death sentence, which sent him on the run.

The last two pages were reviews of the Traven books, to which Tom paid little attention though he sat for minutes staring at the document. He could hardly rise, disheartened as he felt.

Ten minutes ago, he believed that soon he would stand face-to-face with Charlie Hickey. Now, he believed nothing.

A siren, then another, broke the trance. He stood, folded and pocketed the article, and followed the noise, which got ever louder and harsher. He strode up Fifth Street and turned onto Main then saw up ahead what he expected. Yet another of the Red Squad brawls.

Whenever a few union fellows gathered within stone-pitching distance of the Hall of Justice, the Red Squad came out swinging. Tom had observed enough of this action so that he agreed with a definition Les White gave him: "A Communist is anyone who doesn't agree with the chamber of commerce."

Today's clash would make front-page news if a cop suffered a stone bruise to his pinky toe. If any commies got maimed or exterminated, the brief story would run deep in the interior of Hearst's *Examiner* and Chandler's *Times*.

Tom declined to stay and watch. The way he felt, he might've jumped in, on the dangerous side.

When he arrived home, Madeline greeted him with, "Leo phoned. He says I'd best convince you to take an honest to God vacation on Catalina. Be good to me and Elizabeth. Let the past work itself out."

"He's a real pal," Tom said.

He poured a tumbler of Dewar's with a single ice cube. Then he sat in the parlor beside the phone and dialed Leo's number.

Violet Weiss picked up. When Tom asked for her husband, though he tried to pacify his voice, it sounded uncommonly fierce.

Vi said, "You're not going to yell at the old man, are you? He's had a rough day."

"Matter of fact, I am."

"Well then, yell at me instead. I'll pass it along, word for word."

"Sure." Tom's heart began to soften and his voice followed suit. "Tell him I'm going to find Charlie. Tell him to go meddle elsewhere."

"Got it," Vi said. "Our love to your girls."

Madeline, who had observed from the kitchen, sent her husband a dark and ominous glare.

Chapter Twenty-three

Helping Madeline sort and pack her onstage and offstage wardrobes into four steamer trunks cost Tom all afternoon of his first vacation day. At least while they were collaborating on that chore she spoke to him. They both avoided the topic of Charlie Hickey. Tom shopped for and cooked a swordfish supper. Swordfish often appeared on ads for establishments on Catalina. Madeline thanked him, but hardly gushed. Through the meal, she chatted with Elizabeth, and afterwards she helped her daughter pack. When a horn tooted, she hugged and kissed Elizabeth, nodded good-bye to Tom, and ran out to meet Paul Perkins for her ride to rehearsal.

Tom drove his daughter to the Echo Park neighborhood where she would spend the next few days. Then he and the girls held hands as they strolled from Florence's place to the park.

Florence grabbed her brother's elbow. "See that car, Tommy?"

"Yeah. What about it?"

A silver Plymouth had just crossed in front of them on Park Avenue. Before Florence could answer, Tom let go her hand and jogged to the intersection. He watched the Plymouth turn onto Glendale, heading toward downtown.

Florence told him about the little man and his car she'd noticed more than once parked on Lemoyne in an ideal position from which to keep an eye on the girls' dormitory.

Tom said, "I'll bet it's not the girls he's watching. At least not primarily. He's got his eye on you."

He told her about his sightings of the same car, same little man. Florence asked, "Should we worry about him?"

"I've got a spare pistol. You want it?" He didn't tell her his spare was the Browning Chief Davis gave him to use on Danny Katoulis. She didn't need to know everything about the ways of the LAPD.

"I guess not," she said. "I've got your number. That's what you cops are for, isn't it?"

Moonlit lovers, thinkers, and schemers, as well as the usual loud and tipsy boys and girls, occupied the Echo Park benches and shadows. Lanterns flickered in rowboats that glided across the lake. An elderly couple vacated a shoreline bench. Tom and his sister stopped beside it while Elizabeth wandered off to stalk sleepy ducks, intending to pet one, she told them.

"I've been thinking," Florence said, "if the book writer is Charlie himself, what do we do? Say he comes to town and doesn't plan to make a move to look us up. Do we even want such a louse for a daddy? I mean…or do we forget the bum, figure good riddance?"

Tom shrugged and sat on the bench.

Florence seated herself close beside him. "What kind of guy do you figure he is?"

"About all we have to go on is the book."

"That crazy sailor, Wilbur Welch in the manuscript, Gerard Gales in the book, I like the fellow, but…" Florence's chin quivered. Tom waited. She reached out and placed a hand on his knee. "I mean, he never mentions having a kid, Tommy. Not a word about us. Not one."

Tom played defense. "Maybe he figured if he did, he ought to explain why he ditched us, or else readers would take him for a lowdown and give up caring a whit what became of him."

"Or maybe," she offered, "the thought of ditching us hurt him too much." Her lips bent upward, from gloomy to bright. "Maybe he couldn't touch it."

Tom had wondered the same. He reached for his sister's hand. She used her thumb to pet his knuckles. "Our daddy's smart," she said, "and he's read most of the library. Knows the Bible."

"Shakespeare."

"And a whole lot of history. Tommy, are you getting enough sleep, in between all the thinking?"

"Some," Tom said. "You?"

She gave him the smile that always lifted his spirit, the one he found perfectly free of guile, nothing like the impish one of her wilder days. "I get enough," she said. "For now, sleep hardly matters."

But Tom craved sleep, simply to become unconscious. Every waking moment, he labored with restlessness accompanied by a savage desire for action. Get the ball, rush the line, and bust free on the other side.

After Elizabeth wearied of ducks, the three of them walked hand-in-hand past Angelus Temple, out of which issued whoops and amens. Back at Florence's place, Tom sat holding his little girl. Her eyes kept drooping closed then barely opening. With a promise to see her in a day or two, he passed her to his sister. In no time, she fell asleep, cuddled on the sofa with Florence.

He drove in the slow lane like a grandpa just off the farm, up Glendale Boulevard, through downtown and out Wilshire, seeing hardly anything but visions of Gerard Gales as Charlie Hickey. He stopped at the corner market for a new fifth of Dewar's.

The next morning, he had barely started cracking eggs when Florence called. She said, "Sister Aimee's a doll. She says 'Help out your brother. He's not going to ask. He doesn't like to ask for anything.' And she gives me a twinkle of her eye."

Tom knew the look. He'd first seen it on the preacher way back when he grilled her about Milly while investigating the Echo Park lynching of his pal Frank Gaines.

He said, "She gave you the look that means 'It's not me talking, but God'?"

"Yeah, that one. Now tell me what you need me to do."

"I'll call when we get to Avalon. You and my baby have plans?"

"You bet. We're going to the Pike. Can I take her on the Cyclone Racer?"

"Hold her tight, even if she throws up?"

"Promise."

Madeline was still asleep when a Paramount secretary phoned and gave Tom a message from Milton Hopper. The producer and the author who called himself B. Traven would travel to Catalina Island tomorrow on the midmorning ferry out of San Pedro.

Tom was filling a flask to stuff into his overnight bag when Madeline awoke, staggered out to the kitchen, and caught him in the act.

"In case somebody gets seasick," he said.

Chapter Twenty-four

Tom leaned on the rail of the commercial dock in Avalon, Santa Catalina Island, twenty-one nautical miles southwest of where he'd embarked in San Pedro.

The air was crisp, salty, and pure. Not a single solitary car, truck, or oil derrick, the sights most evident around Los Angeles. On Tom's either side stood a fisherperson. A red-haired boy and an Asian grandfather wearing knickers.

As the ferry *Pilgrim* nosed out of an offshore fog bank, Tom pushed away from the rail and stood tall. He kept his eyes keened on the boat at deck level.

Even when the kid hooked something that yanked him crashing into the rail and threatened to snap his rod, and while the boy yelped and a dozen tourists and loiterers hustled closer to witness the match, Tom merely glanced over. Any second Charlie Hickey could materialize on the *Pilgrim*'s bow.

The ferry came ever more slowly, shifting side to side. It caromed off the dock. Ropes flew and deckhands caught and tugged them. At the same moment the ferry appeared to surrender and come to rest in the slip, a hearty cheer rose nearby. For an instant, Tom imagined the cheer signaled his father's arrival.

Then he saw Milton Hopper on the deck beside a lean man a half a head shorter than the producer.

The man's face was a triangle, his shoulders narrow and sloped. Mickey Mouse looked as much like Tom's memories and dreams of Charlie Hickey as this fellow did.

As Tom's heart deflated, he looked sideways and found that the cheering was on account of the red-haired boy, who had landed a grouper about the size of a bull walrus. The fish thrashed and flopped while the boy tried to clobber it, using a gaff the Asian granddad provided.

Tom straightened his posture, attempting to steel himself to prepare for the challenge he faced. Not a reunion but a criminal investigation. Not Charlie Hickey but the louse who stole and published Charlie's book as his own.

And since, Tom believed, Charlie was no dupe or pushover, the thief could also be a murderer.

Deckhands lowered the gangplank. Hopper and the thief stood aside while the other passengers debarked. They were couples from young to ancient and plain to flashy, and a trio of portly young schoolteachers. At the end of the procession, the thief came wobbling, with the producer familiarly close behind him. Once they arrived on the dock, Hopper stepped to one side, reached around the thief's shoulders and guided him.

The producer wore a dubious smile, like someone wary of getting socked.

Before the men came close enough to shake Tom's hand, Hopper said, "Mr. Hickey, meet Hal Croves, the elusive author's secretary."

The man who called himself Croves, Tom suspected was Ret Marut, the socialist pamphleteer who had run from a treason charge in Germany. The article Helga had translated had given a cursory description. And something intangible like instinct seconded the suspicion.

The man had stopped still and shifted from at ease to stiff attention. His eyes darted to take in the whole of Tom.

"I remind you of someone?" Tom asked.

"No." Marut turned menacing eyes on Hopper.

Tom, having witnessed thousands of criminal lies, knew he'd just heard one. "Where's Traven?"

The book thief withheld his response for a dignified moment. Then he said, "Mr. Traven insists upon absolute anonymity. I am his representative, given the authority to speak for him in all artistic, legal, or contractual matters."

Tom gazed out to sea and tried to calculate how best to act. Though his insides writhed, like all good detectives he was skilled in holding his passions in check, at least for a spell. He turned back and reached out his hand.

Marut gave a firm, cursory shake. "You are a director, I presume, or a writer of screenplays?" He pronounced the job titles as if they were lowly occupations.

Tom turned to Hopper. "What did you tell him?"

The producer grimaced.

With a note of petulance, Marut said, "He told me next to nothing, though I asked repeatedly. You will please now explain why Mr. Hopper has brought me to this island."

"Makes for tougher getaway," Tom said.

The book thief nodded as if he caught Tom's full meaning. His upper lip twitched and became a sneer. "And from what, or whom, would I care to get away?"

"From a guy who's going to do what it takes to find out how you stole a book from my father."

"Your father…" Marut said, while his right hand eased across his chest. Before it slid under his corduroy coat, Tom's hand shot out and grabbed the man's wrist.

Tom lifted the coat, revealing a shoulder holster. He plucked out the gun, a Luger 9mm, and shoved it into his own coat pocket. "Yeah," he said, "my father. Charlie Hickey. Alias Gerard Gales."

Tom and the book thief stood squared off, like Tom Mix and Will Hart poised to quick-draw, attempting to read each other's mind.

Hopper said, "Say, fellas, who could use a drink?"

Chapter Twenty-five

Hopper led the way to The Pitcairn, a dockside tavern paneled inside and out in rough pine boards darkened and marred to replicate driftwood. The joint smelled of seaweed, watery beer, and mildew. On the walls hung signed photos of Gable, Laughton, and perhaps every other actor, actress, and extra of *Mutiny on the Bounty*, filmed only last year on and around the island.

A couple weeks ago, Tom and Madeline had obeyed the command of half the billboards on Wilshire Boulevard and spent a Sunday afternoon at the Egyptian Theatre watching the film. Tom approved of it. Madeline thought Gable was swell, but all the way home she belittled the actresses.

The plump schoolteachers had preceded the Hopper party from the *Pilgrim* into the tavern. They perched on stools around a high table fashioned from the top of an oaken cask. They tittered occasionally, sipped colorful beverages, and snuck glances every which way. They appeared all aflutter, as if their principal might have sent spies to catalogue their slightest transgression. Or, with jobs a rare commodity, and saloons off limits to those who shaped the minds of youth, any would-be teacher might rat on them.

After Hopper ushered Tom and Marut onto stools across a plank table from each other, he started toward the bar. But on the way, he peered over his shoulder. The men sat crouched like bare knuckle boxers consigned to their respective corners. So he returned, seated himself, and rested a hand on Marut's shoulder. "Mind I call you Hal?"

"If you prefer."

The producer made a fist as if to reach across and give Tom's arm a good-natured tap, which he then chose not to deliver. "Hal rode the train the whole godawful way. How about that? What, a couple thousand miles, mostly desert."

"Twenty five hundred kilometers."

"Pullman car?"

"Yes."

"Hot as hell?"

"I have known worse." Marut spoke English with a slight Germanic gruffness and diction.

The waiter arrived, costumed in an eye patch and his head wrapped with a bandana. "What'll it be, blokes?" he rasped.

Hopper called for a bottle of Irish whiskey and three tumblers.

Tom had already convicted the man across from him. Back on the dock, on account of Marut's reaction to his appearance and to his mention of Charlie Hickey, he had shed all doubt.

Still, he would need to convince Florence, Madeline, and perhaps a judge and jury. So he continued to collect and memorize evidence, such as the book thief's every expression and move appearing either nervous or sly.

The bottle arrived. The producer poured, two fingers in each tumbler. A long and a short swallow helped Tom speak in level tones. "Let's take it from the top. Charlie Hickey goes to sea, comes back home, and writes about his travels." He shoved the bottle at the man. "Take it from there. Where'd you bump into him, Mr. Traven?"

The man poured a second dose and sipped. "Traven, I am not."

"Then you're going to take me to Traven. Correct? And he's going to take me to Charlie Hickey. Correct?"

"This is not possible," the man said in a voice that hinted of apology.

Tom reached for the bottle. He sensed, or detected from the man's face, what was coming. He closed his eyes.

"Mr. Hickey, I am Traven's confidante. As such, I have heard stories not yet written. One of these regards a seafarer whose friendship inspired the novel in question. If this man was your father, it grieves me to tell you, he is dead these many years."

Tom reached for the .38 Colt holstered under his left arm.

Chapter Twenty-six

Tom slammed the gun broadside onto the table.

All three schoolteachers yipped then heaved themselves up and hastened toward the powder room. The bartender ducked behind the counter. A shotgun barrel rose in his place.

Troubled by his own fury, Tom snatched up the .38 and rushed out of the Pitcairn. He double-timed across Crescent Avenue and up Metropole Avenue, past the Hotel Atwater where Madeline probably still lay asleep.

Last night Madeline and her bandleader Paul Perkins went on a busman's holiday. Dancing to Kay Kaiser at the Avalon Casino Ballroom, while Tom pored over *The Death Ship*, in book form, once again.

Metropole Avenue, the steepest climb on the island's west side, hardly slowed Tom's pace. He had reached the golf course, altitude 1,000 feet, before his blood cooled to simmer and a reasonable thought overtook him.

The article Helga the librarian translated noted that young Ret Marut had worked as an actor. Which meant that Tom should not only doubt the man's words, he also shouldn't count on expressions or gestures to give him away.

And Marut could well be a desperate character. Not only did he carry a Luger. Anybody coming from Mexico, where the revolution never ended, might habitually pack hardware. But also—like Wall Street big shots ruined by the crash who preferred leaping out of windows to witnessing their own fall from grace—a fellow with his sights on fame and fortune can lose all perspective when his career's touchdown pass gets intercepted. Once the reading world learned Charlie Hickey wrote *The Death Ship*, B. Traven would plummet from the literary heights. From reviews that compared him to Joseph Conrad and Miguel Cervantes, to the pit where even hacks would mock him.

Besides, Germans were inclined to venerate honor. Marut might rather become a corpse than an outcast. If so, whatever threats Tom delivered could look puny compared to the fate of a pariah.

All of which meant, Tom reasoned, cunning would likely serve better than pistol whippings and other shortcuts preferred by Chief Davis' LAPD. To get the truth, Tom recognized, he might even need to cut a deal. He stiffened his shoulders and drew deeper breaths to fight the onset of nausea.

On the way down Metropole Avenue, he counted his steps and watched the calming, white-capped sea crisscrossed by a rainbow pallet of sails. He turned onto the sidewalk of Crescent Avenue and spotted Hopper and the thief standing outside the Pitcairn. Hopper waved and hustled across the street. "Now Tom," he said, "granted you're the detective, but might I suggest that if you want the fellow to talk, you ought to quit scaring the bejesus out of him?"

Tom nodded.

"Maybe you ought to let me hold your gun."

"Not on your life," Tom said.

"Funny, Croves gave the same answer about his."

"He's got another?"

"Fished it out of his valise."

"Thanks."

"Fair's fair," Hopper said. "What would you say to a spin on the glass-bottom boat?"

"That your bright idea?"

"Croves' idea. My guess, he thinks nobody's apt to shoot when the bullet might go awry, bust the glass, and sink the vessel. Or else he thinks looking at the pretty fish will lower his blood pressure, or yours."

The thief had followed Hopper. Now he stood at attention directly in front of Tom. "Do you intend, at some point, to shoot me?"

Tom managed a flat smile. "It's an option. Another is, you're going to make me rich."

"Rich?" Marut's sharp hazel eyes darted back and forth between Tom and the producer.

Clearly he now believed Tom and Hopper were in cahoots, out to blackmail.

Chapter Twenty-seven

Hopper chose the only glass-bottom boat without a wait or reservation. Named *Wendy Lee*, the groaning tub reminded Tom of the *Yorrike*, one of the death ships Wilbur Welch alias Gerard Gales labored upon. A relic, the novelist asserted, from the age when galley slaves rowed ships built of rough planks, some rotted, others petrified.

Wendy Lee's pilot stood high on the bow. Below, in the deck-less hull, passengers occupied wood and canvas director' chairs around a rectangular frame that Tom, once an architecture student, placed as having once been the window of a Beaux Arts mansion. Perhaps a neighbor of the Pasadena digs of Mr. Wrigley, the gum and baseball tycoon, and creator of Avalon and most all of Santa Catalina except the dirt.

Aside from Tom, Hopper, and Marut, the passengers were three couples and the children who accompanied two of them. The boy of a couple who announced they'd come all the way from Maine stared daggers at the son of an Iowa farm couple. The farm boy brandished a fist. The boy from Maine stuck out his tongue. The father from Maine boxed his son's ear.

Through the thick antique glass, the sea appeared milky. Still, the view of sizeable crabs, calico bass, stingrays, and bright orange garibaldi relieved some of Tom's agitation.

"All right, Mr. Croves," he said, "have it your way. Make believe you're not Traven, and give me the story. From the moment Traven met my father."

Marut sat still, gazing down as though fascinated by the twin eels or the quartet of sand sharks that circled them. Now and then his lips moved, rehearsing.

At last he shifted his chair in Tom's direction. "Long before the Yankee sailor came to Mexico, during the early years of the revolution, your William Randolph Hearst feared the *campesinos* might overrun Babicora, his vast and lucrative hacienda in the Mexican state of Chihuahua."

In the patronizing manner of a lecturer to an ill-informed audience, Marut said, "Two thousand meters above sea level, near the primary source of the Yaqui River and surrounded by wooded mountains, grama grasses carpeted the plains and valleys in which cattle, sheep, goats, horses, and mules thrive. Each summer *vaqueros* drove great herds of shorthorn and Hereford to El Paso, financing Lord Hearst's European travels during which he purchased the treasures that adorn his castles."

The fellow from Maine scooted closer to the speaker, farther from his wife and children.

Marut said, "To earth's aristocracy, no borders exist. Long before Villa raised his army, Porfirio Diaz appealed to your President Taft, who sent the Arizona Rangers backed by the United States Fifth Calvary to annihilate the copper miners who dared to strike in Cananea.

"Your Hearst considered the security of his holdings guaranteed by the armies of two governments, all the manpower and firepower his obscene fortune could employ, and the news empire with which he governs, using readers as his proxy."

Marut paused and eyed his audience as though awaiting a challenge. Tom only noted that the thief's opinion of Hearst and his power agreed with Leo's. "Get on with the story," he said.

To exhibit his disdain for Tom's orders, Marut turned his gaze to the fishes and maintained silence for a minute or more. Then he lifted his shoulders to attention and summoned a deeper voice. "When land reforms broke up other Yankee holdings, your Hearst summoned battalions of lawyers. His news syndicate portrayed a Mexico infested by Communists, anarchists, all manner of vermin."

Marut's eyes lit on Hopper then Tom. "Are you acquainted with the work of Ambrose Bierce?"

"Yeah," Tom said, "Now let's hear about Charlie Hickey."

The thief gripped an arm of his chair. "I presumed you wanted the truth, rather than the tabloid version."

Tom leaned forward. "Facts."

The kids from Iowa and Maine had left their seats. They knelt like communicants at the low rail around the windowed bottom. The one little girl squealed and poked the glass, pointing at a lobster.

Marut's expression seemed both studious and so aggravated, Tom supposed he was contemplating the odds for and against drawing his pistol, shooting Tom, taking hostages, and escaping the boat, then the island, then the country.

As he returned to telling his story, his posture relaxed and his face animated. "Nineteen-thirteen, Pancho Villa's *soldados* occupied Babicora. The call for *Tierra y Libertad* echoed from mountain to plain, border to border, sea to sea.

"Into this melee, Hearst sent the eloquent firebrand Ambrose Bierce, his most notable, if least reliable henchman."

Chapter Twenty-eight

Tom knew the work of Ambrose Bierce fairly well. He had learned to read quite young and read whatever he encountered. Favoring news, novels, and history, he read whenever he found the time and peace. Reading earned him the grades that, along with his strength and speed, won him a USC scholarship.

About Hearst and Bierce, he knew enough. He knew that Hearst, after inheriting the *San Francisco Chronicle*, set out to build the world's largest newspaper chain and—as both Leo and Marut maintained— to establish government by media.

After some disappointing attempts to gain a seat in the U.S. Senate, Hearst chose to forgo his quest for the presidency and turn to ruling the nation through his stories. He would glorify democracy, manipulate public opinion, and bend the world to accord with his vision.

When he acquired *The New York Journal*, he challenged Joseph Pulitzer of *The New York World* to a game scrupulous folks called yellow journalism. The rules: true always plays second string behind colorful, scandalous, and shocking.

Hearst won the game. A piece of his strategy was to outbid Pulitzer for writers such as Mark Twain, Stephen Crane, and Ambrose Bierce.

Bierce had fought for the Union in the Civil War, risen to the rank of Major, and applied the experience to a book of short stories Tom had read and reread. And long ago, when Tom mentioned the stories, Leo commented that Ambrose Bierce was the only Hearst writer whose articles—though often caustic, cynical, and muckraking—a reader ought to believe.

Marut said, "Lord Hearst assigned his most eloquent lackey to ferret out General Villa, to ingratiate himself, charm and befriend. In the end, his task would be to convince the General that his master's news empire, personal funds, and loyalists in politics and finance, would serve the revolution as a whole, and Villa in particular.

"To guarantee the General's concurrence, Bierce was to propose an epic tale featuring Pancho Villa, the man and the legend. Bierce would compose an account of such scope and authority—which the Hearst empire would publish and promote with such zeal—the General would join the immortal company of Washington, Napoleon, and Bolivar.

"All this, your Hearst charged Bierce to offer, in exchange for the simple guarantee that Babicora would remain a Hearst possession."

Tom raised a hand, palm out. "Lay off calling him *our* Hearst."

Marut turned and addressed the enraptured fellow from Maine. "As is common among the aristocracy, the belief that all humanity can be swindled, outwitted, or purchased, proved to be a tragic flaw. In Bierce, Lord Hearst met his match. He could not fathom a man of true principle and determination. Mr. Bierce was no one's toady.

"Had he found Villa to be a hero worthy of enshrining, the General might have become the protagonist of a work as memorable as *War and Peace*. Yet after a brief audience with Villa and some weeks of interviews and observation, the author's opinion of the General was far from heroic. Simple distemper, to which Bierce was prone, may have prompted the report Bierce actually composed. Regardless of his reasons, he portrayed the General as arrogant, whimsical, and corrupt."

Marut paused, heightening the drama. The fellow from Maine asked, "Hearst published that?"

Chapter Twenty-nine

Through all the talk, a part of Tom's mind had been assessing the storytelling of this fellow compared to that of *The Death Ship*. On one hand, like the book writer, Marut was out to critique institutions and expose greed and hypocrisy. But the German lacked any trace of humor aside from a smidgen of sarcasm, while the book writer saw a measure of comedy in even the treacherous, vile, and unjust. The book writer was a novelist; Marut a provider of journalistic propaganda.

When the fellow from Maine asked if Hearst had published Bierce's Pancho Villa story, the thief allowed a wry smile. "The courier was shot on the road to Ciudad Chihuahua."

"Villa killed him?" Hopper asked.

"How do you know it all?" Tom demanded.

Marut fixed a stony gaze on his interrogator. After holding it long enough to assure Tom got the message, the thief turned to Hopper. "Does the tour offer refreshments?"

Tom reached for the flask in his hip pocket.

Marut's hand flashed quick as Houdini's across his belly to the coat pocket on the opposite side, where it remained until Tom had produced his flask and passed it over. After two earnest swallows and a rub of his mouth as though to displace bacteria, Marut said, "During Bierce's sojourn with the Villistas, he made the acquaintance of Harry Longabaugh."

"Whoa. Hold on," Hopper said, excitedly as though glimpsing the germ of a film plot. "You're not talking about the Sundance Kid?"

"Indeed I am."

"Well, you've got it all wrong. That desperado got blown to bits in Argentina back before the war."

Marut gave his head a languid shake, as though distressed by ignorance. "You believe this account on what authority?"

"I read a couple of books about the Kid and his pals, that gang that hid out at some hole in the wall."

"These books were academic, documented?"

"Say," Hopper reminded the man, "I'm in the entertainment business. We don't read academic crap."

Tom pointed at Marut. "Who's *your* authority?"

The thief leaned backward, folded his arms and assumed a proud posture, like a preacher about to credit Moses or another irrefutable source. "Traven often recalls and speaks of the robber of trains and banks, alias Sundance, who survived a pitched battle in Bolivia. Not Argentina," he said with a patronizing glance at Hopper. "Bolivia. Now might I continue without interruption?"

"Try it and see," Tom said.

Marut, having failed to return Tom's flask, treated himself to another gulp. After a delayed swallow, he said, "Following the battle in Bolivia, Longabaugh, though severely wounded, escaped to find shelter and care from the family of a local *hacendado* whose sympathies lay with the exploited miners, in opposition to the overlords.

"Longabaugh chose against a premature return to the States, aware that the Pinkerton agency remained doubtful concerning his death. Once he had fully recuperated, he traveled north at his leisure, on horseback, supporting his travels primarily by applying his Celtic charm to the seduction of prosperous women.

"Nineteen twelve, in Oaxaca, he encountered upstart peasant armies in need of training by proficient gunfighters. The revolution provided the vocation to which Longabaugh's heritage inclines. 'Only in the heat of battle,'" Marut obviously recited, "'could the Celts, besieged on all sides by demons, find a sort of repose.'"

Tom rolled his hand. The thief scowled and returned the flask.

"Longabaugh established himself with the Zapatista forces and remained with them until an internal dispute attached him to a rogue band that wandered north, pillaging en route, much like your Civil War's Cantrell and his raiders.

"Throughout the northern states of Mexico, your capitalists had constructed a rail system to cart away Tampico oil and the silver, gold, and copper of Sonora and the Sierra Madre. The revolutionary armies of the north included their share of *desperados*, but few of them had earned such a reputation as Longabaugh. He seized the opportunity, and became a consultant in the craft of train robbery. After proving his worth, he attached himself to General Villa."

The boat struck a piling. Tom dropped his briar pipe, into which he'd been tamping Prince Albert. The stem wedged between floor planks. He wiggled and eased it free, while the wife from Maine, appearing queasy, shooed her boy and two girls toward the ladder-steps. She turned and beckoned her husband.

"I'll be along, Mabel," the man snapped. Marut's story had no doubt inspired him with a call to adventure and freedom.

Chapter Thirty

On the pier, Hopper caught Tom's eye and signaled with a toss of his head. The producer double-timed, leaving behind the fellow from Maine and the thief, who continued his account at the fellow's urging.

As Tom caught up, the producer said, "I'm seeing a film here. Who plays the lead?"

"Chaplin," Tom said.

Hopper's jaw dropped, as if Tom had suggested casting a penguin. After a minute, he said, "Chaplin as the Sundance Kid?"

"Chaplin as Gerard Gales?"

"Oh, you mean the book. I was thinking of Sundance and Pancho Villa." Again he stood looking dumbfounded. "*The Death Ship*'s a comedy, you think? Hmm."

Tom was gazing over the producer's shoulder, watching Marut. He and the fellow from Maine had stopped about a first down's distance back, and while the thief talked, one eye remained keened on Tom.

Hopper tapped Tom's shoulder. "Say, what I hear, you L.A. cops are trigger happy."

"So rumor has it."

"And looks to me like you're mad as a hornet and not about to simmer down."

"Not while I suspect this hogwash peddler of killing my dad."

The producer stroked his chin and glanced behind to assure they were still out of Marut's hearing. He leaned a bit forward and softened his gruff voice. "See, I'm blushing to admit, guns give me the willies. Even phony ones on the set. To tell the truth, a clown shoots a popgun, an umbrella spits out, I'm weak in the knees.

"Thing is, Tom, I did my part on the square. How about a promise to keep that gat of yours out of sight?"

"That'd be a tough promise to keep if Marut reaches for his iron."

"Marut?"

"Traven. Croves. That guy." He pointed.

Hopper breathed deep. "If you shoot him, just wing him, will you please? How about a promise not to make me an accomplice to manslaughter?"

Tom couldn't honestly deliver any such promise. Hopper watched him for a minute then attempted to lighten the air. "Besides," he said with a flat chuckle, "who knows? We might have some use for this guy. Always looking for a good liar. We make screenwriters out of them. Chaplin, you say?"

Tom gave a shrug. "I'll try to keep my head."

Over ten years on with the LAPD, Tom had managed to rarely maim, and not once to kill. Still, he knew better than to trust himself. The last time he'd felt so explosive he was a USC sophomore fullback. As he began to rise after getting leveled by a high tackle, a Bruin guard named Gallo reared back and kicked him full in the face. The rest of the game, Tom felt out of control, murderous, and capable of anything.

Behind them, Marut appeared to conclude his tale. The fellow from Maine pumped his hand and thanked him, then jogged off to catch his wife who was chasing their kids up the sidewalk of Crescent Avenue toward the bathhouse.

Tom thought, since a trek up Metropole had somewhat eased his agitation, another climb might do the same.

Marut had passed by, gone ahead to lean on a piling and stare out to sea. He didn't glance over until Tom stood beside him.

"Let's take a walk," Tom said.

Marut appraised Tom then turned his attention to the producer, who wagged his head with certainty. "Not I," Hopper said. "Thing is, the way you two are behaving, I don't care to witness the outcome. No, you're on your own, boys. I'll be in The Pitcairn in the company of a tall mug and a cauldron of chowder."

Neither Marut nor Tom dared to walk out front of the other. Whenever they met with oncoming pedestrians, Tom stepped off the curb and the thief skirted the sea wall until the folks passed. Then the two men walked side by side again. Short of the casino, they crossed Crescent Avenue, started up Marilla Street, and turned onto Skyline Drive.

The road was the steepest on the island. Talk while trudging upward didn't appeal to either of them. At the end of the road, a goat trail commenced. In straight near-verticals punctuated by zigzags, it took them to an altitude several hundred feet above the road, to the spot Tom supposed was the crest of the island, at least on the Avalon side. He had climbed here yesterday, with hardly a change in his breathing. Today he panted. Pulse throbbed in both temples. Marut, older but wiry and taut as a trapeze artist, didn't appear to have broken a sweat.

At the crest overlook, wooden benches faced each other, a few feet apart, perpendicular to the cliff. The drop-off was straight down, with no relief except a few small manzanitas rooted in crags between granite slabs. Below, several dozen sloop, ketch, and clipper rigged sailboats made a flotilla pattern of red, green, yellow, and blue sails. All the vessels were aimed due east, as though to commence a leisurely attack on San Pedro.

Tom sat on the south bench, Marut on the bench straight across. Over the thief's shoulder, beyond thirty miles of pure sky, Tom spotted the Channel Islands off the Ventura coast. Marut seemed interested in nothing but his adversary. Such alert concentration, Tom supposed, might explain how a political agitator, a thief, and likely a murderer, could live to forty-some years in brutal lands during barbarous times.

"Being from Mexico," Tom said, "you'll know all about *la le de fuga.*"

"The law of fire, generally used to exonerate the cowardly *federale* who shoots a suspect, or an innocent, in the back."

"Shot while escaping, more or less. No?"

"And you bring up this phrase as a threat?"

"Did Hopper tell you I was an L.A. cop?"

"He did. In the saloon."

"Being a writer, a guy who keeps himself informed, you might have heard about our chief, James Davis?"

"I am an author's representative, not a writer," Marut said, with a cunning smile meant to imply Tom had best give up trying to make him fumble. "Still, I have heard of your chief, also known as Two Gun Davis."

"That's him. He's a big fan of *la ley de fuga*. Likes to apply it to all troublemakers. Bootleggers who don't play by the rules. Communists, now there's a sort he won't have congesting our jails or courthouses."

Marut let his smile widen. "I believe you *gringos* define as a Communist any fellow down on his luck who asks for a fair deal."

"Close enough," Tom said.

"And your message is that you could kill a Wobbly author, or his representative, with impunity?"

"Close enough."

Marut leaned his hands on his knees, far from the pistol in his pocket. "You won't kill me."

"Maybe not." Tom reached for his smoking gear. He filled, tamped, and lit the pipe then leaned back and puffed. "Depends on the rest of your story."

The man reset his sly expression. "And perhaps on how determined I, representing Traven, am about keeping all the loot."

"Loot?"

"Book revenues. Advances. Royalties. Motion picture rights."

"Ah," Tom said. "Say, how would you feel about Chaplin in the lead?"

Marut grimaced. "The mime?" he said with acute derision.

"So I figured," Tom said. "Go on with the story."

"At what point did you leave us?"

"The gunslinger just got employed by Pancho Villa."

"Yes, and the gunslinger frequented Babicora during the sojourn of Ambrose Bierce. And Bierce may have been marked for murder by Villa, to prevent the release of his unflattering exposé which the General could not allow, for both personal and political reasons.

"Or, perhaps Longabaugh feared the journalist would put the lie to his tale of dying by ambush in San Vicente, Bolivia, which the Pinkertons had never accepted. Those fellows, lackeys of the Union Pacific, would've caught the first southbound train at the faintest evidence of Longabaugh reappearing.

"Or perhaps Bierce died as the result of a simple argument between the two *gringos*, the cantankerous journalist and the hotheaded outlaw. In any case, the outcome was the death of Ambrose Bierce at the hand of Harry Longabaugh."

"What year?"

"February, nineteen hundred and fourteen."

"So, in nineteen hundred and fourteen, where was Charlie Hickey?"

With a curl of his lip for which Tom could see no reason unless to stoke his adversary's anger, Marut said, "Perhaps on a beach in Spain or Morocco, evading your war."

Tom viewed the implication—Charlie was a coward, an idler, a man without gumption—as evidence, the thief and murderer contending his victim was of little value. But sorrow had, at least for the moment, tamed his fury, so that what most engaged him was the man's admission that he knew plenty about Charlie Hickey.

"And from Morocco…" Tom rolled his hand.

Marut said, "After the European war and the fall of the socialist government of Bavaria, Traven chose Mexico as his new homeland, for the promise of the revolution. His hope lay with General Gildardo Magaña, who had assumed control of the Zapatista forces following their *jefe*'s tragic death at the hands of traitors. Should Magaña lead the army of the south to fulfill the Zapatista dream of *Tierra y Libertad*, Mexico would require wise and seasoned voices.

"While finding his way around this new and turbulent country, in the southern city of Morelos, Traven met Carlos the sailor."

When a grown man discovers that, no matter the armor in which he has sequestered his heart, he remains the same lost boy as ever, his first impulse is to run from the truth until he finds a suitable lie to hide behind. Only those with rare courage can shuck off the armor and make a stand.

Tom sat on the edge of his bench, uncertain which way to go.

Chapter Thirty-one

Tom leaped up and paced to the cliff and back. Marut studied his every move and upon his return, motioned for him to sit. Once Tom complied and a five-count stare down passed, the thief said, "Within months after meeting Carlos, Traven's hopes for true revolution waned. They fell prey to the grim realities facing the people's armies: battle fatigue, shortages of food and ammunition, influenza, and the appointment of de la Huerta as interim *presidente*.

"General Villa, having thrown in with de la Huerta, was granted a vast *hacienda* of his own. Even the election to the presidency of Àlvaro Obregón, the rival who would soon arrange for Villa's assassination, did not summon him back to arms. The deaths of two million countrymen may have tamed his tempestuous spirit.

"Without a cause to lead them, Traven and Carlos became vagabonds and wandered north from Morelos, as mechanics on the railroads, as prospectors in the Sierra Madre, as stevedores in Veracruz, and as roustabouts in the Tampico oil fields.

"After some months they arrived at Babicora, where Carlos found acquaintances of his youth among the Hearst ranch hands."

"Before L.A., he was a Texas cowboy," Tom said listlessly.

"Yes." If Tom had been alert, he might've detected a note of sympathy in Marut's voice. "These *gringos* arranged for the employ of both Carlos and Traven, the Texan as a *vaquero*, the German as a scribe.

"Evenings on Babicora, the two collaborated on a project they had begun during their travels. With Traven, the far more experienced writer, tutoring the sailor in the novelists' craft, they created *The Death Ship* together. Traven composed in German, Carlos in English, each submitting plot and detail, in essence translating the story into both languages as it unfolded."

Tom found himself picturing Charlie and Marut scribbling in the light of a campfire. The vision became a reverie.

"During these months, Harry Longabaugh returned to Babicora. Since the retirement of General Villa, he had gone home to Utah, tried his hand at bootlegging and, through indiscretions prompted by women and liquor, allowed the disclosure of his identity. Though Pinkerton's men, having found strike-breaking more lucrative than hunting *desperados*, no longer hounded him, your federal bureau soon took over.

"On Babicora, the superintendant engaged Longabaugh, now as a cowboy, now as a courier between the Hearst and Villa *haciendas*. Occasionally, under the influence of mescal, the outlaw would reveal his identity while boasting about his more colorful or lascivious escapades.

"Of course, ranch hands told tales, one of which concerned the murder of Ambrose Bierce.

"Carlos, as an admirer of the journalist, allowed these reports to overcome his caution. During the last weeks of collaboration on *The Death Ship*, he began drafting a story with which he intended to ingratiate himself to your Hearst."

Marut paused and watched Tom, no doubt looking for signs of homicidal rage. But Tom had lost all heart for spats. Such a calm had settled in him, he wondered whether it might be the state of those who appeared brave when facing a noose or firing squad.

Marut said, "Carlos compiled a number of interviews into an account that would at last solve the mystery of the vanishing journalist and gain him an introduction to the news mogul, who might then be of assistance in the publication of *The Death Ship*. And," the man leaned forward with a solemn gaze, "he entertained the hope that with Hearst in his corner, he might be safe in returning to Los Angeles, and reuniting with his children."

Tom only glared at the man for an instant, long enough to read Marut's expression and from it accept the truth of his last claim.

He stood, strode to the edge of the cliff, and wondered how flying would feel. He gripped the pleats of his trousers and watched the afternoon ferry split the whitecaps. Then he turned back and rolled his hand.

"One fateful evening," Marut said, "over a bottle, in a bunkhouse, Carlos mentioned his plan to a *compadre*. A man at the table, a miserable fellow, deep in debt, played the role of Judas.

"A day later, Carlos' pinto carried him home to the bunkhouse, with Carlos slumped over the horse's neck, a rifle bullet lodged in his formidable brain. Longabaugh had killed him, from afar."

Tom sat on the ground at the edge of the sheer cliff, legs dangling over. He rapped his pipe on a stone, stuffed it into one pocket, and reached for the flask in another. After one long swallow, he said, "I mean to investigate. You're lying, I'll find you."

"Yes," Marut said. "I believe you would."

The two men descended the mountain side by side, in silence. When they reached sea level, on the sidewalk of Crescent Avenue, Marut offered his hand. "Tom," he said. "I will consult with Traven, concerning a suitable financial arrangement."

Tom listlessly accepted the thief's hand.

Chapter Thirty-two

When Tom returned to the Atwater, he found a note from Madeline. "Gone rehearsing." He replied with a note. "Gone home. Call. Love, Tom"

He spent the ferry ride living in the past, in Mexico. After the drive home landed him in the present, he phoned Leo Weiss. Thirty years on the LAPD had given Leo contacts in departments all over the West. But in this case, he wasn't inclined to use any.

They had been friends since Tom was a neighbor boy. Never before had Leo strongly questioned or criticized any of his decisions. But now, even after Tom gave him the thief's entire story, Leo said, "What makes this Carlos in fact Charlie Hickey?"

"Charlie got a kick out of reading Ambrose Bierce."

"Says who?"

"Bud Gallagher."

"Lots of folks got a kick out of Bitter Bierce."

"Over the years, Bud told me plenty about my father. Not a single item didn't line up with Marut's account. When Charlie was a kid, his favorite horse was a pinto, like the one Marut said carried his corpse back to the hacienda. That enough for you?"

"You've heard the claim there's no such thing as coincidence?"

"Sure."

"Well it's crap," Leo said. "Now let's suppose this Marut gave it to you straight. What makes you think Longabaugh is still above ground?"

"Hope, is all. Look, Marut said when Villa got knocked off, Longabaugh scrammed out of Mexico. Maybe he later drowned in whiskey. Or syphilis got him. Maybe he's gone to Tahiti. Let's find out."

"Suppose you do. Then what?"

"I'll go for a visit. Have a talk. Then take care of him. Shot while escaping, like the Chief would have me do."

"Well," Leo said, "if you can get him back to L.A., on Davis turf, before you plug him, it might get you a medal and make you the star of a dime novel. You think that's worth the risk, go on."

"Which risk?"

"Your life. Your girls. Your goodness. Take your pick."

"Goodness?" Tom said. "What's that mean?"

"How many guys have you bumped off, Tom?"

"Never mind."

"You want to tell me Longabaugh's worse than Donny Katoulis. You let him live, bucking orders, no less."

"Katoulis didn't kill Charlie Hickey."

"Then you're saying the penalty for murder ought to depend upon who you kill. Think that one over," Leo said. "Now, Violet's calling me."

"You'll look into what became of Longabaugh?"

"I might," Leo said, which meant he would, only against his better judgment.

Next Tom called Bud Gallagher and asked if he could bring over some groceries. Though Bud was on doctor's orders to lay off the booze, when Tom offered to stop by the market, the old fellow asked for nothing but Johnny Walker.

Bud's place was a faux-Spanish bungalow. Tile roof, dappled beige panels, arched windows in front. Bud had ordered the bungalow out of the Sears Roebuck catalog and pieced it together with the help of a gang of fellow butchers—Charlie Hickey for one. The place was once a charmer featuring a manicured lawn and beds of posies, its wooden floor always polished and tables and chairs protected with throws and doilies. Since Bud lost Maureen, and lost track of their son, it had gradually descended into a mess of torn upholstery, bare light bulbs in cracked lamps, and so many dishes strewn around, Bud must have bought extra sets to keep from frequent washing.

The old man saw no need to apologize. He started right in on the Johnny Walker, poured a teacup half full and asked Tom if he wanted a dose.

Tom passed. "I got the story," he said, then gave the book thief's account without a single interruption. The last few minutes, Bud sat squirming, but he didn't get up and make his trip to the john until Tom concluded, with the death of Charlie Hickey.

When Bud returned to his chair, he said, "That's a doozy of a tale. Put it together with *The Death Ship*, you've got yourself a regular epic. You buy it?"

Tom repeated what he had told Leo, about the pinto and Charlie's fondness for Bierce.

"I'm with you," Bud said. "Sounds like Charlie all right. Now what?"

"Are you still getting to the library?"

"Most days."

"Think you could sweet talk those admirers of yours into scouring the stacks for leads on the Sundance Kid?"

"Could I?" Bud said, with a wink, as he lifted his glass and drank to the quest.

In Leo and Bud, Tom had enlisted researchers with first-rate connections. But Florence proved their superior.

Tom's sister had abundant resources. During the wild years between graduation from Normal School and settling into her first teaching position, she ran off to San Francisco and supported her nightlife wardrobe with a Dickensian occupation. Ten hours a day, six days a week, she read newspapers for Allen's Press Clipping Bureau, a venerable institution, one of whose founding partners was Mark Twain.

Film studios that wanted to scrapbook every single published mention of their stars hired Allen's. For a tire manufacturer that hoped to glean all the latest innovations concerning the processing of rubber, Allen's was the ticket.

Florence had specialized in newspapers. Each day she read every word of every article in twenty some rags from the Northwest.

Aside from her brains, Florence had a gift for securing favors from men. A supervisor who remembered her well set the current stable of readers on a special project. The very next morning, Tom had his lead, out of the *Sacramento Bee*.

A reader named Brian, a Cal Berkeley Economics major with a photographic memory, recalled an article from March and retrieved it from the archives. He telephoned Florence and dictated while she transcribed in shorthand. That afternoon, she handed him a typed copy.

The article profiled Willie Scranton. Having gotten nabbed for passing bum checks in Lodi, Willie turned snitch. His story, as passed through an unnamed source to the reporter, was as outlandish as the thief's tale.

Scranton claimed to have run with the Weaver gang, who specialized in bank robberies around the plains states and Midwest. During various seasons, the reporter asserted, notable crooks belonged to the Weaver gang. Dillinger, Machine Gun Kelly, Harvey Bailey, Pretty Boy Floyd, Frank O'Bannion, and the Sundance Kid, under the alias Hiram Beebe.

Most of the twenty-some hours between Tom's assigning his sister to research and Florence's delivering the article, he had spent with dime novels provided by the Wilshire branch library. The portraits of Longabaugh he read had left him feeling called to track and slay a demon.

Scranton's claims that the brains of the Weaver gang, Betty Weaver, was lodged at the Congress Hotel in Tucson, Arizona, set Tom's mind awhirl. He slapped the crown of his head.

"Fly?" his sister asked.

"Betty Weaver," he said.

"Who's she?"

"A gal I read about."

"So?"

"Betty Weaver is the daughter of Etta Place."

"Etta who?"

"The dame who had a rough time choosing between two outlaws. Harry Longabaugh and his partner Butch Cassady."

Chapter Thirty-three

Tom phoned Leo, briefed him and asked for the official line on Willie Scranton of Lodi.

Leo promised to phone Sacramento. Though Tom had little hope of getting an answer in less than a day or two, Leo called within an hour. He said, "Scranton's a rube, little man with big stories. First place, Betty Weaver's a pro, wouldn't touch the likes of him. Next, Tucson's the last burg you'll find a gang of hoods, ever since the feds nailed Dillinger there."

"Right," Tom said.

"Meaning what?"

"I'll send you a postcard."

"Don't bother," Leo grumbled.

Chapter Thirty-four

Tom left his Chevy with Florence, as she requested. He caught a cab across town to the San Pedro-Avalon evening ferry, feeling lousy about leaving Elizabeth behind again. But the upcoming skirmish between her mom and dad, he preferred she didn't witness.

Tom was first off the ferry. He hustled up Crescent Avenue, all the way admiring his destination, an architectural wonder. The Casino was Art Deco and fully circular, high as a twelve-story building and surrounded on three sides by the harbor.

At the entrance, he used his badge to impress the lone security guard, a Filipino who appeared too shy for such work. He skirted the ground-floor theatre where, on account of its silver-and-gilded splendor and sublime acoustics, Goldwyn and DeMille often debuted films. Hearing the Paul Perkins orchestra and Madeline's wistful voice all the way, he hustled up the circular ramp, the idea for which Mister Wrigley had gleaned from the layout of his Chicago ballpark.

The ballroom was a musician's Eden. The sky-high domed ceiling clarified every sound. Probably no angel voice could've wrenched Tom's heart as did Madeline's sultriest tones delivering the news about "Stormy Weather." He entered and stood just inside. On the circular dance floor a modest crowd performed the fox trot, only hundreds compared to the several thousand the space could hold. Beyond them, onstage, Tom's wife swayed beneath the spotlights. She wore a lagoon blue, skin-tight gown tinted gold and silver by the ballroom's décor.

Her next number was a whispery "Cheek to Cheek" and then came a heart-rending "Brother Can You Spare a Dime," which until now Tom hadn't heard her sing:

"Once I built a railroad, I made it run, made it race against time. Once I built a railroad; now it's done. Brother, can you spare a dime?"

So far, she and Tom had kept from hitting the skids, but from her performance anybody could see she was an artist who managed to feel even what she hadn't lived.

At least she could feel what, in these years, any artist who fell short of the big-time might know before the final buzzer. Poverty. He only wished she possessed faith like Florence, who trusted both in providence and in Tom.

He met her at the steps leading off stage. With nudges and apologies, he eased her away from a huddle of admirers. He walked her out, through one of the high French doors. On the balcony that overlooked the glittering harbor speckled by lamplight and moon glow, he took both her hands and they faced off.

"Tomorrow, I'm going to Tucson," he said, as softly as could be heard over the talk, laughter, and the boom and crackle of surf outside the harbor.

This morning he had phoned and given her a capsule rendition of the book thief's tale of the sailor and German, how they created *The Death Ship* together, and why he leaned toward believing the man's claim that Harry Longabaugh had gunned down Charlie Hickey.

Maybe, Tom thought, Madeline took her husband as a simpleton for buying such a yarn. Or maybe she couldn't imagine him finding any trace of the Sundance Kid, and supposed that truth would dawn on him before he set out on some quixotic mission.

Whatever her reasons, this morning she had treated Tom gently, sympathized in a voice as if she were inviting him into her arms.

Now she stared as though at an impertinent stranger. "Why the hell?"

He told her about the Sacramento article, Willie Scranton, and Betty Weaver, who might be Longabaugh's daughter.

She said, "Dammit, Tom."

"What's that mean?"

"You figure it out." She wheeled and rushed inside, into a crowd of the privileged few not banished by hard times from such elegant settings.

Madeline cared for the gentry as little as did Tom. She saw most of them as arrogant, conniving, or silly. Still, tonight she wouldn't let Tom pry her away.

Chapter Thirty-five

Tom did most of that night's waiting in the Atwater lobby or the adjoining bar. As Paul Perkins' musicians arrived, beginning soon after two a.m., Tom attempted not to act peeved or worried as he asked for clues to her whereabouts.

Mitch, a trombonist, said, "Clientele thinks she's a dream, Tom. They all want a piece of her, won't cut her loose."

When Louis the drummer suggested going to her rescue, Tom heeded the advice. But by now, the Casino lights were dimmed and the doors locked. He saw nobody except a janitor whom Tom thought he recognized as one of the islanders from *Mutiny on the Bounty*. The man was neither willing to talk nor let him in to look around.

Perkins and a few of the boys were renting a house halfway up Manila Avenue, but if Tom found his wife there, the ensuing scene would likely bring grief to all. He chose to tell himself a story in which she got invited by a married couple of fans to their tourist cottage and by now was asleep in the spare room.

While he wandered, he half convinced himself she was only sending a message, showing him what his future could bring. He pretended to consider his options for the Charlie Hickey business, though he had only one. Never would he find peace, with or without his girls, until he settled with Charlie's killer or knew the murderer was in hell.

At dawn he joined a hardy gang of commuters and caught the day's first ferry to Long Beach. A cab delivered him to Florence's duplex before eight.

Elizabeth leaped, climbed, clung to his neck, and wouldn't let go until he had sat and settled her onto his lap. Then she petted the parrot on his silk tie and asked, "What's the desert, Daddy?"

"A hot and sandy place." He pointed vaguely east. "A few hours that way."

"Aunty won't tell me why you need to go there. Will you tell me?"

"I need to find a guy."

"What guy?"

"A cowboy who knew your grandpa."

"I don't know my grandpa," she said. "Tell me about him, please?"

"When I come home," Tom promised.

"Tomorrow?"

"Maybe, or the next day. I hope so, babe." He squeezed her as tightly as her tender self could bear.

When he let go, she wore an earnest frown. "Daddy. If it's hot and you stay too long, won't you melt?"

Tom managed not to chuckle, but he failed to suppress the grin that possessed him. "I'll be careful."

"If you start to melt, run into the shade."

"You bet."

"And drink iced tea."

"You bet."

"Promise."

"Yes, ma'am, I surely do."

She must have learned more from his expression than from his answers, because the talk left her weepy.

Florence sent her to pick breakfast strawberries.

"How about taking a few days off," Tom suggested, "going out to the island and staying with my girl and Madeline?"

"That's a swell idea," Florence said.

"If you get a chance, stick up for me, would you?"

"The wife's in a snit?"

"My guess is, she's debating between homicide and divorce."

"Then me sticking up for you might backfire, Tommy. Maybe I'd better give her the chance to cut loose and scream about her lousy husband. You know, get it out of her system."

"So long as Elizabeth's absent. A kid doesn't need to know she's got a louse for a dad."

The girl returned with her harvest. They removed to the kitchen. While Florence washed and sliced berries and cooked oatmeal, she said, "Don't kick yourself, Tommy. You're doing the right thing. Matter of fact, you're my hero. Only, would you take some advice?"

"Depends."

"Keep your head. What we're after is the truth about our daddy." She stepped to his side and patted the bulge in the side of his coat. "Put that thing in your suitcase."

"Harry Longabaugh's a gunfighter."

"And, if he's still kicking, he's too smart to gun down a fellow just for asking questions, or else he wouldn't have lived to be seventy."

"You know his age, do you?"

"I can read same as you can."

She dished breakfast, settled them at the table, fetched milk and orange juice, and walked off to the bedroom. When she returned, she handed Tom a manila envelope.

Tom remembered the photo, which he had found long ago underneath the shelf paper of a dresser drawer while he prepared to liquidate Milly's possessions.

It was taken in 1909 by a photographer at the opening celebration of the Santa Monica Pier. Florence was a smiley blond baby with most of her curly locks tucked into a bonnet. Tom was four-year-old with a tough-guy scowl, as if the photographer had pinched him.

Charlie Hickey knelt with strong bare arms tugging them to his sides, sporting a look that reminded Tom of himself, since Elizabeth came. The grin of a proud and grateful father.

If he hadn't been conscious of the hypocrisy of considering prayer only when you're five points down with seconds remaining, or when backed against the firing squad's wall, he might've asked Florence to send one off for him.

Chapter Thirty-six

The day before, while a maintenance fellow from Sister Aimee's L.I.F.E. Bible College changed the oil in Tom's Chevrolet and topped off the radiator, Florence had bought a canvas desert water bag, filled and hung it by the rope around the eagle hood ornament. This morning she uncorked the bag and held it out while Elizabeth dropped in a dozen ice cubes.

Also, Florence gave him a map she'd acquired and marked with the recommended summer route, the one truckers used, which an Auto Club fellow assured her offered the widest, best pavement and the shortest distance between outposts.

Tom drove the girls to the Long Beach ferry landing. For Elizabeth's sake, except that he promised to bring her a Navajo rag doll, he made his good-byes as casual as if he meant to return by suppertime. Florence played along.

As Tom pulled away, he switched on the Motorola. While the signal held and the station wasn't playing any number Madeline performed, his spirits leaned toward confident and hopeful. Assisted by the rank smell and sight of oil derricks like a swarm of invading sea monsters, the bleating horns and needless stops and swerves of novice drivers, and the grace of small boats gliding over the Pacific swells, he kept dread at a distance all the way to San Diego and east to the mountains.

Around midday, he pulled off at the Alpine post office and mercantile and emptied one of the gallon jugs of water Florence had provided down the front of the radiator. Then he climbed

Viejas grade, grumbling curses whenever he needed to ride the shoulder while a truck as wide as the goat-trail road came barreling down at him, spewing a dust storm into his path.

He stopped again at the Guatay Store, for gas and tobacco and to fill the empty jug with water. Even up here, only a couple miles of road and less than a thousand feet of altitude below the summit, a thermometer in the shade indicated ninety-five degrees. The store clerk, a slight graying fellow with a cracked lens on his spectacles, fired questions while he pumped gas. He surmised Tom was from L.A. and grilled him about smog, movie stars, and Okies squatting on the beaches.

Tom said, "You ought to go take a look."

"Where you headed?" the clerk asked.

"Tucson."

The clerk commenced with stories about the perils of the desert. Bands of wild Apaches escaped from the reservations, rattlesnakes climbing into parked cars for shade, hobos getting booted off the train in Gila Bend then stealing guns and becoming highwaymen.

"Desert's a taste of perdition, brother. A blast furnace. Twenty-some dropped dead from the heat in the first month of summer. Say, you sure don't want to try crossing the desert till after sundown."

By now a wiry trucker had joined them, sweating as if he'd climbed the mountains on foot. "Got up to one-thirty yesterday," he said. "What make of tires you running?"

"Goodyear," Tom said.

The trucker wagged his head. "Firestone, you might make it. Others, not on your life."

Tom thanked them for the encouragement and drove on.

A mile beyond Tecate Divide, a fiery gale struck, as if the clerk and trucker were agents of a God who swiftly punished those who dismissed his advice. Leaves, sticks, wrappers, all manner of flotsam whizzed past or smacked the windshield. Tom rolled up the windows and tugged his Stetson fedora down to his ears to lessen the sun's glare.

No sooner did he regain a bit of composure, feel somewhat accustomed to driving in a firestorm, than he reached the downgrade. The road, barely wide enough for a car to pass a bicycle, snaked between stacks and pillars of gray and copper boulders so massive, had Pharaohs discovered them, they could have built even grander pyramids. As this was Tom's first trip on the route, between mopping sweat with his sleeve and attempting to stay on pavement while maneuvering hairpin turns, he gaped at the stark beauty. Teetering rocks the size of piggybacked railroad cars. The valley loomed below, brown and flat with jagged fringes and tiny dots of green, all the way to the end of the world, under the same bleached sky. Only a single, angel-white cloud appeared to rise from the earth into heaven.

As he reached the foot of the grade, the firestorm subsided into gusts. The ominous cloud loomed up ahead, and Tom thought of stories about typhoons out at sea. As he neared the cloud, a taste and smell so bitter greeted him, an instinct suggested he brake, spin the wheel, and scram back up the mountain.

He drove into the cloud, peered around in amazement and horror, and discovered a town of sorts. Plaster City. A quarry from which chalk-white geysers spouted. A cluster of wind-bent shacks, a general store, and a sprawling barn-like structure with a sign: U.S. Gypsum.

Coughing and dabbing grit from his eyes, Tom gaped at the working men and women carrying bundles and boys and girls, all of their movements slow and their flesh, hair, and garments from ghostly white to the gray of peasants' laundry. They looked less like people than like a race especially bred to live in a place where common humans couldn't survive.

Once he left Plaster City behind, the heat felt less sufferable, as long as he kept swilling water, pouring it onto his head, and using the sturdy brim of his Stetson to fan himself.

Not long ago, Tom and Madeline had attended a party thrown by a friend from his time driving a sales and delivery route for Alamo Meat. The friend had a visiting cousin, a salesman for a San Diego wholesaler. Once a week, his route took him over the mountains to El Centro. When his eight-year-old son rode along, after a blistering day and a night in a roach-infested motor hotel, the boy proposed a theory. He said desert-dwellers must all be escaped convicts who had run there because police wouldn't dare chase them into such a place.

Tom considered that theory quite reasonable, and it lifted his hope of meeting the Sundance Kid in Tucson.

At the Texaco in El Centro where he stopped for gas and to refill the water jugs, he vowed to call his sister the minute he reached Tucson and gush his thanks for supplying the jugs. The brackish water, served through a hose, was close to boiling, but at least it was wet.

East of El Centro, he admired the laborers in the lettuce and alfalfa fields along the canals. Tom, who featured himself a stalwart fellow and a willing worker, supposed he was a twerp and slacker compared to those folks.

To his baked and fatigued mind, the Algodones Dunes, mountains ground to dust by an ancient sea, appeared bizarre and majestic as if he had slept and awakened on a far-off planet

He descended into the Rio Colorado Valley. Across the river lay the town of Yuma with its riverside hotels, a winter playground for the Hollywood set. A ghost town from June to October, until two years ago.

Doomsayers called 1934 the beginning of the end, when the Great Plains and Midwest got sentenced to pay for a century of reckless farming. Deep plowing of the virgin topsoil had displaced the natural deep-rooted grasses that secured the soil and retained moisture even through droughts and gale winds. The farmers hadn't bothered with crop rotation. They had allowed fields to lie fallow. They hadn't sown cover crops. So when the drought came, and the gale winds rose, the deep, dry, barren soil turned to dust. With crops dead and blown away or buried, their mortgages foreclosed upon, and their lungs blighted by the dust pneumonia, millions of folks trekked west.

Now, Yuma could boast a year-round population of thousands, on account of the migrant camps where refugees got stalled en route from the Dust Bowl to the Promised Land.

Winterhaven, a cluster of tents and huts on the California side of the river bridge, was the post to which Chief Davis had assigned Tom before the police commission ruled against the deployment of detectives. A half dozen sentries loitered in the shade of a tarpaulin canopy at the western foot of the bridge over which a solid line of pedestrians trod and all manner of jalopies waited, sputtered, occasionally crawled. Two sentries questioned pedestrians. Three sentries halted the vehicles and interrogated the drivers and passengers.

While Tom descended toward the border, he watched the sentries send back across the bridge two pickups loaded with furniture and a stake-bed truck carrying a dozen or so men, a few of whom shouted protests. Along the riverbank downstream and upstream, as far as the shimmering air allowed Tom to see, lawmen on horseback patrolled.

Had Tom cared to stop, he might've found the Winterhaven compound to be an oasis, stocked with beer on ice, electric fans, and a chance to rest among fellow L.A. cops before subjecting himself and his Chevy to the stretch of Sonoran Desert where the hottest temperatures in the nation were common.

Tom didn't stop, knowing the comfort might break his will and convince him to stay and sleep. He had promised his little girl he would hurry and assured Madeline, in a note he gave Florence to deliver, he wouldn't waste a minute on this dubious mission.

No one blocked the lane over the bridge into Arizona. As Tom crossed the border, he checked his Bulova. Twelve minutes after four p.m. Before long, he reasoned, the heat would begin to wane.

An hour later, as he approached the village of Tacna, he revised his reasoning. He had stretched his arms up, accidentally touched the roof, and sizzled his finger. He looked up to check for a burn hole in the headliner.

Then he spotted the boy.

Chapter Thirty-seven

At first, he thought the sight a mirage or the shadow of an ominous desert bird, maybe a vulture. He tapped the brakes and keened his dry, sand-pocked eyes.

The boy was across the road, trudging west. He wore a man-sized woolen coat that hung to his knees. Instead of wearing a hat, he held up a section of newspaper for shade. Though the boy didn't signal him or appear to notice the car passing, Tom wheeled a U-turn and pulled alongside. When he shut off the motor, the radiator spewed steam.

The boy stopped still. He stared with defiance both hard and brittle, as if he might any instant crack and give over to weeping.

Tom slipped out the passenger side of the car. The boy appraised him, then broke into a dash made pitiful by wobbling legs and a list to one side. Tom only had to lope to catch up. When he tapped the boy on the shoulder, the boy attempted a burst of speed.

Tom lunged and tackled him. The boy thrashed. His baggy woolen coat flapped at his side, and something hard in the left lower pocket whopped Tom's elbow. Tom reached in and caught hold of the offending item. An aged Smith and Wesson Model 3 pistol.

The boy quit thrashing and lay on his side.

Tom held the boy down while he checked the cylinders. They were loaded. He said, "Did you get this item from Billy the Kid?"

"Lemmee up," the boy said, as he reached and clutched his knees. He commenced a fit of wheezing. When he recovered, Tom stepped back.

The boy scrambled to his knees. "You a cop, sir?" His voice was mostly breath.

"Never mind me. What brings you out here to the middle of nothing?"

"Coming from Phoenix. Ran out of rides. After a while, my thumb give out."

Tom helped the boy up and to the car, provided a jug of tepid water, and got his name. Clarence. Went by C.J. He was slight, dirty blond, adorned with a million tiny freckles. When Tom asked his destination, he said, "Sir, please give me back my gun?"

"Who do you plan to shoot?"

C.J. wagged his head.

"Jackrabbits?"

"Sure. Rabbits."

"Where do you think you'll find them?"

The boy's gray eyes shifted side-to-side. "Around Yuma, I figure."

"I'll get you there," Tom said. "Next stop east is what?"

"Gila Bend."

"Gila Bend, I'll put you on a bus."

The boy pondered. "And give my pistol back?"

"Not likely."

The boy's face flushed beet red. "Dammit, sir." His eyes pinched shut. Tears seeped out. "Took me a whole week digging ditches in Phoenix to buy it."

Tom only nodded and kept silent. The boy wiped his face. "Sir, can a man go to jail for what he means to do?"

"Could, if he's planning to overthrow the government, rob a bank, murder a big shot. Short of those kind, he's got to do it first."

"You one of the border cops?" he said, like an accusation.

"Nope. Name's Tom. You've got a beef with the border cops?"

The boy sat still and silent for so long, Tom considered driving on just to feel some breeze. Dusk began to pale the glare.

"You ain't going to stop me," C.J. said.

"Stop you?"

"Shooting the cop that's got my sister. You ain't going to stop me, I tell you."

"This cop got a name?"

"Loftus." His lip curled as though preparing to spit. "You know him?"

"Tall, lanky, redhead?"

"That's the one. He a pal of yours?"

"Depends," Tom said. "What'd he do?"

C.J. leaned back into the seat and covered his eyes with one hand. "He's got Missy. Told Ma and Pa they could go on west long as she stayed behind and worked for him. Housekeeper, he called it. A ways up the road, Ma started crying. We pulled over and, well the upshot is, they sent me back to keep an eye out."

The boy's hand pressed harder onto his eyes and he shuddered. "I ain't going to tell you no more."

"No need." Tom reached for the starter button. With the motor at a rough idle, gearbox in neutral, he stepped out and poured half a jug down the front of the radiator.

Then he climbed in and drove west.

Chapter Thirty-eight

Loftus had his own place. Along with a gang of other cops, he rented a wooden shack in a court on the Arizona side, a mile or so upriver from Yuma. The boy said, "Nobody lives out that way but cops and Indians. And Missy."

The court was U-shaped, with a dirt lot for parking on the open end. When Tom pulled in between an LAPD cruiser and a paddy wagon, the men on benches around a long table in the courtyard turned from their poker hands and stared. The moon was a sliver, but abundant stars offered adequate light.

Several men stood and ambled toward them. Tom knew the burly one out front. Marlon Brooks had served with him as a rookie detective. A soft-spoken, diligent cop. While assigned to juvenile division he had questioned an order, got busted back to uniform, and later assigned to the border detail.

Tom and the boy stood in front of the car. From twenty yards away, Brooks said, "Tom Hickey?" He came another few steps but stopped when he recognized the boy at Tom's side. "Oh oh."

"Marlon," Tom said, "you want to take me to Larry Loftus?"

Brooks glanced at each of the two men who flanked him, stiff as bookends. "You fellas know Tom?"

"Heard of him," one man said.

"First off," Marlon said, "this is an official visit?"

Tom didn't answer. "On my way to Tucson, I happened upon C.J. here. I believe you know him."

"Seen him around, sure. First off, Loftus don't beat the girl, nothing like that. He did, we'd of made him pay."

"Swell," Tom said. "Which ones of you keep her from running while Loftus is on duty?"

Brooks glanced at the others then sighed and shrugged. "Mostly Frenchy. You won't find him around tonight. He's on mounted patrol."

Tom motioned toward the bench. "Loftus among the card players?"

"Nope."

"Where do I find him?"

Marlon gazed toward the stars and worked his slit of a mouth like a gambler deciding whether to fold. "You're putting me on the spot here, Tom."

"Can't be helped."

"We could run you off."

"I'd come back."

"That you would." Once again, Marlon glanced both ways then shrugged and sighed. "Number four."

"Thanks," Tom said. "Watch the boy for me, will you?"

"Hell with that," C.J. yelped, and dashed toward shack number four. The man on Brooks' left grabbed and cinched him. The boy thrashed until Tom caught up and laid a firm hand on his shoulder.

"Hold still and you'll get your chance. Keep up the fuss, these fellas are going to hog-tie you."

Tom passed by the card players. Though he knew a few of them, he didn't acknowledge. He stopped in front of number four and tried the knob. Then he leaned back and kicked with the sole of his brogan.

The door flew open and dangled on one hinge.

As Tom rushed in, he drew the Colt .38 automatic from his shoulder holster.

The shack was a single room with a cookstove, icebox, sink, toilet, and a pallet in the corner, from which Loftus had risen to his knees.

He wore army-issue undershorts. The girl beside him lay wrapping a brown serape tighter around herself. She was small and pale with grand round eyes and even more tiny freckles than her brother.

Tom said, "Hold still, Larry. Missy, move off the bed, please. Over here would be best." He motioned toward the front door.

She trembled while she sat and tugged the serape still tighter. Then she bolted up and scampered away from the bed, but opposite to Tom's suggestion. She pressed herself against the wall beside the shack's rear door.

Tom hollered, "Marlon, bring the boy in."

As C.J. entered, escorted by Brooks and another fellow, one on each arm, his sister slid down, her back scraping the wall. She came to rest seated on the floor with her face pressed to her knees. Timid peeps issued out of her.

With the barrel of his pistol, Tom motioned to Loftus. "Off the bed. Face down on the floor."

Loftus only stared, didn't budge. He looked like a wooden Don Quixote topped with a fright wig made of rhubarb. When at last he opened his mouth, a wag of Tom's gun hushed him.

"No need to talk," Tom said. "Off the bed, on your belly."

The man crawled off the bed and lay on the wooden floor, his face turned toward the girl.

Tom managed a gentle voice to call her name. After a minute and his third attempt, she raised her head and looked him in the eye.

"Missy," Tom asked, "what should I do with him?"

The girl shuddered and clutched both sides of her thick, straw-blond hair. Again, she shuddered, but her voice came strong and clear. "Shoot him."

Tom bent forward and sighted the gun on the back of Loftus' skull. The floorboards beside the man's shorts darkened. Tom listened for a whimper from the man but heard nothing.

"Roll over," he commanded.

Loftus obeyed. Tom drew a bead on the man's nose. He glanced at the girl. She had covered her eyes with the blanket.

Tom lifted his right foot hip high, then caught his balance. He slammed the large brogan down hard. The man's kneecap splintered. Loftus' howl filled the room with echo.

While Brooks and another cop dragged Loftus, still wailing and cussing, to a paddy wagon in which they raced off to a hospital, Tom handed a ten and two fives to Marlon Brooks. He said, "Get the kids over the line, to the coast."

Then he sat on the running board of his Chevy and brooded.

He had assured the end of his career with the LAPD. But what troubled him most was that, if he hadn't imagined the girl facing prison for conspiring in a homicide, he would have gladly squeezed the trigger.

Chapter Thirty-nine

As long as the railroad paralleled the highway, Tom spotted flames or sparks from cook-fires, at least one every mile or so. Probably folks booted off the trains. A decent man, he supposed, would stop at least once and offer a few hobos a ride out of the wasteland, or water, or a handout. But he wouldn't risk another errand. Already, stopping for C.J. had cost him a career.

In Gila Bend, the Texaco was open. The attendant was a stooped, aged Mexican who advised him to drive all night. He said, "One twenty-three today. Tomorrow," he predicted, "mucho hot."

A few miles northeast, Tom braked for an unworldly sight. A small army of sidewinders, fifty or more, slithered across the pavement as though fleeing a disastrous battle. The next eerie sight was a cluster of shooting stars that whizzed like fire-arrows attacking a settlement just beyond a craggy mountain range. And when Tom's eyes returned to the road, bright yellow eyes greeted him. Something scampered away before he reached it. Though he had little knowledge of desert wildlife, he imagined an armadillo.

As the stars began to blur into pools of light, he pulled off at a turnout beside the first grove of saguaros he had noticed. He shut the motor, waited for the dieseling to halt, then gathered his pipe and tobacco. He climbed out, stretched, and rounded the car, eyes cast down on the lookout for sidewinders, scorpions, tarantulas, armadillos, and any other mysterious creature that might inhabit these badlands. Nothing moved. As he reached for his zipper, he spotted a sign, small and half covered by a creosote bush.

After he zipped up, he stepped closer to the sign and bent to read: *Beware of Javelina.*

"Javelina?" he mumbled.

He hustled back to the car, climbed in through the rear door and sprawled as best a six-two man could on seat four-five door to door. After he squirmed into the least annoying posture, he tried to imagine a javelina. He conjured a vision of a giant sidewinder with armor-plated scales, yellow eyes bright as a noon sun, and a gaping mouth out of which shot tongues of fire. Then the vision became something more human that recalled the palooka named Rusty, in east Burbank, the pimp he had watched Milo Saropian thrash. A shiver crept through him.

Even after he banished the vision, he listened for rustling through the creosote and tumbleweeds. He rolled his shoulders, reached around and massaged his neck, counted backward from fifty, and at last drifted into the weird, hazy thoughts that set the stage for sleep.

Then he remembered Larry Loftus, the screams and curses, and most of all the pleasure of delivering justice. As close as he could describe, the feeling was release, a sudden burst of freedom. Much like one Stanford game when a horde of Goliath-sized linemen bore down on him, and somehow, magically, he broke through and ran for a touchdown.

He wondered if such pleasure from maiming a fellow meant he was as wicked as his mother. Maybe all along he had fooled himself into playing by rules that didn't apply in any world except the one Florence and her Bible thumpers dreamed of. Maybe forgiveness and mercy were only illusions conjured out of weakness.

Maybe a fierce joy awaited, once he caught up with Charlie Hickey's killer.

Chapter Forty

Going southeast during the first few hours after sunrise, the stands of saguaros and mesquite got denser, the sky went from silver-brown to deep blue, and either the air cooled a bit or Tom was rapidly becoming a desert rat.

Once again, he vowed to call Florence the minute he booked a room in Tucson. This morning his gratitude was over the thermos she had packed in her wicker picnic basket, along with the water jugs, a bear claw, and several bananas.

Madeline usually awoke before eleven. He would call her at noon Mountain Time, and hope she hadn't given orders to the hotel switchboard to block any calls from Arizona.

As the climb leveled to a plateau, sand gave way to pasture, cotton fields, orange groves crowded with pickers, and camps where gangs of barefoot children lugged buckets, peddled eggs or apples, or chased each other alongside the irrigation ditches.

The first signs of a city were clusters of the flat-roofed adobe cottages that had inspired half the architects in L.A. Tom had appreciated the style until developers littered Los Angeles and Orange counties with endless tracts of flimsy imitations.

Following the Tucson map the Auto Club provided, upon which he had marked an X, Tom left the highway at Broadway, then merged onto Congress Street and passed several brownstone and brick office buildings higher than he had expected in a frontier town. A block beyond the Fox Theatre, he parked in front of the Congress Hotel.

Though he knew better, as he stepped out of the car, he wondered if there might be a kernel of truth in a Hearst news account
that implied the ghost of John Dillinger haunted the place.
Dillinger had captured lots of imaginations.

After the stock market crashed, and then Prohibition got
repealed, a breed of shrewd and ruthless men who might've
otherwise made their fortunes in stocks or booze turned to
bank robbery.

John Dillinger was a prodigy. Among the stories, Tom's favorite had the gang entering a bank in the guise of a Hollywood
crew filming a robbery scene and leaving with a real $100,000.

Two years ago, a murderous escape from prison in Lima,
Ohio, landed Dillinger at the top of the FBI's most-wanted list.
Then, a dozen bank jobs later, he and some pals sought to lay
low in Tucson.

In January of last year, a fire in the Congress Hotel basement
climbed the elevator shaft to the third floor, where the Dillinger
gang resided. The switchboard operator alerted guests, and the
gang escaped out the windows on rope ladders. Where Dillinger
went wrong was giving a hefty tip to the firemen, who then
retrieved and delivered the gang's luggage, which included an
arsenal and better than $20,000 in cash. The gang relocated to a
house on North Second Avenue. But one of the firemen, a reader of
True Detective Magazine, recognized some faces and called the law.

The *Tucson Citizen* reported, "In five hours, without firing a
single shot, our police accomplished what the combined forces
of several states and the FBI had failed to do over many months."
When they nabbed him, Dillinger said, "Well, I'll be damned!"

Since then, Dillinger had escaped once again, gathered
another gang, and knocked off banks around Illinois, Wisconsin,
Indiana, and Ohio before he got fingered by a Chicago madam.
Feds and local cops caught him leaving a movie theater. One
of them fired a shot that severed his spinal cord and ripped
through his brain.

But a different story circulated around the LAPD, where
respect for the FBI was rare. In this version, the dead guy wasn't

Dillinger, but one Jimmy Lawrence, whose fingerprints didn't match Dillinger's, who was a bit taller, whose eyes were a different shade, and who had a rheumatic heart, which the autopsy clearly showed.

By Tom's estimate, one of life's thorniest problems was knowing who to believe, since too many people, maybe most, were born or bred liars. For all Tom knew, Dillinger might still be running free.

Chapter Forty-one

The Santa Fe came rattling and screeching, only a block from the Congress Hotel. Tom, who found the racket and sight of trains calming, stood on the sidewalk in front of the entrance and watched fifty-some boxcars and flatbeds rumble past.

Inside, the hotel was the dark wood of an Old West saloon. A wide archway led from the lobby to a lounge with a theatrical motif, including drama masks, comedy and tragedy, and mannequins in flapper costumes Tom supposed came from the Rialto Theater across the street.

Before his arrival, Tom had intended to book a room, call Florence and Madeline, and rest or nap an hour or two before investigating. But the desk clerk was a curly brunette with large twinkling green eyes. Her breasts, in a frilly white blouse, posed lovingly on the counter. She flashed him a coy smile.

Well aware that flirty gals often loved to talk even at the risk of telling secrets, Tom strolled over. He gripped his bag in his left hand, and leaned his right elbow on the counter.

"Mister," the gal said with concern, "you look a bit done in."

"Long drive. All night long."

"Passing through?"

"Nope. Stopping over."

"Business?"

Tom nodded.

"Well, you've come to the right place. Now what all can *I* do for you?" Her voice was melodic, uncannily like Madeline's singing.

"I'd better start with a room."

"We've got a few of those. Single?" She offered an ivory smile. Tom said, "Just me."

She reached under the counter, lifted out a leather-bound volume and opened it to the bookmark. "Need your autograph." She handed him a fountain pen.

After he signed, he gazed straight into her twinkling eyes. "Maybe you could tell me how to go about sending a message to Betty Weaver."

The girl leaned back off the counter, stood tall and loosed a belly laugh. "Somebody tell you this is the mob headquarters?"

"Matter of fact."

She turned the register around and read his name. "Tom, if I knew that kind of dope, a smart kid like me would go out and sell it to the highest bidder. Local cops, state cops, feds. Am I right?"

"Depends."

"On what?"

"On whether you're looking for trouble."

She paused to observe him up and down. "Say, what are you? Let me guess. I got it, you're a bounty hunter."

"Buy you a drink after work?"

"Show me your other hand."

Tom set down his bag and complied. The girl eyed his wedding band, wagged her head and sighed. "Another good man gone wrong," she said, and replaced the registration volume under the counter.

A bellhop had materialized directly behind him. When Tom glanced that way, the kid, around eighteen and broomstick-thin, surprised him with a sly wink. Then, before Tom could stop him, he hoisted the flowered canvas suitcase borrowed from Madeline.

The desk clerk tossed the room key to the bellhop. "Take good care of him, Sammy," she said. "That lucky girl of his ever dumps him, he's going to drive all night and buy me a drink."

"You betcha." Sammy hustled toward the stairs.

The room was on the second floor. The bellhop bounded up two steps at a time. By the time Tom caught up, the kid had already set the suitcase atop the mahogany highboy, turned back the covers on the full bed that monopolized the room, and pulled the cord to open the louvered blinds.

"You look like a fella needs some shut-eye."

"On the nose," Tom said, as he sat on the edge of the springy bed.

Sammy went to the door, but failed to do the expected—either leave or turn and hold out for a tip. Instead, he shut the door and asked, "You a cop?" He pulled a comb and ran it through his pomaded hair.

"Used to be," Tom said, "until last night."

"Troubles?"

"Some," Tom said. "You got a question?"

"You betcha."

"Let's hear it."

"Betty Weaver," the kid said. "You want to know about her, am I right?"

Tom stood. "You know her?"

"You got the wrong hotel. She comes to town, she rooms at the Arizona Inn."

Tom shook the kid's hand, and reached into his billfold for a ten.

Chapter Forty-two

The Arizona Inn was across town, up Stone Avenue along the streetcar line, past a bowling alley and a tire and auto repair shop where Tom decided to take his Chevy for an oil change and new radiator hoses before the drive home. That would be if he survived this trip into the world of Old West gunslingers and New West gangsters.

He made a right onto Speedway Boulevard. As he passed the university, he remembered the story of an Arizona quarterback who spoke his last words, after an auto wreck, to Coach "Pop" McKale. He said, "Tell the team to *bear down*." As Tom swung left onto Campbell, he wondered what his own final words should be.

He turned right onto Elm, in as shady a neighborhood as the street name suggested, and pulled up in front of the Inn. A valet jogged out to meet him, a cheery young fellow, beefy and graceful. Juan Carlos, according to his badge.

Tom said, "You play football."

"Yep. For the U."

"Fullback?"

Juan Carlos flashed a grin. "How'd you know?"

Tom didn't feel sociable. But making friends with a tough guy felt worthwhile. "That was my position, at USC, nineteen twenty-three, twenty-four."

"I'll be," the valet said, "I mighta heard you on the radio."

Just as Tom would've asked about Betty Weaver, another car pulled up behind. He decided to wait for later, catch the valet unoccupied, and slip his queries into a sports conversation. Before he let the valet into his car, he got directions to the lot around the corner where he could, if he chose, find the car on his own. He kept his key on the ring and gave the valet a spare. The grounds were a sheik's oasis featuring plentiful water in pools, ponds, and gurgling fountains. Paths wove between cactus gardens, cottages, and the shade of mesquite picnic trees.

The lobby bustled with bejewled dames in luncheon garb and a staggering variety of hairstyles and hats, from simple berets to derbies laden with a bounty of crepe-paper fruit. Tom paused in his preoccupations to feel thankful he was a man, who could dress without much premeditation. If he chose to exhibit some flair, he only needed to sort through his collection of hand-painted ties.

The desk clerk, copper-skinned, prim and businesslike, greeted Tom with a look he read as an order to wipe the smile off his face and skip the small talk. She got his signature, took his money, and traced a path to his cottage on a map of the grounds.

Rather than wait for a bellhop, he preferred to ditch the lobby and its shrill cacophony. He left through the garden door, skirted a garden of cactus with thorns that deserved to be outlawed, passed a pond teeming with flashes of gold, a swimming pool around which only a few pink bathers lay, and a patch of yellow, sapphire, and vermillion wildflowers.

His cottage was actually a duplex, one unit facing west, the other facing east, each fronted with a sitting porch. The porches were draped in bougainvillea. Across the walkway grew a tree so wickedly gnarled it could mark the entrance to a witch's forest.

Fatigue had begun to weigh him down. He would have staggered straight across the buffed wood floor that matched the knotty pine walls to the bed, upon which a small bouquet and a wrapped bonbon awaited, had he not vowed to phone Florence first thing. He kicked off his shoes and sank into the leather easy chair beside the one-drawer desk. He picked up the telephone and rang the switchboard.

He gave the operator the number of the Angelus Temple office. The woman who picked up might've done time in acting school to achieve her dramatically obliging manner. She promised Tom to seek out his sister and urge her to return his call promptly.

Next, the Inn operator connected Tom to the switchboard of the Santa Catalina Atwater Hotel. The phone in Madeline's room rang a dozen times before he gave up and left a message with the hotel operator.

He peeled off his socks, unsnapped and shook off his suspenders, and slipped out of the shoulder holster and shirt. He looped the holster over a bedpost and tossed the shirt and socks into the corner for room service to pick up and launder. Then he dove onto the bed, its mattress soft and sheets velvety. He intended to reach across to the radio on the nightstand, in case he could tune in a lullaby or the tail end of a Yankees day game. Had he sought out news about tomorrow's commencement of the Berlin Olympics, after Leo's rants, he would've felt like a traitor.

"Good night," he muttered. He might've set the alarm for a short nap if he hadn't expected that before long, a return call from Florence would wake him.

What woke him was no phone call, but rather a sharp tap on the crown of his head. He had gone so deep, he wondered why the bed didn't feel like his own. He propped up on an elbow and crooked his head to get his bearings.

Whether he looked right or left, he found himself staring up the barrel of a Colt .380 pocket gun.

Chapter Forty-three

They had caught him lying on the bed facedown, and cuffed and cinched his hands behind his back before he caught on.

His captors were a tall, beefy Indian and a shorter flaxen-haired man, sharp-featured and pale, who gave the orders. With the towhead out front, the Indian behind and poking Tom's spine with the barrel of his pocket gun, they led him through the grounds without the slightest objection from any of the half dozen guests they encountered, or from a bellhop out for a smoke.

In a dirt alley behind the Inn's grounds, the Indian crammed Tom into the rear of a Chrysler Imperial and fixed him with a blindfold of the sort light sleepers commonly wear. Then he looped a bandana around Tom's head, over the blindfold, and tied it in back.

The towhead drove for about five minutes. He stopped twice at intersections, made three left and two right turns and parked on gravel. The Indian helped Tom out of the car, held him rather gently by the arm, and led him on a blind forced march through a gate and around some obstacle.

When the Indian removed the bandana and blindfold, Tom saw the interior of a place much like his cottage at the Arizona Inn. One spacious room with a bed, dresser, knotty pine wardrobe, a flower-print easy chair, and a mirrored door leading into a bathroom.

The Indian appeared as listless as a fellow who has outgrown his occupation. Only his eyes remained alert, on the lookout for either an opportunity or a blindside attack.

The towhead affected a sneer. With a single gold tooth, second from center on the right side, his head appeared slightly off balance. The slide of his bolo tie featured a sizable chunk of turquoise.

He shoved Tom into the easy chair. "You a cop?"

As they had ignored every question Tom had thrown out during the drive, he didn't feel inclined to answer.

The towhead nodded at the Indian, who made a listless fist and boxed Tom square and hard on the ear.

"Yeah, I'm a cop," Tom growled. "What are you?"

"Then you ain't no friend of Miz Betty Weaver's."

"That's a fact."

"So what business you got with the lady?"

"I don't give a hoot about her, except insofar as she can lead me to Harry Longabaugh."

"Insofar. What're you, educated?"

"Somewhat."

"Somewhat. Aren't you a pip," the man said with a grin. "Who's this Longbow?"

"Try Hiram Beebe."

The towhead stepped back and studied Tom with a puzzled gaze. After a minute, he turned to the Indian and hitched his chin. The Indian made another fist and walloped the crown of Tom's head, drove it down and forward enough so the towhead could aim and deliver a vicious kick, which snapped Tom's head back and ripped a gash in his cheek.

Tom wouldn't let himself reach for the gash. He attempted to scorch the towhead with his eyes. "Why the kick?"

"Why, you say?" The man laughed and glanced at the Indian, who delivered severe blow to Tom's back, directly between the shoulder blades.

When Tom looked up, the towhead held out a glass. "Drink."

After some moments, Tom decided to comply rather than decline and get walloped until they could pour the stuff down his throat. He took the glass, which was half full of brackish water laced with a bitter substance. He slugged it down. "What sort of mickey is it?"

The towhead hitched his thumb toward the door. "C'mon, Geronimo." He led the way. After the Indian closed the door behind him, Tom heard the lock click.

Chapter Forty-four

Left alone, Tom attempted to consider his options, if any existed. But his condition made thinking into hard labor. His head still whirled from the blows, the wound between his shoulders stabbed, his cheek throbbed, blood dripped onto his trousers, and a leaden numbness was spreading upward and downward from his belly.

Outside, not far off, a high-pitched laugh sounded.

Tom heaved himself up and stumbled to the picture window. He nudged the curtain aside with his shoulder. He saw a twilight gathering of monsoon clouds in rose and vermillion streaks, a house with Spanish iron grates over the windows, a mesquite with a bench beneath, and a guitar-shaped swimming pool upon which inner tubes floated. He looked for people but soon gave up, stumbled to the bed and lay on his left side, to keep his mangled cheek from touching anything but air.

If the thugs had stayed around, he might have thanked them for the dope. Already, his cheek throbbed less viciously, the whirling of his head had eased, and the stab between his shoulder blades had gone sporadic. And soon enough, sleep delivered him to Echo Park, where he watched Elizabeth chase a herd of panicky ducks. She was laughing, which pleased him so, he didn't attempt to make out what a woman nearby shouted. He imagined the woman was Florence, until she slapped his forehead.

"Sit him up," the woman said to the Indian, who stood beside her, close enough to Tom to deliver a sudden blow should the order come.

Watching the Indian's hand for any sign of a fist, Tom rolled off the bed on the far side and sat up on his own. He peered over his shoulder and watched the woman come around the bed. She was tall and buxom, shapely though rather thick through the waist and hips. Partly on account of the denim skirt and plaid blouse, Tom might've cast her as Annie Oakley. Her brownish face looked soft, more naturally colored than suntanned. Her bobbed hair was midnight brown. In an Okie drawl she said, "What's your story, chum?"

Tom surprised himself with his ability to speak, his lips and tongue felt so heavy. "You Betty Weaver?"

"Your business," she said, calmly. "Out with it."

"I'm looking for Hiram Beebe."

"Ain't what I heard. Told Bradley you were after Longabaugh."

"That I did."

"And just what the blazes brings Detective Tom Hickey of the LAPD to Arizona looking for a fella been, these thirty years, six feet deep someplace in Bolivia?"

Even while doped, Tom knew to give away as little as he needed to. "It's about a murder in Mexico, around nineteen twenty-two. Suspect is a German called Ret Marut."

The woman's dark and steady eyes studied him for a minute. "Michael, it's too damn hot in here. Take him poolside."

Tom stood, gave the Indian a back-off glare, stumbled around the bed and to the door. He waited until the woman, whom he would presume was Betty Weaver unless he learned otherwise, passed him and stepped outside. As she passed, he caught a whiff of lilac through the rain-sweetened air.

The yard's adobe pavers were slick, the spaces between them like rivulets. The drips off leaves of mesquite, paloverde, and lemon trees shone silver from the stars and gold from the hovering moon. A log fire crackled in a poolside fire pit covered by a wooden awning and surrounded by Adirondack chairs. The Indian pointed to one of the chairs. Tom complied. Betty Weaver took the chair facing him, on the far side of the pit.

The Indian, named Michael, and Bradley, the towhead, occupied the other chairs.

"Now, boys," said Betty Weaver, "this detective is either going to tell us a dandy story or go for his last swim. And if he thinks we would hesitate to drown a cop, tell him who we mean to pin the homicide on."

Bradley the towhead gave Tom a vicious smirk. "Name's Larry Loftus."

Chapter Forty-five

Tom had no problem inventing a story. Though he was no storyteller by trade, he knew what he liked to read.

He led with a hook. "No doubt you all have heard of Pancho Villa."

"Heard of him?" the woman said. "Hell, I met up with him."

Bradley rose from his slouch. "That so, ma'am?"

Even aloof Michael the Indian showed a morsel of interest and scooted his chair a few inches closer.

The woman said, "Yessir. Got raised up some on Uncle Wesley's spread, downriver from El Paso. Believe it was nineteen eighteen when Villa rode in with maybe fifty of his boys.

"Black Jack Pershing had got done chasing Pancho by then, give up I suppose, and Pancho tells my uncle he's going to seize the rancho, set up some of his *vaqueros* to run the place. He says, acting like the prince of hospitality, we all can stick around a few days to pack up before we move on.

"Uncle Wes, he was a horse trader. And happened he owned a couple of the first Kodaks, awful rare in West Texas. Fixed-focus, single-shutter jobs, came loaded with film for about a hundred shots. Shoot all the pictures and send the whole camera back to the factory. The film gets developed. The camera gets reloaded.

"Well, Pancho spotted a camera, the one called Brownie, and told us take his picture with the pilfered livestock before we move on.

"Uncle Wes shoots a whole gallery worth, then he says, 'General, it's going to require some months to get the shots back developed. You take the ranch and run us off, I can't see how you mean to get your photos.'

"Well, Pancho gives the matter some thought, and he decides to run off with the horses and cattle, and leave us be for the present. Half a year later, he comes back for his photos and to seize the ranch. By this time Uncle Wes had employed a platoon of fighting cowboys. They drove off those Mexicans. But not before Pancho got his photos. Uncle Wes figured handing over the photos was the only way to make that pesky fellow scoot."

Bradley was still chuckling and slapping his leg, and Michael had cracked a meager smile, when the ringing of a phone interrupted.

Chapter Forty-six

Bradley hustled into the house through the back door. Soon he came out and announced, "Ma'am, you've got a call waiting in here."

Betty Weaver rose. While she walked toward the house, she hitched a thumb over her shoulder, which sent Bradley hustling back to poolside. He sat and produced a pack of brown Mexican cigarettes, pulled one out and lit it.

He blew a couple smoke rings then leaned toward Tom. "Hickey," he said, and shook his head. "You do something to earn that moniker?"

"Got born," Tom said.

The towhead sneered as though responding to an insult. He turned to the Indian. "A sorehead, ain't he?"

"You say so." The Indian yawned.

"I'm betting he can't swim. You in for a sawbuck?"

"You're on," Michael said. "What's the odds a fella from L.A. can't swim?"

"That's why you're giving me three to one."

The Indian shrugged. Bradley stroked his chin. "What've we got can work for an anchor?"

"Look what you're sitting on top of."

"A chair?"

"Under the chair."

Bradley leaned forward and leaned down. "Oh yeah, the pavers. Sling a few in a gunny, rope it on. Then watch close, see what a guy does when he's drowning. Two to one he'll kick and thrash like a choke chicken."

"Three to one," the Indian said.

The way Bradley jumped up and threw his hands out might've signaled the proclamation of a discovery that could render Mr. Einstein's trivial.

"Suppose we hold off till tomorrow's monsoon, and figure out a way to hitch a tall rod to him, and we sit back and wait for the lightning. What a sight."

Despite the dope and Tom's suspicion that the towhead was in charge of nothing, the talk delivered some nightmarish thoughts.

Betty Weaver returned from the house and came straight to him. She reached down and gave him a warm pat on the shoulder. He thought either she possessed a good, kind heart or a soft spot for men she was about to kill.

She said, "Let's hear what you got to tell."

The Indian yawned.

Bradley stood and said, "Care for a nightcap, ma'am?"

She waved him away. In a sullen posture, he walked to the house.

"Go on," she said to Tom.

He sat up tall. "The story begins like one of your Old West feuds, Lincoln County or Tombstone. The trouble started with land. Mr. William Randolph Hearst—you must know about him."

"Who doesn't?"

The way her eyes lit, Tom considered asking if she had any Hearst stories to share. But he decided she might take offense, believe he was critiquing her Villa tale with sarcasm.

"Much like your Uncle Wes, Hearst wasn't charmed by the idea of Mexicans running him off his million-acre spread in the state of Chihuahua. No matter that it was their country.

"First he tried playing politics and propaganda, but those schemes bought him no assurance. So he sent a writer, name of Ambrose Bierce, down to make a lot of promises to Villa, who had bivouacked some of his troops on Hearst's hacienda. Babicora, he called the place.

"Now Bierce was the sort who makes up his own mind about things. Despite what assignment the boss gave him, he made up his own mind. And he made Villa for a blowhard politician. He wrote up his story accordingly.

"Where he went wrong, Villa got wind of his plans and enlisted a *gringo*. Winchester was his name." Tom enlivened his tale with the name Winchester in honor of an L.A. crook and snitch he considered the most obsequious of all lowlifes. "Winchester cozied up to Bierce, and bumped him off.

"A few years passed. Hearst bribed enough politicos so he held onto Babicora. After the big war a fellow by the name of Charlie Challender showed up on the rancho." With some reservation, Tom had saddled Charlie with his evil wife Milly's maiden name. "Charlie had come home from the war in France with big plans."

To engage and please his audience, Tom made Charlie an outlaw. "Back in L.A. he landed a job running Canadian liquor from the Channel Islands by boat to a drop around Santa Barbara.

"One night, as Charlie beached the landing skiff, a swarm of headlights flashed a greeting. And a copper on a bullhorn shouted out his name. He was a powerful swimmer, so he dove into the surf and got back to the cruiser while the coppers thought he was hiding low in the skiff. He roared off in the cruiser, dodged the Coast Guard, and didn't stop until he docked in Ensenada.

"This was nineteen twenty-one, and the Mexicans weren't done squabbling between one brand of revolutionaries and another. Charlie knew of an old pal or two in the employ of Mr. Hearst, on his spread in Chihuahua, and Charlie grew up as a Texas cowboy, as did you, Miz Weaver."

The lady barely reacted to her name, only lifted her eyes to meet his. They gave away nothing. Tom said, "Babicora suited Charlie fine. Still, he would lie awake wishing the Mexicans would wind up their revolution so he'd feel right about sending for his wife and kids to join him. Or he would try to dream up a way he could return to L.A. without doing time. "

"And just how do you know so much about what went on in this chap's head?"

"I'm guessing," Tom said. "You wanted a good story."

The lady smiled, big enough to give herself a dimple.

"One day this Winchester shows up, come as a messenger from Villa to make a deal with the Babicora manager about joining a herd together with one from Pancho's *hacienda* for a drive to El Paso. By now, Villa had got granted a spread of his own, and settled in.

"A Mexican old-timer pointed Winchester out to Charlie as the *cabrón* that shot old Bierce.

"Well, Charlie used to read the *Examiner* for nothing more than to get a kick out of Bierce's orneriness. Seeing Winchester run free riled him plenty. Besides, he surmised if he prowled around, got the whole story and wrote it up, Mr. Hearst might trade the solution to the Bierce case for the expunging of the files about a certain Canadian whiskey runner.

"Where Charlie went wrong, he had a writer pal, name of Ret Marut. A German who favored mescal, and who we suspect got juiced and spilled the beans. Next time Winchester came to Babicora, Charlie went missing, for good."

"That's it," Tom said. "I'm after Winchester."

Through the whole story, Betty Weaver had sat attentive with folded arms uplifting her ample bosom. Now she leaned back and clasped her hands atop her head as though making them into a bonnet. "You telling us the L.A. coppers sent you to snoop a murder happened in Mexico, to a whiskey runner, some dozen years back?"

Tom found himself required to think harder than he felt capable of, with the dope that left him limp, dizzy, and soft-headed. Still, he needed to try.

He supposed that since the lady seemed to know about Tom's assaulting Larry Loftus, from which anyone could deduce that Tom was now a renegade, she would more likely buy that Tom had set out on his own.

He said, "Truth is, Challender's kid is a gal of mine. See, Ret Marut is loaded, and got a reputation to lose. The more evidence I dig up, the more I can take to Hearst, or forget about taking it to Hearst if Marut decides to play ball. This gal and I, we mean to buy a certain roadhouse that's for sale on the coast above Ventura, near the turnoff to Ojai."

Betty Weaver's ample pink lips twisted left and right. "Say again, what's Hearst's stake in this game?"

"Winchester not only bumped off Hearst's best writer, he also whacked the guy that would've brought him the goods on Winchester. Mr. Hearst doesn't abide getting crossed, if he can help it."

The lady said, "Your gal. Her name?"

"Um, Elizabeth."

"What's your wife have to say?" She was gazing at Tom's wedding band.

Tom attempted to disguise his wince with a scowl. "Ran off with a movie producer."

Betty Weaver turned and looked from the towhead to the Indian. "Well boys, what do you say?"

Chapter Forty-seven

The Indian shrugged. Bradley turned thumbs down. "Drown him."

"Bring him a glass of water," Betty Weaver said to the Indian. "Make it a stiff one." While he was gone, she asked Tom, "And what's your reason for hunting down Hiram?"

"He was on Babicora, with Charlie and Marut. Knows the whole story."

"Says who?"

"Elizabeth got it from the widow of a Mexican, longtime Babicora ranch hand. After the husband dropped dead, the widow came to live with a son in L.A. She looked up Charlie's daughter to pay respects."

"Well," the lady drew out the word as long as her breath held, "I reckon your story's good enough to buy you one decent night's sleep, before we drown you."

Tom watched her expression, in hopes she would crack a smile to let him know she was pulling his leg. All he saw was a poker face.

When the Indian returned with a tall glass and held it up to Tom's mouth, Tom said, "How about undoing the cuffs?"

The Indian glanced at Weaver. She said, "He's a joker, right, Michael?"

Michael shrugged.

Tom only needed a sip to know the water was laced with dope, a heavier dose than the first one. He leaned back, away from the glass. Weaver said, "Tucson in summer, you drink plenty or you dry up and die."

If he had wanted to escape, Tom would have fought to keep from drinking anymore. But escape wasn't his goal. He sipped and swallowed half the glassful before the thought occurred that the dope might act as a truth serum. Then he wished he hadn't spun a web of lies.

The Indian motioned with his head toward the pool house. Tom stood and led the way back inside.

Once alone, he reviewed the story he had given them. He was hoping to relieve himself of the nagging sense that Weaver had only played along with his tall tale, for her own mysterious reasons, when she appeared at his bedside. He hadn't heard her come in.

She was holding a small bottle and a damp cloth. "Don't flinch," she commanded. She held the bottle out close and he read "Mercurochrome."

The lady daubed and wiped at his cheek. He didn't flinch. She was gentle, and he was fairly numb. From a pocket in her skirt, she produced two large Band-Aids.

After she applied them, she kissed her forefinger and touched him between the eyes.

Chapter Forty-eight

The morning was already hot when the Indian entered. On a tray he carried a bowl of oatmeal topped with sliced banana, half a grapefruit, and a cup of something that looked like coffee but, as Tom would soon learn, was a vile herbal concoction. The Indian pulled the easy chair close to the bed, scooped a spoonful of oatmeal and held it out.

"Be a pal," Tom said. "And save yourself some trouble. Just fix the cuffs in front of me."

The Indian's mouth crinkled in what he might've considered a smile.

Tom sat up on the edge of the bed and got spoon-fed. After a sip of the herbal concoction, he made a gagging face. "More dope?"

The Indian nodded toward the mug. "Don't matter though, the other's bad all by itself."

"What is it?"

"She calls it tea, makes it out of cactus leaves."

"And what're you doping me with?"

"Like it?"

"Tastes like rot. The effect's not bad."

"Mexican laudanum. The bottle says it's to stove up diarrhea."

"Even if I drink it with this swill?"

The Indian crinkled another smile and stood to leave.

Except at around noon when Michael showed again with a tall glass of water, Tom spent the day alone, splitting his time between the easy chair, the bed, and pacing the length of the room. His most demanding effort was in shouldering the curtain aside, giving himself a view through the picture window. The pool, silver and gold in the sky's white glare. Lemon, olive, and mesquite trees around which starlings fluttered. A curtained window and the rear door of the house, and a tall wooden fence that denied him any clues about the neighborhood beyond the fence except the top of a tall willow, to which a flock of small parrots came and perched, and offered a brash concert.

The laudanum provided entertainment. He saw a mastodon and a saber-toothed tiger rising out of the LaBrea tar pits into which, after Charlie Hickey disappeared, Milly often threatened to dispose of her children. He found himself in the grim boiler room of a death ship, and flying over Echo Park while Elizabeth fought off a battalion of savage ducks. With each of his attempts to swoop and rescue her, he only rose higher into the oily sky.

He would've preferred making plans about how, if Longabaugh were to arrive, he should handle the desperado. He thought it best to give no hint, at least in the beginning, that he knew Longabaugh was the killer. But each time he attempted to collect and organize his thoughts about meeting with the outlaw, some wild vision interrupted.

When he tried to imagine his reunion with Madeline, in hopes of finding the words to banish the hard feelings this quest of his would no doubt leave behind, no matter the outcome, along came a horde of memories in Technicolor. A shootout he had witnessed before he joined the force, between Leo Weiss and a cop gone overly bad. A slow motion close-up of his brogan mashing Larry Loftus' knee. Madeline singing "My Man," a favorite of the Paul Perkins Orchestra's audiences. He laid himself down and let her winsome voice guide him into a spell of sleep.

The pool had gone bluish and the willow rustled from a breeze when Michael brought him a bowl of stew along with his evening water ration. The Indian set the food and drink on the coffee table beside the easy chair, then stepped outside and returned with a radio. He found a receptacle near the bed, set the radio on the floor, and plugged it in.

"Hitler games coming tomorrow," he said.

Tom nodded and thought about Leo, whose scorn had wounded him bone-deep.

"Baseball fan?" the Indian asked Tom.

"Yep."

While the Indian spoon-fed him and treated him to gulps of water that tasted strangely pure, they listened to the Boston Braves and the Yankees. Lefty Gomez shut out Boston until the top of the eighth inning, when the Babe socked a three-run homer. After Huck Betts shut the Yankees down, Michael unplugged the radio and walked to the door. "Drink?"

"Scotch?"

The Indian shrugged. In short order, he returned with a double in a crystal glass.

Tom sipped. "Lousy Scotch, or one part laudanum?"

"Both."

He gulped it, since Michael's solemn face assured him that, either with or without further persuasion, he would imbibe the concoction.

As the Indian opened the door to leave, a pack of dogs on the hunt commenced with their yelps and howls. The laudanum helped Tom discover that even such a racket could become symphonic, in this case a sort of lullaby.

Then he opened his eyes and saw daylight and Betty Weaver standing beside an old man.

Chapter Forty-nine

With a sweep of her arm, the lady said, "Tom, Hiram Beebe."

He could've played the role of a desert prospector with his burro tied up outside. "Nuts, Betty," he said, and reached out a large spotted and weathered hand. "Harry Longabaugh. Pleased to meet you, Tom Hickey."

He zeroed deep-set topaz eyes and studied Tom for a lengthy moment, then turned away and surveyed the room. "Bring me an honest chair, will you doll? The softy there would break my back."

Weaver hustled to the door and out. The old man turned and shuffled to the window. While he stood looking out, his head jerked to his right, more like a signal than a twitch.

Tom's heart pounded as though, rather than sleeping, he had been running sprints all night long.

The Indian delivered a high-backed rolling desk chair. Longabaugh appraised it then turned to Tom and pointed to the easy chair. He waited until Tom heaved himself off the bed and got seated where he was told.

"You Charlie's kid?"

Even if Tom's mind weren't confounded with fury in the presence of his father's killer, the question would have stumped him. In the story he'd told Betty Weaver, Charlie had gone by another name. But then, doped as he was, he surely might've slipped and called him Hickey.

Tom said, "You know a Charlie Hickey?"

"Did."

Tom glimpsed a hint of sorrow in the man's eyes. Maybe the desperado couldn't quite pardon himself for cold-blooded murders.

Tom wouldn't yet trust himself to speak. He sat still and watched while the old man stiffly eased himself into the roller.

"Here's the rules, son," Longabaugh said. "The gal's got feelers out. She gets a notion you're working with the G-men, I go on home and Betty's friends send you off to the basement of the devil's cave, the place he keeps special for cops. Fair enough?"

Tom only shrugged.

"What's that supposed to mean?"

"Means what's fair got to do with it?" Tom mumbled.

"Speak up, son. You're the one wanted to talk to me, no?"

Tom caught his breath and swallowed. "One question, is all." He couldn't keep the tremble out of his voice.

"Spit it out, then."

"Who killed Charlie Hickey?"

Chapter Fifty

Tom sat rigid on the edge of the easy chair, feeling certain Long-abaugh would say "I did." Then Tom would leap, rush, bowl the man over and stomp him until Weaver gang bullets intervened.

Longabaugh scowled. "Winchester," he said. "Like you told Betty."

Tom sat gaping, baffled for as long as the old man held the scowl. Then a belly laugh broke out of him. "Son, any *gringo* stayed in Chihuahua from the death of Mr. Bierce to the killing of Charlie Hickey, I'd known of him. Wasn't any Winchester." The outlaw leaned back, lifted fingers to his mouth and gave a piercing whistle of the kind Tom, as a high school baseball infielder, had wished he could produce.

Michael entered and sauntered over. With a frown, the old man censured the Indian's leisurely pace. He said, "You got the games on?"

"Yep."

"Owens sets foot on the track, you'll come fetch me. Meantime, hustle us *refrescos*."

The Indian sauntered off to his errand. The old man asked, "How much you got riding on Jesse?"

"Not a dime."

"Shame. I got a king's ransom down on he's going to break the record in the one and two hundred both. Take a guess what odds the wetback bookmaker gave me?"

Tom shook his head.

"Not much of a talker, are you?"

"Depends."

"A little worried, are you?"

"Nope."

"Ought to be. You are, after all, in the hands of a pack of desperados. Reckon you would care to hear from the horse's mouth the God's truth about the Sundance Kid."

Tom supposed if he played along, his odds of survival might rise. "Sure."

"You mighta heard the Kid's one of the bloodthirsty kind. Well, that is by no means a fair call. Though I will admit to a hot temper. Tom, my life is comparable to that of most men. We find us a suitable vocation, and from then on, we got expectations to live up to and procedures the profession calls for.

"I had to kill a few. Likewise, not all the bounty I reaped came from the bankers, financiers, captains of industry, all them that harness the workingman and connive a variety of means to rob him of his pay. Most, but not all, of my income has been pinched from the takers."

The Indian entered carrying two tall glasses of the herbal concoction Tom had suffered yesterday. He placed Tom's glass, with a straw inserted, on the coffee table next to the easy chair. Tom leaned, reached it and sipped. He found it even more vile today when it wasn't laced with laudanum.

The old man said, "General Villa and I were *simpatico*, made of similar stuff. In Don Pancho, I found a reason to sojourn in that bloody land and do my share for the revolution. Which is how I came to Babicora."

Longabaugh set his glass on the floor and leaned forward. "Son, how much do you know about Mr. William Randolph Hearst?"

"Some."

"Born to a silver spoon," Longabaugh said. "Along the line, he picks up the notion he's here on Earth to achieve a grand destiny. And who's going to argue? Who's willing to slap him around or cut him down to size? Not a soul, until Mr. Bierce comes along.

"Even that old gentleman, took a woman to call him out, dare him to write his beliefs, no more, no less, consequences be damned."

Longabaugh cocked his head and gazed out the window. The pool already shimmered with golden streaks. A pair of doves fluttered, side by side on a mesquite branch.

When the old man spoke again, his voice carried a hint of snarl. "The takeaway is, Mr. Bierce writes up what you call an exposé." He picked up his drink and studied Tom. "It was a fine piece of work, I'll assure you, though I am not the literary sort."

"You read it?"

"I surely did. A masterpiece, in my opinion. Told God's truth about the plight of the *campesinos*, the greed of the *hacendados,* and the rape of a nation by the oilers and cattle barons and all manner of *gringos*. Including, make that especially, William Randolph Hearst.

"Did I read it?" the outlaw said, "Not only did Mr. Bierce invite me to read it, he asked my opinion. I told him, 'You had best make tracks, sir, get yourself up to New York City, to the offices of a magazine such as *Life* or *Esquire* or the *Saturday Post*, one that Hearst don't own.

"Mr. Bierce replied with a hearty laugh. 'I already wired it to Hearst,' says he. And to that, I replied, 'Well then, I fear you're a goner.'

"Very next day, I set off with Don Pancho on an expedition, else I would surely have kept watch on the old gentleman, and covered his back."

"Who killed him?"

Longabaugh raised his hands face out, meaning hold your peace until I get there.

Chapter Fifty-one

The way Tom would remember the details of Longabaugh's windy account:

In December, 1913, half a year before the declaration of war in Europe, Ambrose Bierce crossed the border from El Paso, Texas, into Ciudad Juarez in time to witness Villa's army whip the *federales* at Tierra Blanca.

The *federales* retreated south along the Rio Grande and after a week holed up in Ojinaga. Their strategy was to revive the army of the north with money, provisions, and military assistance arranged by their *gringo* supporters, among them William Randolph Hearst, who would pay dearly to save Babicora.

Hearst had long pressed for U.S. intervention, and his news empire had persuaded millions of readers that Villa, who had made off with sixty thousand of Hearst's herefords and shorthorns, was akin to Ghengis Khan, the fiendish boss of a barbarian horde.

But neither support from across the river nor the arrival of Luis Terraza, Mexico's wealthiest *hacendado*, along with a thousand bodyguards, sufficiently encouraged the *federale* troops. With the approach of three thousand *Villistas*, the *federales* threatened mutiny.

Meanwhile, enterprising *gringos* constructed bleachers along the north bank of the Rio Grande, to accommodate the impending battle's throng of spectators. By now, the revolution was a media war. Loyalists and rebel generals faced off not only on the battlefield, but also in the newspapers and in cinema newsreels, gaming for the hearts and minds of the U.S. citizenry. Presidente Huerta, as well as Villa and Zapata, were selling access to U.S. newsmen, trading inconvenience for the chance to position themselves as worthy recipients of foreign aid. Scores of journalists and cameramen crossed the river into Ojinaga by bridge or ferry. Once the spectators and *federale* deserters were in place, the fireworks commenced.

Now Longabaugh pursed his lips and scratched his head and cheek, his eyes narrowed and keened as though peering with regret at long ago. "Son," he said, "when I returned from my own expedition and inquired about Mr. Bierce, I learned he had left Babicora, returned to Chihuahua City, and boarded the Northern railroad with a troop of Villa's boys.

"You can bet the house the old man didn't get to Ojinaga. Though I played no part in the battle, being otherwise occupied, I kept my ears open, got the testimony of a dozen men. Hell, I went so far as to wire a certain reporter with a reputation for calling a spade a spade, same as Mr. Bierce. That fella, Jack Reed, wired back he had not encountered Mr. Bierce nor heard tell of anyone in Ojinaga that did."

Longabaugh leaned closer and stared like a prosecutor. "You were how old, last you saw Charlie?"

"Five."

"And why do you suppose he run off?"

Tom glowered.

"That's no suitable answer."

"It's the best I've got."

The door opened and Michael sauntered in. "Owens took the hundred."

"Record time?"

"Yessir. Ten point two."

Longabaugh slapped his leg. "Call up the wetback, tell him scoop my winnings and put the whole pile on the two hundred. Same deal, got to break the record. Same odds."

"What if he argues over the odds?"

The outlaw turned his head sideways from Tom, facing the Indian. "Kill him," he said.

Tom caught the shadow of a wink.

As Longabaugh turned back to Tom, he stroked his stubbly chin. "Where'd I leave off? Was it springtime nineteen and twenty-one Charlie Hickey come to Babicora?"

"Alone?" Tom demanded.

The outlaw's frown darkened. "A fella in handcuffs ought to mind his manners."

Tom leaned back, caught a long breath and rolled his shoulders. "*There's* a rule to live by."

"That it is. Charlie brought a German along. Face like a crow. Steely eyes. About yea high." He reached a hand out at the height of a dwarf. "I'll grant, after some months in France, where I served a year or so of the big war with the Canada regulars, I had my fill of Germans, no matter whose side they claimed to be on.

"Rumor got around Babicora this German was the bastard son of the Kaiser. I reckon folks cooked up that story on account of the Kraut's uppity act. This Moroot seemed to count himself mighty noble."

"Moroot?"

"Red Moroot." Longabaugh whistled, called out for another beverage, then sat rapping the side of his hand on the chair arm.

During the intermission, Tom thought surely Marut had outwitted him. Sent him to hunt a gunslinger whose bullets might pull Tom out of the game.

The Indian delivered a tumbler then sauntered away. After a swallow, Longabaugh said, "Now I can't say I knew all there was about Charlie Hickey or the Kraut. Those days, my home was in Canutillo, a *hacienda* General Villa had purchased. Trips to Babicora came along when the general deemed an errand best suited to an English-speaking man with discretion.

"Next trip I learned Charlie had met his maker. Seemed he got nosy, inquiring after the fate of Mr. Bierce. Got the notion to dig up the facts and present them to Hearst himself. Damned if I could tell you what he figured that endeavor would buy him. Nor can I tell you what conclusion he reached. After pestering all the old-timers on Babicora and tracking down others of them in Chihuahua City, what I do know is, Charlie brought a request to the foreman."

"His name," Tom demanded.

Longabaugh studied a moment and apparently decided a fellow hearing about his father's death had earned a pass to act rude. "Could've been Mendoza."

"Request for what?"

"Don't know. Could've been to deliver the story he wrote. On account of, the next day, in the morning Charlie gets sent to round up straggling shorthorns. Around twilight, riders go out searching for him, find him shot, back of the head. From afar."

Tom heaved himself up and plodded to the window. If he could have wrenched his hands around front, he might have pounded the glass to powder. Instead, he stared at the silver blue sky and followed the circling path of a graceful bird, a hawk or eagle, while part of him died.

He felt the path of death, like a hotwire from his heart to his brain, sizzling, then going cold. Now that a second source, far removed from the first, confirmed he would never on Earth see his father, he could only hope Florence and her employer had the lowdown on eternity.

The bird swooped and vanished. Tom swung around and faced the old man. "The German might've killed him?"

While Longabaugh pondered, he scratched various parts of his face and head. "Can't see a motive."

"I've got one."

Tom leaned against the wall beside the window and briefed Longabaugh on Marut's story about the creation of *The Death Ship*. All through the account, the outlaw nodded as though piecing in the last few parts of a jigsaw puzzle.

After Tom finished, for a minute or more, Longabaugh's thin, pursed lips shifted side-to-side. "Care to know where I would seek retribution, were I you and I lived past this afternoon, and were Charlie Hickey one of my own?"

"Go on," Tom said.

"The way I see, it was Mendoza shot your old man, or more likely sent out the gunmen, Mendoza being elderly."

"He still in Mexico?"

"Died a few years back. Only one man alive can testify who gave the orders. Way it looks to me, if Betty rules in your favor and you live past today, you had best go settle with the eminent Mr. William Randolph Hearst."

Whether from shock or confusion, Tom couldn't determine, but the strength to stand failed him. He staggered a few steps and launched for the easy chair.

The outlaw gave him a minute to settle. Then he said, "Tell me, son, what's your opinion of bankers and the like?"

"Why?"

"Could be I know a lady might be inclined to cut a fellow in on a job or two, once he proved himself by ridding our troubled nation of a stuffed-shirt lying publisher. Now, give me an answer, which I'll consider before I lodge my recommendation concerning your fate."

Tom's answer might've been that all people—bankers and bank robbers included—to whom the quest for money was the highest motive, he considered equally lowdown.

So he declined to answer at all. Instead, he confessed, "Marut said you killed Charlie Hickey. That's what brought me here."

The outlaw turned his palms out, low as if to catch a lateral. "Serves you right, taking the word of a German." He stood and leaned in Tom's direction. "You got nerve enough, boy, accusing me." Nothing about him implied either threat or denial. For some moments, he stared down at Tom. Then he said, "Ten to one Adolf won't shake the black hand of the great Jesse Owens. I can't wait to see the newsreels, study the look on that Rhine Monkey's face when he hands over the trophy."

Chapter Fifty-two

As Harry Longabaugh walked toward the door, he turned and gave Tom a stern salute. Whether he meant it as a friendly gesture or as a token of respect for one soon to be executed, Tom couldn't guess.

The door had only just shut behind the old man when it swung open and the towhead entered, followed by the Indian. Bradley carried a short tumbler. He flashed a wry grin as he knelt in front of Tom and held out the glass, brought it close and then pressed it hard against Tom's lips. "A pick-me-up, from the lady of the house."

Tom loosed his lips and allowed a taste. As it reached his tongue, he detected the laudanum and leaned away from the glass.

"What's the trouble?"

"Not my brand," Tom muttered.

Bradley turned to the Indian, who stood behind Tom. "Know what I hate?"

"Most everything," the Indian said.

"A guy that don't appreciate hospitality."

Tom had gotten clobbered by a sap before, but never quite so hard. Michael landed a blow dead center and a couple inches above Tom's neck. As he slumped back into the chair, along with the pain and dizziness, he felt strangely betrayed, having let himself believe the Indian rather liked him.

"You got one hard head, buster," Bradley said, and bent close to admire the swelling bump.

The Indian held Tom steady by the shoulders. Using the blade of a hunting knife, which he inserted between Tom's lips and teeth, he wedged Tom's mouth open.

He might've spat out the stuff Bradley poured into him, except Charlie Hickey was dead, and his son had become somebody Tom didn't recognize, who didn't care enough to fight.

Chapter Fifty-three

Tom awoke in the dark to a noise like snare drums and a barrage of stinging pokes up and down his legs, as if he had riled a tribe of Amazon bees.

When he heaved up to sitting, his forehead cracked against the felt and metal molding around the rear door of his Chevy. Soon he recognized the snare drum and stinging as hail. Hot hail. Desert summer hail, which he had heard of but never known firsthand.

He scooted back, drew his legs up inside the car, and tried to ascertain where he was, how he arrived here, why he was half inside, half outside the car, why the open door.

His throbbing head soon lost its will to abide the drumming on the roof. He slid out of the car and stood in the midst of a fusillade of pellets, some mushy, some hard, all of them at least lukewarm.

The air smelled akin to Betty Weaver's tea, only double on the sage. The night was pure dark except when spikes of lightning attacked the ragged mountains toward which the highway appeared to aim. He wondered if they were the Superstition Mountains, a place he had wanted to visit since as a boy he read a book about them. A German prospector discovered a lode of gold then lost his bearings, and left the lode to be claimed by an adventurous boy such as Tom, whose insistent dream was to steal away, taking Florence, and put endless miles between them and their demon mother.

When Tom heard something like a twig snapping, he shot glances all around but saw nothing except shadowy brush and the outline of a fat saguaro. The drum and splatter of the hail defied him to place where the snap came from. He turned to the car, opened the front passenger door, and reached for the overhead light switch.

Madeline's cloth suitcase lay on the floorboard. On the seat was a pile of the gear he had worn or brought into the Arizona Inn, piled on the front seat. Sport coat, brogans, shirt and tie, and at the bottom of the pile, his Colt .38.

He reached for the gun, backed out and closed the door. He stood in the downpour with the gun at his side, wondering what on earth javelinas are and about the sign in another clearing warning about them. A minute passed before a low but sharp crack sounded to his right. He turned and bent forward, peered through the hail and dark until he saw the faint rustling of a creosote bush. His gun jerked upward and fired.

The rustling ceased. He didn't go to see what life he had wasted, only stood still and shuddered with a vision of the East Burbank pimp called Rusty. This time he was laughing.

He spent minutes gazing toward the mountains, and wondered what he had become since Bud handed him Charlie's story. And what it might mean that tonight he'd broken a golden rule. Not some rule handed out by Chief Davis or the system—the alliance of swindlers, bullies, and glad-handers that ran Los Angeles. Their kind probably ran every burg, county, state, and nation.

This time, he'd broken a rule of his own making, which he had followed strictly over ten years as a cop. Never shoot, or even aim, blind.

He remembered the Browning, which he kept under wraps in the trunk, at least until the Weaver bunch got their hands on his car. As he rounded the car, he thought that if it were gone, since Betty Weaver had spared him—for which he owed some goodwill—he could write her in care of the Congress Hotel's Judas bellhop and let her know that any damage it did they might seek to pin on Capone's Benny Katoulis. But he found the Browning still in its wrappings.

Water was cascading out of his hair, pouring off his chin and sleeves and out of his trouser cuffs, before he attempted to light-step over the rocks around the car. As a boy, he had spent whole summers barefoot. These days his spoiled feet might've belonged to Lord Fauntleroy.

The key was in the ignition, so he didn't need to root in the glove compartment for his spare. He glanced at the gas gauge. Half full.

He reached for his brogans and slipped them over his water-logged argyles, then turned the key, tender-footed the clutch, jammed the gear lever forward and set off toward the mountains. A road as wide as this one, on which a truck could pass a truck, and featuring a skunk stripe down the middle, was no doubt the route to Phoenix and on to California.

He set the throttle for sixty mph and leaned back to drive. By now, more accustomed to the hail's clatter and the throbbing of his head, which by now was mostly depleted of laudanum, he found himself able to think. Not clearly, but perhaps steadily enough to decide upon a destination.

He opted to consider the suspects one by one.

Ret Marut, he knew, was a liar of the first order. Claiming to be the representative of a fellow, most likely himself, who claimed to have written a book he might have stolen or even killed for, or at best, collaborated on.

Even when most dimwitted from laudanum, Tom had recognized why Marut might've sent him after Longabaugh. How better to rid yourself of a pest than convince him to hunt down a gunslinger?

That Tom had leaned toward believing the German when he when fingered Longabaugh as the killer might only mean that Tom had gotten desperate for a guy to pin Charlie's murder on.

Still, suppose Marut had come clean and hit the mark, and the old man in Tucson was in fact the Sundance Kid?

That the Kid would call Tom to run a Hail Mary play to rid the world of Hearst might have little to do with Charlie's death. The outlaw's grudge against Hearst, or against the tycoon and all his kind, ran mighty deep. Beefs against the privileged often did, especially during these wicked-hard times.

That the old man was actually Longabaugh, Tom didn't care to stake his life on. But whether Longabaugh had survived a shootout in Bolivia or an imposter took advantage of the gunslinger's reputation to establish himself in Mexico, no doubt this fellow knew Charlie Hickey.

A few pieces of the mystery, Tom had solved beyond reasonable doubt. Charlie Hickey and a German wrote *The Death Ship*. They both had lived and worked on Babicora, as had the old gambler who claimed to be Harry Longabaugh alias Hiram Beebe.

What's more, Tom felt assured that the murders of Ambrose Bierce and Charlie Hickey, both fine men and masterful writers, got instigated by stories whose telling would've displeased William Randolph Hearst.

Chapter Fifty-four

Hearst—more so even than Marut, by Tom's assessment—was a dedicated liar, by trade and inclination. Ten years ago, Sister Aimee promoted an upcoming sermon that promised to name the biggest liar in Los Angeles. No doubt half the public in the know would've bet on Hearst to win the title.

Maybe he wasn't a natural liar, the kind like churchgoers accused the devil of being. Those kind simply preferred lies. Tom made Hearst as more like what Florence had been at sixteen. Back then, he had once sat her down and demanded to know why she so frequently lied to him, though his only aim was to protect her. With a coy smile, she said, "Gosh, Tommy. If I told the truth, I wouldn't get to do what I want."

The difference between Florence and Hearst was, Florence grew up. Florence came to understand that the sun didn't rise and fall just for her. That the word *good* might not always be a synonym for what Florence found pleasing or expedient.

Hearst, around Bud Gallagher's age, by all indications still wasn't about to let the truth prevent him from getting whatever he desired, or from his attempt to shape the world according to his every belief or whim.

Leo maintained that Hearst hadn't changed his MO over the thirty years since he incited the Spanish-American War.

Cuban rebels had resisted the Spanish government for years before Spain sent General Weyler to put down the insurrection.

The tactic Weyler used was to isolate suspects in relocation camps. Hearst decided, probably on account of the copies the headlines would sell, that the Spanish were fully to blame for the insurrection. He devoted the front pages to lucid accounts of atrocities the Spanish allegedly committed against the Cuban prisoners and their supporters. Torture, rape, pillage, bodies piled along the roads and left for carrion.

When Hearst sent his illustrator Frederic Remington to document the savagery in pictures and Remington advised him that conditions weren't by any means bad enough to warrant intervention, Hearst replied, "You furnish the pictures and I'll furnish the war."

For miles, Tom wondered whether Leo so despised Hearst, he might opt to be the backup or lookout for a one-man firing squad.

Chapter Fifty-five

All night, through alternately sharp and slushy hail and later beneath an obsidian sky wearing a fine lace garment of stars, Tom puzzled about the old man who claimed to be Harry Longabaugh and about the German who denied he was B. Traven. He reviewed each story, looking deeper each review for items he might verify or disprove through news accounts or by consulting professors at USC, where he could still call in favors on account of the nine touchdowns he scored during his sophomore year.

At a Marathon all-night gas stop and diner near enough to Phoenix so the city lights tinted the northern sky, he filled the Chevy's tank and bought a ham sandwich, a pack of Anacin, and a thermos of coffee as thick and bitter as Betty Weaver's herb and laudanum brew. Out front, he noticed an Indian woman wrapped in a shawl, sitting in shadow and leaning against the diner wall. He approached, intending to ask if she might know of a place open so late where he could buy an Indian rag doll. He stood over her and gazed down long enough to suspect she was asleep. But as he turned to leave, she looked up. Her eyes, large and vertically oval, surprised him with their brilliance, as if they were lit from inside.

For a moment he considered taking a seat beside her, telling his story, asking for advice, just in case she was a soothsayer. But she reached out a hand, palm up and fingers curled. The index finger twitched in constant spasm.

"Hungry?"

"Hungry," she said.

He reached into the sack he carried, handed over his sandwich, then filled the cup of his thermos with coffee and passed it to her.

After he returned inside for another ham sandwich, he counted the money in his billfold and decided to postpone buying Elizabeth's gift until he reached L.A. The PD would likely withhold his final pay. And he wouldn't risk any more of Madeline's pique by tapping the family's modest savings. But Florence would spot him whatever he needed. Or Leo might, now that the search for Charlie Hickey's killer had become a vendetta against William Randolph Hearst.

He returned to the Indian and gave her all he could afford, two dollars. She muttered something he hoped was a blessing.

Then he drove on, continued his review until he could no longer think about Marut or the outlaw or their stories, which hadn't so much clarified as perplexed him. Most significantly, they had shattered his hope that given enough interrogation, testimony, and introspection the truth would come clear. Instead of delivering him the confidence to judge, all he heard from Marut and the outlaw had delivered him to a state of mind like Alice encountered in Wonderland, in the loco book he often read to Elizabeth. In Wonderland, where everybody lied, the whole concept of truth was nonsense. Maybe, Tom thought, that children's story was a fount of wisdom, the everyday world in sharp relief.

He consumed every drop left in the thermos and pulled off the road twice to relieve himself, one eye out for the mysterious javelina.

At dawn, he raced a long train upon which he spotted at least twenty hobos, one sitting in the doorway of a boxcar strumming a guitar as if serenading the rattlers, prairie dogs, lizards, and drivers.

He arrived on the outskirts of Yuma soon after eight a.m. From the booth outside the Sinclair station, for thirty-five cents, a receptionist with the voice of a squirrel connected him to the office of Angelus Temple. The receptionist sent a runner and soon he was talking to Florence.

She was panting. "Thank God, thank God," she said, then began grilling him, asking whether he found the outlaw, what was he like, did Tom have to beat him up, and "What the hell—oops—heck became of our daddy?"

Tom wouldn't say over the phone, when she might have no one close to lean and weep upon, that the Marut and Longabaugh stories agreed. That as sure as could be, Charlie got murdered in Chihuahua. He said, "I'll be there before dinnertime. We'll eat supper in the park. When Elizabeth runs off with the ducks, I'll tell it all. Now I'm out of nickels. What I need you to do is locate Mr. Hearst."

"The Mr. Hearst?"

"Yeah, find out where he'll be tomorrow."

"What for, Tommy?"

"He and I have got business to settle. That's all for now, babe. Is my little girl with you?"

"She's over in the Bible school, getting a fancy hairdo, ribbons, and curls. Tommy, Madeline called, said she got word you beat up a cop. He had it coming, right?"

"You bet he did."

"Good for you, then. Now get a move on. But first, sure you won't tell me?"

"Ask Sister Aimee how she feels about the virtue of patience."

"Patience, phooey."

In midtown Yuma, as Tom passed a drugstore behind a dirt parking lot, he noticed a silver Plymouth. He braked. The horn of a tailgating jalopy blasted at him. To save a few seconds, he resisted reaching out the window and shaking his fist. He hoped the cars in the oncoming lane had good brakes, as he cut into that lane and wheeled a U-turn. In less than a minute, he was pulling into the lot in front of the drugstore.

The Plymouth was gone. Or he'd lost his marbles and started seeing phantoms, maybe a lasting effect from using laudanum.

When Tom crossed the Rio Colorado, bone thin men, women, and youngsters from the migrant camps perched on the shore, upriver and down, fishing for breakfast before the sun rose, the water boiled, and the catfish fish went to nap in deep pools.

He got stalled on the bridge at the rear of a dozen-vehicle lineup. Dusty and bug-splattered as it had gotten crossing the desert, his four-year-old Chevy was easily the most presentable crate. Most of the others were farm pickups loaded with sofas and washing machines or pens crammed with clucking chickens, or billowing with blankets tied to bent poles that formed Quonset-shaped shelters.

The first ten minutes he waited behind the wheel, mustering the patience he'd advised Florence to exhibit, and only inched forward when another car got sent to the turnaround and shooed back over the bridge. After smelling his burnt clutch, he learned from the migrants. He turned off the engine, stood outside and when the chance to move came, he pushed, one hand on the steering wheel, the other on the doorjamb.

By the time he reached the checkpoint, a small gang of cops had gathered. A couple of them nodded in his direction. But even the nods were more sorrowful than friendly, even from the one man Tom recognized, a veteran beat cop named Bosley.

The interrogating officer at the front of the gang, whose Armenian scowl looked frozen in place, wore the state trooper get up. "You would be Tom Hickey."

"Pleased to meet you," Tom said.

"Now, I don't know this, else I would arrest you, but these fellas tell me you might want to turn around, head east and keep driving."

From behind the trooper, Bosley wagged his head so hard, his jowls wiggled. "Davis put out a warrant."

"Nothing to do but turn myself in," Tom said.

He saluted thanks and drove on, wondering whether one of Madeline's Hollywood connections could land her an audition with a Chicago or New York orchestra, and if Davis would go to the trouble of interstate extradition.

But all such speculation meant nothing if he intended to act on Harry Longabaugh's advice and set out to get justice against the man Leo consider the actual ruler of the world.

He called Madeline from the El Centro Shell station. Her room phone rang until the snippy hotel operator cut him off with a wry "Sorry, as usual, Mister."

Chapter Fifty-six

William Randolph Hearst got around. Aside from residing in his home in Los Angeles, the mansion he had built for Marion Davies on the beach in Santa Monica, a retreat in the northern California woods, and his castle up the coast, he was inclined to spend months of each year in Europe collecting art.

On the road out of the desert, across the mountains, and following the coastline to L.A. along El Camino Real, Tom considered all those possibilities. And he contemplated strategies for avoiding the LAPD. Cops in the city weren't as likely as those in Yuma, who knew the lowdown on Larry Loftus, to give Tom a pass.

He decided to drop off his car on the outskirts and use the streetcar.

From Highway 101, he caught Firestone Boulevard east and soon arrived at a butcher shop, proprietor Ralph Clifton, a pal from his Alamo Meat salesman years. Ralph had a fenced parking lot, which Tom entered through the alley. He pulled in between the incinerator and a delivery van.

He stepped out, stretched, and noticed a police cruiser making the turn off Alameda Boulevard. As the cruiser drove out of sight, Tom noticed the street sign above the corner. Florence Avenue. Next, while digging through the miscellany in his Chevy's glove compartment in case it held something he ought not to leave behind, he came upon an envelope Florence had given him months ago. He had meant to take it from the car to the box where he kept mementoes. Apparently he'd forgotten.

Inside the envelope was a studio portrait, a colorized photo of his sister, himself, and Charlie Hickey.

Tom, at four years old, wore a lacy blouse Milly the seamstress had crafted. He was perched on the right knee of his dad, aged twenty-four. Charlie's wavy hair looked mussed, his bright blue eyes and broad smile beamed with love. His arms, muscular and sinewed, wrapped around his children's shoulders and pressed them to his sides, with their faces turned slightly toward him. Florence, on the left knee, was half Tom's size. Her hair was wavier, more golden, and her eyes bluer and bigger. A tiny replica of Charlie.

Tom stood in the hazy sunlight staring at the photo and realizing anew that what became of their father, of his murderer, and of Tom himself, meant as much to Florence as it did to him.

Whether or not some ghostly force had delivered him to the corner of Alameda and Florence and then to the photo, he knew that from now on, he and Florence were a team.

Chapter Fifty-seven

After a brief chat with Ralph about their mutual pal Bud Gallagher, Tom hustled to catch the Alameda streetcar. Downtown he connected to the Glendale Boulevard route. He reached Angelus Temple soon after four.

As he crossed Echo Park, he used the cover of oaks and the shade they cast, avoided the wide sunny clearing near the lake, and kept watch far ahead. A platoon of chattering squirrels tailed him until he crossed the road to the sidewalk that bordered the Angelus Temple sanctuary.

Florence's desk was on the ground floor of the parsonage, between the sanctuary and the Bible college. Tom hadn't entered the parsonage in ten years, since he went there to question Sister Aimee about the Echo Park lynching of Frank Gaines, a great man without whom Tom might have gotten lost in darkness during his dreadful childhood. The year Frank got lynched, Sister Aimee was dueling with accusers in the Grand Jury inquiry over her allegedly staged kidnap and rescue. Reporters swarmed all around the parsonage, while guards blocked the entry. Now, Tom simply turned the knob and walked in.

A girl wearing the blue and white Bible school uniform sat at the desk beside the circular stairway, brushing her hair and reading *The Bridal Call*, a magazine Sister Aimee wrote and published. When Tom cleared his throat, she looked up and gasped.

She rose and peeped, "One minute, please," then tore up

the spiral staircase. As she reached the top, she called out, "Miss Florence, come quick."

In seconds, Florence appeared and came rushing down the stairs. She didn't bother to greet her brother, only grabbed him by the wrist and pulled him toward an interior doorway behind the stairs.

"Whoa." He reached to pick up Madeline's daisy print suitcase, which he had set down beside him, then allowed Florence to tow him through a room stacked nearly wall to wall and floor to ceiling with Foursquare evangelical tracts and magazines. She towed him out a back door that led to a parking area, a loading dock, and the rollup warehouse doors at the rear entrance to the sanctuary, through which crews delivered the elaborate stage sets the preacher used to dramatize her sermons.

Florence dragged her brother to the preacher's 1934 Packard 1108 Dietrich convertible, cream-beige with a white top and four doors, whitewall tires, and plenty of chrome. When they reached it, she grabbed his suitcase, tossed it into the backseat, and steered him around to the driver's door.

"You're driving, Tommy." She flung the door open, gave him a firm push, then ran around the car, flung open the passenger door and dove in.

As she settled herself on the passenger seat, she said, "Anybody sees a blond gal driving something like this, they figure it's got to be a movie star. We don't want a bunch of fans chasing after our autographs." She reached into her purse and shoved a key at him. "Get a move on."

"Are we stealing this ocean liner?"

"I'll tell you once we're out of here. I've had the girls watching out for cops, Tommy. The little guy in the Plymouth, he didn't even go home last night. He's camped out in the shade of the same oak they hung Frank Gaines on. I don't know how you got by him."

"You sure he's a cop?"

"Well, no matter. He's not the only one. A cruiser rolls by every ten minutes or so. Circling the neighborhood."

Tom had often daydreamed about driving such a vehicle as this Packard. When the motor kicked in, he gave it a few revs. Florence reached for the chauffer's cap sitting on the dashboard and tossed it to her brother. "Put this on," she ordered.

Tom switched headgear. Then he eased the clutch out. Still the Packard lurched. On the driveway up the slope between the parsonage and the Bible school, they did more bouncing than rolling.

A block away, at the intersection of Lemoyne Street and Echo Park Boulevard, they turned left in front of the cruiser occupied by two uniformed cops Tom didn't recognize. Florence gave them a smile and wave. "The driver's a regular at the temple," she said. "Sits in the third row."

Tom was about to turn left onto Glendale when he hit the brake. "Hold it. Where's Elizabeth?"

Chapter Fifty-eight

Supposing his daughter would be in the Bible school getting spoiled by a crew of mothers-to-be, he said, "I'll park and hunker down out of sight while you run back and fetch her."

"She's not here, Tommy. Madeline came for her this morning."

Tom sat a minute weighing the potential meanings of Madeline coming for her girl. "Are they going back to Catalina?"

A Ford behind them blasted its horn. Tom, who considered a toot polite, a blast inflammatory, shook a fist out the window before he pulled away and made the turn.

Florence said, "Couldn't tell you where they went. I was out when Madeline showed up. Elizabeth was cutting paper dolls with Rachel, at the front desk in the parsonage. Rachel didn't ask questions on account of Madeline acted like, you cross her, she'll bite your nose off."

"We'll drive by the house," Tom said. "Look for any sign of them."

"Okay, but a couple blocks before we get there, pull over and let me drive. That's when you better hunker down. The cops are sure to have your place staked out. I'll run in and out, look around. And on the way to Leo's, I'll keep an eye out, see if we've picked up a tail."

"Leo's? Why Leo's?"

"He made me promise to bring you, first thing. Say, you don't suppose he's turned on us, do you? I mean, he *is* a cop, Tommy."

Tom didn't answer. He felt a ghastly solitude descending upon him. A week ago, he would've trusted Leo with his life. Today he trusted no one except his own blood. Not Leo, not Bud, not even Madeline.

"By the way," he asked, "are we stealing this swanky machine?"

"Not exactly. I mean, Sister's with us. Only, if they nab us, we cop to stealing it. She can't afford to get nailed for helping out desperados. That's the deal."

"Great. I not only do five to ten in Quentin for assaulting an officer, but they tack on another ten or so for grand theft, and you go to Corona for abetting."

Florence gave him a wink. "That settles it. They're not going to take us alive."

Tom only hoped she was teasing. With women in general, Florence in particular, he could never feel certain.

Along Glendale, he spent minutes deliberating whether Leo was on their team or had defected to Chief Davis'. At last he said, "I don't trust Leo."

She cast a woeful eye his way. "Ah, Tommy. If we can't trust Leo, who *can* we trust?"

"Nobody, except each other."

"Gosh," she said. "That's lousy. If that's the case, why bother to keep on living?"

"We've got work to do, is why. How about Hearst?"

"What about him?"

"Did you pin down his whereabouts?"

"Oh, that was a cinch. I read it on the *Times* society page. Seems old Harry Chandler keeps a sharp eye on his competitor. Mr. Hearst and pretty Marion left town a few days ago, on their way to San Simeon."

Chapter Fifty-nine

The drive-by of the Hickeys' Hobart Place cottage gained them nothing except an assurance Madeline hadn't so much as stopped there. Florence got that news from a neighbor, the ancient but spry Mrs. Evelyn, who could be found most any day as twilight approached watering her tomatoes, strawberries, and petunias. She assured Florence neither Tom nor his wife had come or gone from the cottage these past several days.

When his sister returned to the car, Tom took the wheel. Florence sat sideways, legs curled on the seat. On the way out of the neighborhood, for a couple miles up Wilshire past the Ambassador Hotel and the Coconut Grove, where Tom had promised to take Madeline for her upcoming birthday, and into the Fairfax district, she kept a sharp eye out for a tail.

She gave Tom an all-clear as they neared the Weiss residence, an older but shipshape Craftsman three blocks northwest of Wilshire and LaBrea. A mile from the tar pits and nearest derrick, the easterly breeze carried an oily smell and flavor. Bougainvillea, summer lush and in full bloom, masked the view of the next-door rental where Tom, Florence, and their mother had lived for a spell, before Violet caught Milly whipping her kids' bare backs with a garden hose.

On the porch, as expected, Tom kissed Violet's cheek, round and firm as a ripe nectarine. She was plump in a curvy fashion, and given to cheerful ways. But today, a sad dull patina tinted her eyes and clued Tom that she knew plenty about his predicaments, and how he'd landed in them.

He asked to use the telephone and left his sister to field Violet's questions. He carried the phone from the parlor as far as the cord allowed into the alcove Leo called his library, between the parlor and dining room. He perched on the window seat across from the built-in mahogany bookshelves and fished from his billfold the number of the Hotel Atwater.

When, as before, nobody answered the phone in her room, he asked the snippy operator if she had seen Mrs. Hickey and her daughter this afternoon.

"I'm s'posed to know what she looks like?"

"The lady's a dish, auburn hair, wide eyes, walks a bit swishy. She's the singer at the casino. The girl, prettier still, age five, curly, blondish."

"Nope."

He asked for the front desk. The clerk named Bruce, a pale, thin, bespeckled youngster whom Tom had noticed gazing starstruck when Madeline passed by, denied having seen Elizabeth. "Mrs. Madeline went out this morning, sir, accompanied by a gentleman."

"What did the gentleman look like?" Tom asked, supposing it was the bandleader Paul Perkins.

"Pudgy fellow. Clean shaven. Reddish hair."

Perkins was trim, had dark curly hair. The gentleman could well be Milton Hopper.

"She hasn't come back," the clerk said. "I would of noticed."

"I bet you would," Tom said. "She comes in, tell her to call Leo, leave a message, when I can reach her."

"Got it. Leo."

Tom wouldn't have used Leo as a message drop if he had known what the next few minutes would bring.

When he returned the phone to the parlor, Leo was on the edge of his easy chair, stiff and leaning forward. His face, stone still with an outthrust jaw, meant trouble. Whenever Tom had seen him wearing that look, somebody got hurt or at least gravely accused.

He motioned Tom to the love seat Florence already occupied. She slid to one side and patted the velvet cushion.

Violet took her leave, with a claim she was preparing supper. "Anyone care for a drink or a snack, just holler."

Tom sat. He noticed a folder beside Leo, wedged between the easy chair's arm and seat.

"Got something for me?"

After a silent few moments, Leo said, "That I do,"

"Hand it over."

"You won't like it."

Tom attempted a chuckle. "Can't say I've liked a thing I've got handed this past week or so. Listen, just in case you're not the right guy I make you for, you're not setting us up, are you?"

"What in hell does that mean?" Leo growled.

"Means I should trust you're not expecting a visit from the gang in blue?"

Though Leo glowered and shook his head, the gesture appeared more of chagrin than of denial. Florence scooted closer to her brother and looped her arm under his.

"Loftus isn't necessarily the end of the world," Leo said, "or even the end of your job."

"What do you think, Kent Parrot's going keep bailing me out forever?"

"Might not have to. A number of the boys on the Yuma detail wouldn't mind standing up for you. The way I hear, plenty of them would've done the same if they had been as stupid as you currently are. Getting you back on the force is a long shot, but worth considering."

"One in a million," Tom said, "even if I were to forgo what I'm bound to do next."

Florence said, "We, Tommy."

"Yeah, we." He glanced over and patted her hand then turned back to Leo. "Well, I'm proud to know I've got some friends. Now," he pointed, "what's in the folder?"

Leo sighed as he leaned back into the easy chair. "First, are both of you truth-seekers willing to know it all, no matter if it's going to break your heart?"

Tom looked long and hard at his sister and read terror in her eyes even while she sat nodding. "No matter what," he said.

Leo heaved himself out of the chair, picked up the file, and delivered it.

Chapter Sixty

The file was about an inch think. Tom set it resting half on his pant leg, half on the thigh of Florence's rosy skirt.

Page one led off with a summary of the particulars of the victim. Terence Poole, son of Talbot Poole, founder of Suncoast Oil. Age 24, height 5'9", weight 170, brown eyes, sandy hair, no scars or other distinguishing marks. Cause of death, puncture wounds that severed the aorta.

The Hickeys leaned together and read in silence that Poole died outside the home he shared with two other young men, one of whom, Raul Webb, witnessed the altercation. According to Webb and Victor LeBlanc, the neighbor from across Kingsley Street who phoned the police, a man had stood outside the Poole and Webb residence shouting challenges and threats, demanding that Poole come outside. When Poole complied, the man shouted accusations LeBlanc, who was older and hard of hearing, failed to make out, but Webb caught enough to infer that the man was claiming an affair between Poole and his wife. Webb, when questioned after the fact, denied having any knowledge of said affair.

According to Webb, Poole was unarmed. LeBlanc, however, claimed Terence Poole was waving a pistol when the man lunged at him and plunged the knife into his chest.

The assailant then threw down his weapon and fled on foot, around the corner onto Council Street. No one followed. Webb attempted to stanch the victim's wound. LeBlanc ran to his telephone.

A patrol car arrived in five minutes. They, and subsequently a pair of detectives, searched the lawn and porch of the victim's home and seized as evidence the bloody knife with which Poole got stabbed. The search continued well into the night, through the house and nearby yards, but failed to produce the pistol neighbor LeBlanc contended Poole had waved at his assailant.

Both Webb and LeBlanc were escorted downtown and their statements were taken. LeBlanc never relented from his assertion that Poole had waved a pistol, and that the killer had dark brown hair and stood shorter than Poole.

However, the detective in charge, Marino, noted that Raul Webb was younger, with presumably keener eyesight, and had witnessed the crime from only yards, while LeBlanc viewed the scene in twilight from across the street. According to Webb, the murderer was inches taller, more slender, and lighter of complexion and hair color than Poole. Tom noted that these details fit the particulars of Charlie Hickey.

Near the bottom of the stack they found a report asserting that along with Poole's blood, the knife had shown traces of blood from a cow.

Charlie Hickey was a butcher.

Subsequent pages featured a summary by Detective Marino about the steps in his investigation that determined, beginning with a serial number on the knife handle, that the weapon came from Alamo Meat.

The last and longest document was a transcript of an interview with Millicent Hickey, wife of suspect Charles Hickey.

Tom only read the first paragraph, in which his mother claimed that Charlie became savagely jealous when he learned that she and Terence Poole had gone out for drinks after they met at a film audition.

At that point, the folder and its contents went flying, as Florence leaped up and lunged across the room toward Leo with her arms thrashing.

Leo sprang to his feet and caught hold of her head in both hands, while Tom rushed in and cinched his arms around her waist. The curses she screeched sounded like the Florence of a dozen years past, at the climax of her worst night. She was sixteen. Tom had caught up with her in a Santa Monica speakeasy, found her lit up on gin and dancing the Charleston with a notorious procurer of call girls, who soon found himself hospitalized with a concussion and broken ribs.

Tom warned Leo away and dragged his sister, still thrashing and screaming, to the front door. He kicked it open, and then stopped. Holding Florence tight around the waist and shoulders, he faced back toward Leo. "I've got to ask, what's all that phony evidence have to do with who killed Charlie?"

Leo barely shook his head. "Don't make me say it."

In the Packard, Florence braced herself on the dashboard. She wailed and sobbed for minutes, while Tom kneaded her neck and shoulders. At last, she tamed her fury and sat another minute gathering her thoughts. Then she asked, "That crack, 'Don't make me say it'. Did he mean what I think?"

"You're thinking what?"

"Don't make him say that since our daddy murdered a guy, why should we care who murdered our daddy?"

"I suppose he meant just that."

She used another minute to catch her breath and smooth the rosy woolen dress around her breasts and legs. "What do you make of it all, Tommy?"

"Hearst," he said.

"What about him? You mean he was in on the Terence Poole murder?"

"I mean, Hearst got wind of what we're up to, and he's out to put a lid on it before we get started."

"He got to Leo?"

"My guess is he got to somebody who got to Leo."

Florence let go of the dashboard and settled into the cushiony seat. "Okay, but Hearst got wind of us how?"

"Could be that lousy producer. Say Hopper ran off flapping his jaw about the murder of Ambrose Bierce, and the way things get around, a Hearst reporter intercepted and ran to the boss."

"Sure, I like it. And, Mr. Hearst knows any investigation of the Bierce murder is apt to lead straight to him. Think we better talk to Hopper?"

Chapter Sixty-one

As they drove out of the shady Fairfax side streets and turned onto Wilshire Boulevard, where the sun's glare ricocheted off the multitude of picture windows, a torrent of questions attacked Tom. Foremost, he wondered how he was liable to react if he caught Madeline with the producer.

And who was Marino, the detective who had allegedly traced the murder weapon to Alamo Meat, and where could Marino be found? Could Milly's connections have gone deep enough into the system, or her talons sunk deep enough into a cop, such as this Marino, to get the cop or department to deliver false evidence? Where was Bud when the cops descended upon Alamo Meat, as they no doubt would have, and why hadn't Bud, when he gave Tom the story, come clean about the Alamo Meat butcher knife they called evidence against Charlie?

And was Leo part of the Terence Poole murder investigation? Tom berated himself for leaving the file behind instead of waiting in the car for Florence's fit to pass, then going back and gathering what she had scattered.

His mind shifted from one question to the other so fast, they deflected the anger and worry. He couldn't dwell on the fright Florence had given him, that the peace she seemed to have found might be only skin-deep. He couldn't wrestle with the notion that Hearst might be onto their moves and playing the LAPD against them. He couldn't wallow in the fear that his willful exploits had sent Madeline running into the arms of

Milton Hopper. Nor could he ask himself to consider whether the Charlie Hickey he remembered, or the one he knew from stories, could have murdered.

He stopped for gas at the Richfield on the corner of Rampart and Wilshire, his regular stop because it offered a view of the both Lafayette and Westlake parks, each with its mansion row, and the Elks Lodge, a spectacular Egyptian Revival colossus featuring plinths that morphed into behemoth angels. According to Les White, half the system's conniving got done in the Elks Lodge.

A lanky attendant who looked cross, as though itching for a fistfight, came running to their service. While he pumped gas and checked the air pressure and oil and washed the windows, every other second he appeared to shift his admiration from the car to the knockout blonde in the passenger seat with her door open, even though Florence was hardly at her best. She slumped and looked severely downcast, her soft curls tangled and flyaway.

Tom, who had gone to the telephone booth, returned to the car with an address for Milton Hopper. The attendant pointed to the price on the gas pump.

"Good God," Tom mumbled. "How many gallons does this dirigible hold?"

"That's what you get with twelve cylinders, pal," the attendant said as though daring Tom to offer a comeback. Tom handed him a ten, waited for the change, and tipped the fellow a quarter.

They took Vermont to Sunset Boulevard, and turned right on Sunset Plaza Drive, maneuvered the S-curves and upsweeps to Apian Way, and found Cyprian Drive. By then, Florence's demeanor had cheered a bit.

She reached for her brother's arm, inviting him to stay another moment in the car. "You going to be okay, Tommy?"

"I'm holding up," he said.

"I mean, with this producer, maybe you want me to go to the door and ask the questions? I've got ways of getting men to talk."

"So do I. Let's go."

The Hopper place was a low-slung Oriental model perched on a cutout in the slope. Beyond a hedge on the downhill side, lights glanced off a swimming pool. The front yard featured a chinaberry tree that rustled in the tangy breeze that drifted up from the Pacific, a curving flagstone walkway between patches of tuft grass, and two fishponds with silvery creatures the size of sardines flashing around.

A chain activated the doorbell, which played a xylophone tune. Tom and Florence waited until his patience expired, then he pounded the door with the side of his fist.

Eyes appeared on the other side of the peek window.

"Open up," Tom said, loud and harsh enough to clue her that he would just as soon kick the door down.

The woman who opened the door wore a Japanese housecoat. In Tom's appraisal, she had the face of a starlet gone halfway to seed. Her lipstick wasn't smeared but was carelessly applied. Her platinum hair probably hadn't gotten brushed since morning, and then only a few strokes. Her eyes were pale, the whites nearly gray as the pupils. She glanced at Florence but addressed Tom. "Are we acquainted?" Since she gave so little sign of fright or concern, he made her for someone who had given up caring.

Tom used the title detective along with his name. "I'd like a word with Milton."

"So would I," she said. "Say, you detectives always bring your girl along?" In one of the rooms behind the woman, two children argued over some trifle. "Milton do something naughty?"

Tom gave her the look cops use to remind folks which of them is supposed to ask the questions.

She replied with a sigh. "Well, he's not here. Not for a few days, now."

"You want to tell me where he went?"

"Santa Catalina. On business," she said with an uptick on the last word, like somebody trying to assure herself.

Chapter Sixty-two

At the intersection of Sunset Plaza Drive and Sunset Boulevard, at the stop sign when Tom glanced right, his sister laid a hand on his arm. "Tommy, we go to Catalina, we're probably giving up on our daddy, aren't we? I mean, giving up on knowing the truth about him?"

"How do you figure?"

"I'm no cop, but my guess would be they've got the ferries staked out, and the Atwater Hotel and the Casino, if not the whole island."

"What makes me that important?"

"Like you said, maybe Hearst got to them."

Tom nodded as he eased the clutch out and swung west on Sunset. His sister left her hand on his arm. He said, "Forget Catalina. We'll make a right on the Coast route."

Most vigilantly through West Hollywood and Santa Monica, Florence kept her eye out for cruisers and silver Plymouths. North of Malibu, she allowed some distraction and persuaded Tom to give her a play-by-play of his trip to the desert, beginning with a full account of his metamorphosis from a cop to an outlaw.

Tom was glad to talk, a reprieve from brooding over Leo's damned file, or picturing Madeline and Elizabeth frolicking on a sailboat with Milton Hopper, or imagining how a desperate nobody could gain a private audience with the high and mighty William Randolph Hearst.

He described the boy C.J. and his sister, told their story, and recalled in detail the court of shacks, the cops playing poker, the presence of Marlon Brooks. He confessed to feeling not a dash of mercy and, in cold blood, shattering Loftus' knee. A touch of guilt put him on defense. He said, "Eye for an eye, more or less," and glanced over for his sister's reaction.

She only tossed a grimace his way, and Tom reminded himself to leave the Bible alone. On that topic, if she disputed, he would punt. She was way out of his league.

He told her about the Judas bellhop at the Congress Hotel who pretended to clue him to Betty Weaver's whereabouts then ratted on him. About the Indian who did him a couple favors, and the towhead so pointlessly ornery he gave thugs a bad name, and the enigmatic Betty Weaver with her vile herbal concoction. He voiced his opinion of both the pleasant and the wretched effects of laudanum.

He described the old man who called himself Hiram Beebe and Harry Longabaugh. After he launched into the outlaw's story, he noticed Florence crumpling the hem of her skirt, brushing it flat, and crumpling it again. She also gnawed her lower lip with her upper teeth, as if she meant to draw blood. He reached over and put a finger to her lips. From then on, all through his account of the Longabaugh version of the Bierce and Charlie Hickey murders, she held her face taut and still. Only at the end, a deep moan issued out of her. Storm clouds appeared in her sky blue eyes and painted a dark veil over them. While she wept, Tom pulled off and stopped beneath the sparking neon Vacancy sign between a diner and a row of overnight cottages.

He was opening Florence's door, thinking this place could be the site of one of his lies in the story he told Betty Weaver, when a highway patrol cruiser came rattling over the ruts and gravel.

Chapter Sixty-three

The diner served as the motor-lodge office.

The patrolman, a straw-haired youngster built as if he had grown up hoisting hay bales, shuffled along behind Tom and Florence, no doubt enjoying the view.

Inside, the lone waitress, dark and voluptuous, refilled the patrolman's thermos with coffee and absorbed the fellow's attention. His only glance in Tom's direction was for a peek at Florence, which earned him a sneer from the waitress.

The proprietor, a swarthy Greek slightly upward from middle age, maintained his hearty smile while the Hickeys checked in. Tom gave his name as Tommy Wayne, the aka under which he led a dance orchestra. The name Hickey too often drew smirks and wisecracks.

The Greek led them out to the porch, pointed to the nearest cottage, and handed over a key. "Now you better eat, righto?"

"Yep, we'd better," Florence said. Both she and her brother had skipped the whole day's mealtimes.

Back inside, the Greek recited a short menu, took their order and called into the kitchen for tuna sandwiches and cans of strawberry nectar. He showed them to the largest of three tables, sat with them and quizzed Tom about the gadgetry of his snazzy Packard. Tom knew little about gear ratios or carburetion. He had to bluff a few answers, which unnerved him. For all he knew, the LAPD had caught on to the fugitives driving the evangelist's boat and broadcast the news statewide. The highway patrolman might've opted to simply observe them checking in. Right now, he might be summoning the posse.

The waitress delivered their sandwiches and nectar, gave Tom an eyelash flutter, and dismissed Florence with a toss of her chin.

Florence suggested they eat in the cottage. The Greek was standing nearby and overheard. "Okey doke," he said. "Anastasia, she's a good girl. A flirt, you betcha, but a good girl, no kidding." He went behind the counter and fetched a paper sack for their sandwiches.

The cottage walls were whitewashed boards. A coat rack, pole lamp, and two full beds with a floor model Motorola radio in between so filled the place, that when they perched on the sides of the beds that faced each other, their knees touched. They kept their own council while they ate, until Tom asked, "What are you thinking, babe?"

"Oh, stuff about Charlie. Like, are we sure he's dead? Like, do we know for certain he didn't stab Terence Poole?" She let herself collapse backward onto the bed. "How about it, Tommy?"

"What we've got," Tom said, "is stories. That's all."

"I'm with you. Like Harry Longabaugh gets bushwhacked in Bolivia and buried down there. Whole books testify he did. Now, he shows up. Same as Charlie could."

"There's a happy thought to sleep on."

Once they had visited the bathroom, peeled off a layer of clothes, and settled under the patchwork quilts and dingy sheets, Florence said, "Tommy, about tomorrow?"

"Uh huh."

"Think about what Mr. Hearst does for a living."

"Peddles lies?"

"Dreams up stories, anyway."

"That he does."

"What I mean is don't let him do the talking. We've already got our fill of stories. Don't ask him anything. Turn the tables. *You* tell *him*. You've heard enough to make up your own story."

"*Our* own story," Tom said. "So you say I tell him how Bierce and then Charlie got in his way, and he gave the order to rub them out. And all the while I watch close, and he gives himself away?"

"Yessir, unless he's got no heart at all."

"Then I kill him?"

She only rose up a little, braced with her elbow, smiled and blew him a kiss. "Good night, Tommy."

Chapter Sixty-four

Tom dozed an hour or so. Then he lay wondering what chilling dreams sent Florence into fits of writhing and uttering fearful yips and gasps. He would have woken her except he supposed a troubled sleep was better than none.

All his questions twisted and tangled around each other. Supposing the worst, that something convinced him to believe Charlie Hickey killed Terence Poole, should he pass the same judgment on his father's killer as if Charlie were innocent?

And regarding judgment, could the offspring of two murderers prove of sound mind enough to correctly judge anybody?

Then, if he convicted Charlie, should he keep the judgment to himself or pass the verdict along to his girls? What would become of Elizabeth as the grandchild of two murderers and the daughter of another, as Tom might become an assassin within hours?

He had left the curtain open enough to allow a shaft of daylight in. Florence woke at the first hint of dawn. She used a shower to wake up while Tom sat on the porch watching sunrise and counting miles on a map. From their location along a stretch where the coast highway jogged inland, Tom estimated another hour to Santa Barbara, at least two hours from there to Pismo Beach, and no more than two the rest of the way to Hearst's compound at San Simeon.

Chapter Sixty-five

From age ten, when Tom first rode his bicycle along the boulevards, he delighted in watching the builders erect graceful edifices such as the Art Deco Bullock's Wilshire and the Wilshire Temple with its majestic dome. If not for Florence, whom he valued far above any career, he would've become an architect. He'd spent two glorious years as a USC architecture major.

On account of his passion, he'd learned plenty about Hearst's projects, especially the one up the coast halfway between L.A. and San Francisco.

Once the tycoon inherited a quarter million acres on the chaparral hills that rose from the coastal plain around San Simeon Bay, he had contacted architect Julia Morgan, advised her that he and his guests were tired of camping out, and asked her to design and build a little something.

Julia Morgan was a hero of Tom's, California-born, Paris-trained, the first female architect licensed in California. During college, Tom had ridden a bus all day and night to visit her Beaux Arts Fairmont Hotel on San Francisco's Nob Hill. Later, as a route salesman for Alamo Meat, he often stopped during lunch to watch the construction of her Neo-Renaissance Hollywood Studio Club. Since he'd become a husband, cop, and father, he'd given up making excursions on his own, or else he surely would've gone to snoop around San Simeon.

He'd read of the eclectic integration of southern European design and of the marble statues of lions, classical busts, and goddesses, bas-reliefs adorning the colonnades, entire walls featuring classical and pastoral murals bought in Europe and shipped intact.

He had viewed a gallery of photographs. His favorites were the third-century marble *Sarcophagus of the Nine Muses*, and a mosaic of the *Three Graces*, Beauty, Charm, and Joy, the daughters of Zeus, who sang and danced for the gods on Mount Olympus.

As he drove through Cambria, Tom felt dismay at the thought that the guy in whose case he would play judge and jury was a lover of beauty. Better to consider the man a wretch clear-through. Maybe he just bought masterpieces to prove that he could.

A mile short of the destination, Tom pulled off, stepped out of the car and went to the trunk, to the suitcase for his holster and .38. He strapped it on, climbed back into the car and tried to ignore his sister's frown.

"You've got a plan, Tommy?"

"Wouldn't help if I did. Who knows what we're up against?"

The road to Hearst's compound ran straight uphill from the coast highway then leveled off and became a lengthy circular drive. Tom let the Packard ease around the circle to the front. He parked at the curb a long field goal away from the entrance. He caught a deep breath, glanced over at Florence and nodded. He climbed out and gazed through an archway at the Casa Grande, with its towers like those of Spanish cathedrals.

What charmed Florence was the ocean view. They stood side by side in front of the Packard, facing opposite directions, both so engaged they didn't hear the guard approaching until he demanded, "Your business?"

Florence left the men and strolled to a patch of begonias, where a Mexican fellow squatted, plucking tiny weeds while he eyed her with brazen admiration.

The guard looked Hawaiian. Not particularly tall, but with shoulders as wide as two middle linemen.

"Appointment with Mr. Hearst," Tom said.

The guard laughed like a sadist at a hanging. "Nice try, bucko."

Tom attempted calm and confidence. "Mr. Hearst and I go way back. See, Miss Davies is a family friend. So you hustle on in and let W.R. know Tom Hickey came to talk."

When Tom gave his name, the guard's eyebrows raised.

Tom said, "You give him my name, he'll want to talk, all right. On the other hand, there's this." He attempted to slip the billfold from his inside coat pocket without revealing the packed shoulder holster. A twitch of the Hawaiian's eye proved Tom's attempt hadn't succeeded.

He opened the billfold and let sunlight flash off his badge. While the Hawaiian made a study of the badge and its possessor, he wore a look as though perplexed about whether to kneel in front of Tom or to punch him in the nose. "Mr. Hearst left early," he said. "First thing."

Tom sighed. "Where to?"

"Say, I'm nobody's private secretary."

"What'll it take for you to run inside and ask around?"

The man rolled his massive shoulders. "Bribe, or threat?"

"Take your pick."

Before the guard could summon a response, Florence was at her brother's side, her arm on his shoulder. "How about lunch? I'm famished."

Tom glanced over and saw the pursed lips, her version of a telling wink. He walked her around the car, opened her door, and closed it behind her.

He leaned across the Packard's roof and said to the guard, "We'll be back." He slid in behind the wheel.

"What did you get?" he asked Florence.

"Well, Paco's nicer than the big guy, and he got straight from the chambermaid that a secretary brought in a message while Miss Davies was dressing, and next thing, the charming couple decided to rough it. Set off in a Bentley, Davies driving. By now they ought to be halfway to the family fish camp on the McCloud River, up north. Over the hills and far away."

Chapter Sixty-six

Tom was driving with one eye, consulting his map with the other in hopes of choosing the swiftest route through the foothills, when a patrol car headed south wheeled a U-turn and raced up onto their tail.

Tom cussed. Florence said, "Ditto."

He slowed and pulled onto the gravel shoulder.

The patrolman walked with nervous stutter steps to Tom's window, his left hand on the butt of his sidearm. Rather than squatting, he stooped and kept a yard of air between himself and the window.

"Since I wasn't speeding," Tom said, "I'm at a loss here."

Florence leaned close to her brother and graced the officer with a sweet hello.

Up close, he appeared frail, timid, and sunburned. His sharp nose was peeling in strips. "License."

"Care to see my badge while you're at it?"

"Suit yourself."

As Tom reached inside his coat, the officer cross-drew his weapon, a black Walther-like one Leo had favored before Hitler came to power.

Tom removed his right hand from the coat and laid it atop his head. With his left hand, he pulled back the lapel and showed the inside pocket. He passed his billfold to the officer.

After a glance at the license, the officer said, "I heard you city boys take a cut here and there. Guess that's how a cop comes to afford a Dietrich ragtop."

"It's a swell crate, all right. My sister here borrowed it."

She leaned across Tom. "My employer's the generous sort."

"Got papers on it?"

"Sure do." Florence slid back to her side and opened the glove compartment.

"You a churchgoer?" Tom asked but got no answer. "Might of heard about Sister Aimee Semple McPherson. Florence is a trusted associate."

If the fellow hadn't asked for papers, Tom wouldn't have offered the Sister Aimee connection, as the multitude who adored her was outnumbered by those who called her a fake and a swindler.

The officer only glanced at the papers Florence passed to him then handed them back. "About a mile up ahead, you'll come to a roadhouse. You pull in, have a soda while I telephone your employer. She vouches for you, you're jake. Now, before we get moving, you best show me what's under that coat."

Tom lifted the right lapel.

"Like I thought. Now step out here, unstrap, carry it around back, and stow it in the trunk while you're showing me what else you've got in there."

The trunk only held two suitcases, a ratcheting jack, a tool kit, and a canvas bag for water. Florence's leather suitcase, the officer merely peeked into. He dug deep into Tom's flowered one and brought out the Katoulis Browning.

The officer's soft eyes sharpened and drilled Tom's.

"Our daddy lives out in the woods, east of Weed," Florence said, "all alone. Needs protection, desperate as some folks are these days."

The officer gave her a gradually widening smile and laid the Browning on top of Tom's spare trousers.

As they pulled back onto the road, Tom said, "Weed?"

"Up north somewhere. I saw it on the map."

"And there's woods east of the place?"

"I hope so. Tommy, one of those fellas back at the Hearst place ratted us out. I hope it wasn't Paco. I liked him."

She turned and waved to the officer behind them. "You know, when we pick up today's or tomorrow's *Examiner,* we're liable find our names in a headline. Maybe we ought not to be Hickey for now."

"Last night, at the motor lodge, we were Mr. and Mrs. Tommy Wayne."

"That's no good," she said. "You were a famous bandleader"

"Famous, was I?"

"Sort of. Anyhow, let's pick a new one.

Over the mile to the roadhouse, they settled on Jasper and Minnie Arbuckle.

The roadhouse had walls of adobe blocks, which Tom suspected might've gone up before the Mexican settlers got run out by the *gringos.* Inside was a telephone and seating of benches at long redwood park tables. The waitress, a señorita with a smile wider than her face, recommended the albondigas. Florence ordered a bowl. Tom settled for coffee and a sweet roll. Ever since Betty Weaver's herbal concoction, he hadn't digested well.

Florence was considering a second bowl when the officer dropped the phone into its cradle, gave a thumbs-up, walked over and straddled the bench across from her. "Sister Aimee thinks you're a peach. She even put in a word for your rough-neck brother."

He turned to Tom. "Now how's about your version of the incident in Yuma? And make it a doozy, so I don't go around feeling like a chump about sending a rogue cop on his way."

Chapter Sixty-seven

By sundown they had navigated the winding ups and downs through the oak and chaparral coastal range into the sticky heat and festering odors of the San Joaquin Valley. Cattle stood with necks stretching over the barbed wire and gaped as if hoping a kind motorist would stop and offer a cool drink. Field hands plodded, stooped and rubbery, along the shoulder toward camps of tents and Quonset barracks.

Tom said, "Mostly Okies." Last count, according to the news, which Tom rarely believed without corroboration, a quarter million workers had gotten deported to Mexico. About half of them U.S. citizens. Deportation was a cause the mighty Hearst promoted.

The gas gauge bottomed out as they approached Lemoore. A gray-bearded fellow came hopping out of the office shack to pump gas and run around scrubbing the windows in cheery haste, as if the tip he might earn for filling the Packard's tank would stake him to a flush retirement. During a pause, he said, "Be cooler if you cranked the top down."

Tom nodded and declined to follow the suggestion. He preferred to sweat rather than attract the attention top-down convertibles did.

Before they pulled away, Tom counted what paper was left in his billfold and asked Florence to do likewise. Then he drove on. She totaled their numbers and tallied the likely costs. When she gave the result, he said, "Could be we'll escape from McCloud on stolen bicycles."

"Horses would be faster," Florence said.

"Felony. Bicycle's a misdemeanor."

In midtown Fresno they met the north-south highway. In the gentler air of twilight, traffic slowed through neighborhoods where couples strolled and singles prowled and preened, and where the Packard got too much notice.

Any observer might have read or heard a news clip and go running for the nearest phone. Tom attempted to relax by looking out for stone buildings, remains from the gold rush years, and for Mono Street, where his last rookie partner Milo Saropian used to live.

As they neared the outskirts, Florence grabbed his arm and pointed at a silver Plymouth. Parked at a curb. All they could see of the driver was a brown fedora. Tom lead-footed the gas, cut into the opposite lane and passed two cars.

The state's inland highway paralleled the Sierra Nevada range. While they drove, still windows down though dark had fallen, a three quarter moon and plenty of stars allowed views of the grape, peach, and almond orchards.

Tom scolded himself for failing to buy a *Fresno Bee* off one of the newsboys they had passed. He reasoned that if Hearst got word of them driving Sister Aimee's hay burner and the Hawaiian had snitched on Paco for clueing Florence to the boss man's next destination, every news reader in California could not only be on the lookout for the Packard and its gorgeous blonde cargo, they could know the likely routes on which to spot it.

He roused Florence out of a pastoral reverie. "If we were smart, we'd ditch this swell bucket and steal an old Ford."

Having recently left behind the aromas of a dairy and fertilized pasture, Florence drew a couple deep, luxurious breaths. "Except we're not car thieves, and this boat's awful comfy."

Chapter Sixty-eight

Tom calculated that driving straight through would land them in McCloud well before dawn.

Florence wanted to stop for a real supper. As they neared Merced, he spotted a log cabin structure. The signage included a neon cocktail glass alongside the name, Little Jim's Chuck Wagon.

Inside, overhead fans clacked, dim lights and candles flickered, and a troop of cowboys at the bar joked and howled laughs and curses. A few of them made eyes or low whistles at Florence. One of them shot Tom a dare that meant, "Come on, big boy, let's see you object to our manners."

Tom met the dare with a deep yawn then led his sister to the far side of the room. She said, "If any of those rubes come over, you let me handle them. I'm a bit out of practice, since my speakeasy days and I could use the drill."

She devoured a mountain of fried chicken and potatoes. Tom couldn't manage any more of his T-bone than the filet, even with a double Scotch to settle his stomach. The phonograph behind the bar offered Bill Monroe, Jimmie Rogers, and the Carter Family. Even that good music didn't help. He carved the steak into bite-sized chunks and saved them in a sack the waitress brought. On the way out, Florence waved a gracious farewell to the cowboys. Wistful gazes followed her out the door.

In the lot, Tom tripped over a begging dog. A skinny young man in ragged overalls came slinking, grabbed the dog by the collar and apologized. Tom handed the fellow his sack of beef and pointed to the dog. "Looks like he could use a bite."

Florence convinced her brother to give up the wheel. He slipped out of his brogans, curled up as best he could and closed his eyes. But even with his window open wide, sweat trickled out of his hair and ran down his forehead and cheeks. Every time he began to doze, he awoke to a vision of Charlie Hickey dashing across Kingsley Street, his right hand raised high, clutching a butcher knife. In one vision, he spotted Rusty the East Burbank pimp on a neighboring lawn. He was grinning. The next instant he was gone, and Tom wondered if the pimp Milo had thrashed wasn't human at all but a disguise of the demon that had possessed Milly Hickey and a few other villains he'd known.

Maybe, he thought, Rusty was what became of the worst when they landed in eternity.

Then, and for a long while, he felt out of his mind, suspended in a place that offered the knowledge of everything but appeared in no hurry to deliver.

As Florence pulled away from a stop sign on a Sacramento avenue of willows and houses with plantation facades, he glided back into time, bringing a story with him.

The story rang staggeringly true.

He bolted up. "I've got it, Sis."

"Huh?" Florence patted a yawn with her pretty red-tipped forefinger. "You've got what?"

"Maybe it was Bud."

"Huh?"

"Maybe Charlie didn't kill anybody. Maybe Terence Poole was making whoopee with Maureen Gallagher."

"Gallagher?"

"Yes, Bud's wife. She was a knockout, looked like a kid at forty, and was none too stuck on being married. Say Bud got wind of it, went after Poole, the boy had a pistol. Bud got him first, with the knife. You see."

Tom fell back into his seat, wrestling with the portion of shame he felt for accusing Bud.

"Sure, Tommy, I see. I do. That's why our daddy ran away. If he beat the murder wrap, he would've sent Bud to the gallows."

"Damn it all," Tom muttered.

"What a guy, our daddy." She drove slowly, shaking her head, while Tom hoped she was changing inside like he was, from the child of a monster and a murderer, into the child of a monster and a hero.

They were already outside the city, where the highway ran on a berm between rice paddies, when she said, "How'd you figure it out, Tommy?"

"I didn't," he said. "Couldn't think straight enough. The story just came to me, like special delivery from one of those muses."

"Maybe from the Holy Spirit."

"Maybe so, maybe not."

"Now what?" she asked.

Tom pointed through the windshield. "Step on it."

Chapter Sixty-nine

Florence began nodding and running the Packard onto the shoulder. When Tom spotted a saloon, he advised his sister to pull into the graveled lot. As he climbed out, she scooted over to the passenger side and closed her eyes. A grateful sigh issued from her. "Night, Tommy."

He went to the backseat for his shoes and laced them on. He left her in the car, entered the saloon, and became an anomaly amongst sleepy but dedicated drinkers by asking the bartender for a thermos of coffee.

The bartender rubbed his gray-whiskered chin then shuffled to a back room and returned with a tall thermos, dented and bruised. When the fellow asked for five dollars, Tom said, "You're wasting a talent. You ought to be a banker."

"I oughta charge you eight dollars," the man said.

Tom passed him a five and pointed to a *Sacramento Bee* on a shelf behind the bar. "Throw in the newspaper?"

"Don't come out till morning."

"Yesterday's will do the trick."

He read by the Packard's overhead light. What he dreaded, he found in the interior, in the California section.

The write-up was brief and concise. Detective Tom Hickey, wanted on a charge of assault, thought to be driving north in a stolen Packard. No mention of the model, or Florence, or of Hearst. But, he realized, the *Bee* wasn't a Hearst publication.

Coffee powered him across several bends of the Sacramento River, through Redding and over the Cascade range on a treacherous two-lane engineered so that a Packard and a delivery truck could pass with an inch or so to spare.

His Bulova's radium dial read 3:45, which Tom calculated as two hours before sunrise, when a sign welcomed them to Dunsmuir and the gas gauge warned him to fill the tank. He pulled off and parked in the lot of a closed Mobil service station. There, with his head his sister's lap, he managed to discard every thought.

Dawn woke him. Waking to the sight of a woman's lovely face offered a strange and delicious moment of peace, even though the face belonged to his sister.

He sat up and helped himself to the rest of the lukewarm coffee. Caffeine had never been a vice of Florence's. She yawned and stretched. "Where are we, Tommy?"

"About twenty miles short of McCloud."

She gazed out the windshield. "Lots of big trees. I'll bet they smell good." She rolled down her window and breathed deep. "Pine with a hint of cedar, am I right?"

"Sure," Tom said, though he didn't smell any cedar.

Across the highway and down a steep drop, a train whistle blew then a long freight came rattling. Tom stepped out of the car and walked to an outhouse. While using it, he decided to make a difficult phone call.

The phone booth was between the service station office and a vehicle Tom, a native Angelino, only guessed was a snowplow. He stopped at the car for Bud Gallagher's number, on a list in his billfold.

He supposed Bud would be awake. Pain didn't allow the old man to sleep much. The phone rang a half dozen times. Then Bud said, "Who the hell is this?"

Tom attempted to say, "Tell me something," but slurred so even he couldn't have understood.

"This Tom Hickey?"

"Yeah."

"Tell me you found that gunslinger and took care of him."
Tom's eyes began to water and the lump in his throat swelled.
"How about it?" Bud demanded.
"Did you murder Terence Poole?"
Bud didn't answer. He hung up. But not before a choking
noise gave him away.

Chapter Seventy

In McCloud, a few minutes before 7 a.m., a waitress at Minerva's, the village's crowded diner, sent Tom and Florence to the Rexall Drug and Sundries in their quest for a pay phone. The Rexall was the only establishment open so early, aside from the diner.

In the Rexall, Florence found a candy aisle while Tom seated himself on the phone booth stool. He imagined that by now Elizabeth would've woken her mother and gotten a few smooches then a mild command to go play with Chewy while Mommy catches a couple more winks.

He sat a minute staring at the phone. His heart thumped with a fear that if Madeline failed to answer, he would know his wife had run off with Milton Hopper.

The producer was no dreamboat. But he was amiable, seemed decent enough, and he had all the contacts an entertainer required. Especially these days when dolls from everywhere rolled into Hollywood by the thousands. They figured landing a movie role couldn't be much tougher than finding a secretary job in Des Moines.

Maybe he ought to wait and call after he had dispatched the Hearst business. But who could say whether he would survive the Hearst business? Besides, he simply missed his girls, every minute.

His finger slipped twice as he dialed. When the connection came through, he said, "Madeline Hickey, please."

Either the snippy switchboard gal was psychic or in the know about Madeline's affairs, or Tom's voice had gone weak enough to earn her sympathy. For once she sounded kind. "Are you all right, sir?"

"Swell, thanks," he said with effort. "Hook me to room twelve."

On the fifth ring, Madeline answered, "Mr. Parrot?"

"Huh?"

"Tom?"

"Yeah, babe. It's me all right."

"Where are you?"

"A little town up north."

"What for?"

"I need to talk to a man."

"Not the mighty Hearst, I hope to God." In Tom's recollection, she had never before used the word God except in vain.

"Where'd you get that idea?"

"Leo. Now quit stalling."

"Yeah, I'm going to visit Mr. Hearst."

She treated Tom to a long silent spell. "So you won't be coming home."

"Says who?"

"They're onto you Tom. You might as well be out to murder the president."

"We'll see."

"Is Florence with you?"

"Yeah."

"And you're going to risk the life of your precious sister?"

"Babe," Tom said, and paused while trying to conjure the best words, "I don't know what we're going to do, how far we're going to take all this. Could be we'll decide to skip Hearst, come home and deal with the guy who called this play and sent me out to run it."

"Huh? Who's that?"

"Never mind, for now. Look, I may be sort of overwrought by it all. But I'm not stupid, or crazy." He paused to consider the dubious truth of the final words. "And in a day or so, I'll be home," he said wistfully. He couldn't force himself to add the *I hope* that would have made the statement true. "Your voice sounds a little scratchy, babe. You'd better suck on lemons."

She said, "I got a letter for you. Milton delivered it."

He winced at the name Milton. A week ago, she called him Hopper.

"You want me to read it to you? It's from a Hal Croves."

"Sure."

"Who is he?"

"Ret Marut. Go on, please."

"Let's see. Okay. Here goes. 'Dear Mr. Hickey, In regard to our negotiation…' Oh, who am I kidding? I already read it. What it says is, the fellow claims a guy he represents wants to give you ten grand, as long as you agree to keep your mitts off the rights to what he calls a property created as a joint effort between the guy and Charlie Hickey. He means the book?"

"That's what he means."

"I read the book," she said.

For reasons that went too deep to explore now, knowing that Madeline had read Charlie's tale warmed his heart.

"It's one hell of a story," she said. "You can sure be proud of him. So can Elizabeth."

He wanted to tell her about Terence Poole, and Charlie covering for Bud Gallagher. But now wasn't the time. First, before he told anyone, he needed to settle with Bud. He said, "Thanks, babe."

"What do you think? About the man's offer, I mean."

"Ten grand is a chunk."

"Oh, there's a provision that joint authorship won't be revealed and so on, blah blah blah."

"Tell you what. How about you field this one for me?"

"I suppose I could."

"You like the deal, don't you?"

"We need the money, Tom, with you out of a job. Why'd you stomp that fellow in Yuma anyway?"

He gave the briefest version of the C.J, Missy, and Larry Loftus incidents. Rather than satisfy her, he supposed it reminded her that in throwing away his career, though he might've felt like a white knight, he had tossed the future of his wife and little girl to the wind. Because all she said was, "Damn it, Tom."

Then she added, "Okay, I'll deal with Croves."

"You think ten grand will keep the two of you in beans and bloomers while I go off to prison?"

She made him endure another long silent spell. Then she answered with surprising fervor. "No matter how stupid you are, I won't let you go to prison. I mean, not for what you've done so far. That's why I'm waiting for a call back from your pal Kent Parrot."

Tom wagged his head, forgetting she couldn't see him. He said, "Only, I'm not asking him for another favor. He's done plenty."

"Well, this one's Leo's idea. He says tell Parrot to frame it like this when he talks to the chief: Drop the charges about stomping the guy and, one, Tom won't go public about an L.A. cop holding a minor slave girl in Yuma, and two, he resigns so you get rid of him forevermore. Leo says Mr. Parrot will enjoy cutting that deal."

Tom might've imagined the chief's consternation and gotten a laugh, if he'd had a laugh in him. But the thought of accepting a favor from Leo revolted him.

As far as Tom could determine, Leo had probably gone a dozen years, more or less, suspecting Charlie of murder without snooping until he dug up the truth. Had he followed the leads and angles until they led him to Bud Gallagher, Charlie could've come home. Had Leo been a true pal, or even a diligent cop, Charlie might never have landed on Babicora, never given the tycoon a reason to kill him.

"Yeah," he said, "deals are what Parrot loves, all right."

Florence appeared at his side. She waited until Tom said good-bye then slipped him the morning *San Francisco Examiner,* early edition, and a Hershey bar. "A guy on a mission needs a nutritious breakfast."

Chapter Seventy-one

Across the street, a large man in overalls was unlocking the door to Robbie's Bait and Tackle. He turned and watched Tom and Florence approach, though he may not have noticed the former until Tom asked, "You Robbie?"

"Hmmm. Oh, sure am." After the briefest sideways glance at Tom, he turned back to Florence.

"I'll need a rod, reel, tackle," Tom said. "The McCloud's good fishing, I hear."

"Hmmm." Robbie, whose girth, complexion, and pointed nose reminded Tom of a snowman, turned only halfway, as if losing sight of Florence would mean forsaking an angelic vision. "Good fishing? The McCloud. What are you, a comic? Christ." He winced and said, "Pardon, ma'am."

"I'm Florence."

As he observed her smile, his jaw went slack.

"Fishing," Tom said.

"Sure." Robbie gave the door a shove and stood aside to watch Florence enter. Tom brought up the rear.

Robbie went to the counter and leaned against it, eyeing Florence as she studied a wall decorated with stuffed fish. He inspected her as intently as if she were dancing burlesque and ready to peel.

She wore a modest sundress hemmed below the knees, but a burnoose wouldn't flatten Florence's curves, and Robbie surveyed them all. If Tom hadn't come here for information, he might've offered a lesson in manners. "Fishing," he said.

"Take a look." Robbie waved toward the wall beyond Florence. "You ever seen the likes of those Dolly Varden trout?"

"Which ones are Dolly Varden?"

"Hmmm? Say, what are you, a rookie?"

"Yeah, that's me, a rookie that heard the fishing's good enough so well-heeled folks come here to build their fishing lodges."

"Yep," Robbie said. "And here's where they buy their gear."

"They who?" Tom asked.

"Hmmm?"

"Who buys their gear here?"

"Why, the Hearst family, for one." He spoke the name as if the acquaintance made him a noble.

Tom allowed the man a few moments to gawk in peace, while he studied a map displayed beneath glass on the section of the counter Robbie didn't cover. Then he interrupted the man's reveries and pointed to a spot on the map. "Shows the only road that leads to the lake branches off from there."

Robbie gave the map a glance. "That's so."

"Which way to the big shots? Up or downriver."

"Say what?"

"The big shots' lodges, up or downriver?"

"Big shots?"

"Hearst and the rest."

"Why, hell…Pardon, ma'am. Of course they're downriver. Ain't nothing upriver but waterfalls and feeder streams. Say, streams are the place for fly-fishing rookies. You interested in flies?"

"Bait will do."

Tom went to the rack of rods and picked out a cheap one, bamboo, and a three-dollar casting reel rigged with line. He stepped behind the counter. From the shelves, he selected one hook, one weight, and a copy of the map under glass. An ice chest on the floor featured cups filled with mossy dirt through which night crawlers squirmed. Tom picked out a cup.

By now Florence had turned from the stuffed fish to a counter by the street-facing window. She faced Tom and looked about to speak, but reconsidered and opened a photograph album of proud anglers.

Tom handed Robbie a ten and waited for the man to break from his fantasies and fetch change. He allowed a minute then gave up. "Ready, Sis?"

"Hmmm?" Robbie noticed the ten and returned to the world of business.

Tom carried the sack and pole. Florence led the way to the door then stopped, looked back and blessed the big fellow with a smile and wink. "Bye, Robbie."

As they walked to the car, she said, "It's funny, Tommy. Sometimes, a guy like that, you want to bust him in the nose. Other times, you kind of wish you could give him what he wants. I mean, maybe not all he wants, but some of it."

"Depending on his looks?"

She stopped and squinted at him. "I guess. But not the handsome ones. Phooey on them and their trophies. Sometimes it depends on how sad a guy looks. Don't you ever wish you could cheer up sad girls?"

Today, with all that burdened his mind, he didn't like feeling stumped by a simple question. His only answer was a scowl.

Florence said, "That silver Plymouth rolled by while we were in the shop. Same little guy in brown." She pointed up the highway in the direction of the river and Wyntoon. "You think he's been tailing us or just reading the papers?"

"This time, we take him out," Tom said.

Chapter Seventy-two

Over coffee, eggs, and toast in Minerva's Diner, Florence took charge of the *Examiner*, scanning every headline. "Nothing in section one." She tossed that section aside. "Look here. Jesse Owens again. This time he ran the final leg of the four hundred-meter relay. I'll bet Leo drank a toast to that one. Oops, we'd best not talk about Leo."

She passed the sports section to Tom. A minute later, she said, "Mr. Hearst forgot about us, Tommy. Not a word in State or Local. What do you make of it?"

"Trouble."

"How so?" she asked.

"Either it means Chief Davis and Hearst held a powwow and decided not to raise a fuss over little matters like assaulting an officer, and flight to avoid prosecution, and whatever else we might be up to. Or, they've got us covered all the way and they're biding their time until they can nab us pulling a caper that can justify their using what the Mexicans call *la ley de fuga*."

"The law of fire?"

"Translates best as 'shot while escaping'."

"Whew," Florence said. "I'm rooting for the first possibility."

"Go ahead and root, just don't bet on it."

"Tommy, then what's our game plan?"

Tom pointed out the window.

"Robbie?"

"Second floor of the Mercantile looks to be a hotel. We'll get a room."

"Okay. Then what?"

"Did you bring any books to read?"

"Huh?" Her puzzled gaze slowly drooped into a frown. "Hold on." She shoved the paper aside and slapped her hands palms down on the table. "You're not talking about going it alone."

"Afraid so."

She leaned his way until they were nose to nose. "Are you going to knock me out, or tie me to a bed post, or what? Otherwise, Brother, you go off without me, I'm right on your tail."

Tom closed his eyes and remembered Florence's wild years. When he locked her in her room, she broke the window latch and vanished for days. He tried hiring a neighbor to stand guard. Later she confessed it took a bit of smooching with the neighbor before she broke his will, found an opening, and ran.

Chapter Seventy-three

According to the map, a road to the lower McCloud River branched off the highway that ran southeast from the village of McCloud toward Susanville. But after driving ten miles, when Tom felt sure they had missed the turnoff, he swung a U-turn and crept the Packard back toward the village. The second time he pulled to the shoulder to let a logging truck pass like a hurricane, he spotted a narrow trail that branched off the highway.

He couldn't imagine the mighty Hearst and his kind making do with such a rough and narrow route. This road, he deduced from the map, must lead to the river and likely to a wider, less pitted road along the eastern shore.

He had failed to spot the trail on their first pass-by because a long, low wooden structure blocked the view. The building, which Tom guessed was a garage for road-graders and snowplows, offered plenty of cover for a car to hide behind.

Florence agreed to wait in the Packard. Tom climbed out and strolled into the woods, then juked about fifty yards through a maze of lodgepole pine and waist-high manzanita. When he ducked out of the woods, he sprinted across the road at a diagonal, a straight line to the nearest point of the building. He crept around the corner and along the wall. At the southwest corner, he leaned out and peeked, and found himself peering at the rear end of the silver Plymouth.

He reached beneath his coat and lifted the .38 from its holster. The little man who leaned against the siding at the southeast corner didn't move. He might've been asleep on his feet.

Tom lifted and braced his pistol then whistled loud and shrill. The little man jumped and turned in one motion. He stopped still, facing the trained .38. A black pistol hung at his side.

"Drop the gat," Tom called out. The little man complied. "Now don't budge." Tom reached him in a dozen strides.

The top of the man's hat came level with Tom's nose. Every visible item he wore was brown wool except the worn brown oxfords, beige cotton shirt, and silk tie hand-painted with a belly dancer. His suit coat was padded high and inches too wide at the shoulders. The coat had been brushed and laundered until threadbare.

As Tom watched the little man's watery hazel eyes, he thought of C.J. This fellow could be the boy's brother only a few years older. His eyelashes and brows were pale and sparse. A deep, narrow scar angled down from his right ear. In Tom's assessment, the little man was as worn down as his suit, and desperate. Another farm boy displaced by drought and dust. Tom picked up and pocketed the Luger semi-automatic. Then he patted the little man down. In coat pockets, he found a sap, carved with the same initials as those in the arsenal of L.A. cops, and a sheathed knife with a formed grip and a six-inch serrated blade. He found no billfold, only a money clip with a half dozen singles.

He tickled the man's chin with the tip of the knife. "Going fishing?"

"Drop dead."

"Whoa," Tom said. "Let's be friends."

"You ain't no friend."

Tom flipped the .38 to his left hand, and held out his right. "Tom Hickey."

"Smart guy," the little man mumbled.

"What do we call you?"

"Nuts to you."

"Turn and march," Tom said.

While he nudged and followed the little man into the open and across the road, he said, "My sister's going to want to know your name."

"Call me Stupid," the little man said, "on account of getting nabbed by a dumb dick."

Florence was waiting perched on the Packard's front fender. As the men approached, Tom said, "The gentleman prefers we call him Stupid. No need to shake his hand."

She smiled. "What's his story, Tommy?"

Tom pointed at the running board. "Have a seat, Stupid."

The little man declined and stood watching with hooded eyes while Tom asked Florence to go to the trunk and fetch the handcuffs out of his suitcase. When she returned, she held the .38 while Tom did the honors. The little man didn't resist, only added a sneer of disdain to his scowl.

"Let's get down to business," Tom said. "What's your game, Stupid?"

Since the little man didn't answer, Tom gave his sister a go-ahead glance.

She said, "What he means is, we've got to decide what to do with you, and that could be anywhere from setting you free to God knows what awful things. With that in mind, I'll bet you can tell us at least who you're working for."

"You lose, sister."

"Chief Davis?"

He gave Florence a lewd and impossible suggestion. Tom reached into his pocket for the little man's sap. "That one crack's all you get."

Florence said, "Mr. Hearst?"

"Pffft," the little man said.

"Okay then. Don't hit him too hard, Tommy. Just a little."

Tom passed his pistol to Florence, and juggled the sap from one hand to the other. But he used a fist, threw an uppercut to the man's belly, which felt so slight and fragile, as the man doubled over, Tom grimaced from a dose of shame.

Soon the little man looked up. His watery eyes flashed a challenge.

Tom led his sister a few yards away and spoke low, hoping the man couldn't hear. "A guy like him, figures what's he got to lose. I could beat him to death, ten to one he'd clam up all the way."

Chapter Seventy-four

Florence suggested what her brother was thinking, that they should waste no more time grilling the little man, but should take him along for the ride. Not that he would make a valuable hostage, but if his employers refused to deal for him, he might turn and spill some of their plans.

"And the Plymouth," Tom said. "We'd better take it along. A spare car could come in handy."

"I can ride in the back," Florence said, "keep him covered."

Tom shook his head. "I need you with me."

"But say he makes a break, then what?"

Tom reached for the Luger in his pocket. "Think you can handle this item?"

A couple years ago, when an Angelus Temple violin soloist got inflamed with a notion that God meant Florence to be his, her brother had met with the fellow and explained that God's actual will was for him to fiddle at a mission in Tasmania. The violinist complained to Sister Aimee, who assured him that not only was Tom's suggestion Godly, but that Florence often visited the police shooting range where Tom and other cops happily coached her.

Florence took and inspected the Luger while Tom crossed the road and went to the door of the building, where he hoped to find a tow cable. The double doors were secured with a chain and padlock Tom disengaged by a few whacks with the butt of his .38. He held up the door chain and deemed it too short for his purpose. Rather than search for a lamp in the windowless building, he returned to the Packard and dug in the glove compartment for his flashlight.

The building was indeed an equipment garage, housing two snowplows, a grader, a 'dozer, and a machine he couldn't identify. He shined the flash all around one snowplow and then the other before he found, under the driver's bench, a long, heavy tow chain, and even a hank of wire he could use to cinch the chain ends together.

He delivered the chain to the Packard trunk, then ushered the others into the car, Florence in back. "Don't get used to the luxury," he advised the little man. "You'll be driving the Plymouth, and minding your manners. You think about any funny business, remember we've got three guns and three free hands to shoot them with, and all you've got is one clumsy hand with ten fingers."

Across the highway, Tom chained the vehicles bumper to bumper, the Plymouth in front. He then delivered the little man to his coupe, and gave orders for him to follow the trail.

Florence offered no objection to the bumps and jolts, or to the gnashing squeals of manzanita branches slapping and dragging against the Packard's shell, which only yesterday had looked pristine. She didn't object when the tow chain caused the Packard front bumper to tap or ram the trunk of the Plymouth. Tom supposed his sister was less concerned with the abuse of Sister Aimee's fine automobile than with the homicide her brother might soon perform. After all, the man whose wisdom she most believed in had prayed, while dying, that his own murderers be forgiven.

Tom wondered how he would feel should his heart and gut command him to put an appropriate end to the mighty Hearst, while the tycoon, his enchanting mistress, and Tom's own sister begged him to show mercy.

She looked oblivious, entranced by her preoccupations, until a doe nosed onto the road in front of the Plymouth. Then she grabbed Tom's arm. He braked. The tow chain held, the Plymouth bumper stretched and bent. After Tom gave a toot on the horn, the hitched cars crawled past the doe, which was followed by three fawns.

"You okay, Sis?"

She nodded. "Thinking is all."

"Thinking what?"

"You know. Life. How soon do we meet up with the boys Mr. Hearst has waiting to ambush us? Are we on the right road? Does our friend Stupid work for Chief Davis and how big is the posse the chief rounded up? And, you know, what's heaven all about? And, why did we forget to pack a lunch? How about you, Tommy? What're you thinking?"

"Charlie," Tom said. "Mostly I'm thinking about Charlie. How, the way I see it, he ran off to save Bud from a murder rap. How he chased around the world and still found time to write a book or two."

"Two?"

"Who knows how many?"

"That B. Traven Marut fellow, he knows."

"Yeah."

Florence said, "Anyway, our daddy was quite a guy."

Tom nodded, slowed to a crawl, and gazed at his sister. He started to speak but choked on his words. He braked, stopped the car, and caught a deep breath. "He must've been quite a guy to create, even in cahoots with a demon like Millie, an angel like you."

Florence turned full toward him. Tears formed and sparkled turquoise then swelled and ran down her cheeks. Without a word, she leaned and kissed Tom's brow.

She laid her head on his shoulder and rode in that posture for most of an hour, despite bumps, wicked sways, and the jolting racket from slapping brush, cedar branches, and a sputtering Plymouth jalopy.

The forest gave way to meadows where Hereford cattle grazed. The Packard, which had yesterday appeared indestructible, rattled like a can of bolts. Tom checked his Bulova. Over an hour and twenty minutes since the highway, they hadn't passed, or anyway hadn't seen, a single human. Neither had they noticed even one dwelling. Another couple minutes, Tom vowed, he would find a turnaround and unchain the cars. He would deliver the little man into the Packard's trunk, then go back to McCloud for lunch, a pint of Scotch, and a chance to punch Robbie in the nose.

Maybe the letch had steered them into a dead end to ensure they would return, which would allow him another eyeful of Florence. Or, Robbie might've outfoxed him. He had a telephone. No doubt the local operator could connect by radio to the big shot's retreat. Robbie, or for that matter every citizen of McCloud and vicinity, might be onto and allied against them.

He rounded a bend and spotted a turnaround, about a ball-field length ahead. He didn't see the stake-bed truck in the shade of an oak until he was a middling end-run away.

Then he saw three men, and their dogs, and their rifles.

Chapter Seventy-five

He braked. Once both cars were still, he nudged Florence. She sat tall and picked up the Luger from the floorboard. "Hearst's boys?"

"Let's see."

She opened the glove compartment and passed Tom his .38. "Tommy, don't shoot anybody on account of me. I mean, you know, if they're horny like Robbie only meaner."

He glanced over and saw her lift from her purse what he thought at first was a vial of makeup. But as she cupped it into her hand, on her lap, he saw it was a push-button knife.

"Whoa," Tom said, having before only known such a weapon in the hands of pimps and burglars. "Where did you get that nasty piece?"

"A fella."

Tom motioned for his sister to follow then climbed out of the car. They both walked ahead, one on each side of the Plymouth. The little man had his window down. Tom said, "We're switching cars. I'll tow, you leave the big one in neutral. No brakes for any reason. If we stop and they come your way to talk, keep your hands out of sight and play dumb. Got it?"

The little man only scowled but when Tom opened his door, he climbed out. Once he settled into the Packard behind the wheel, Tom and Florence took their seats in the coupe.

Tom gave the Plymouth too much gas. The rear wheels slipped and spun. He let up then eased the throttle and clutch until the tires caught traction. The Plymouth resisted and felt like a model train required to pull an actual loaded boxcar but, after a near stall, it inched ahead.

As they neared the armed men around the flatbed, Florence said, "Tommy, get a whiff, will you? We might as well be in the Top Hat."

Tom hadn't gotten as familiar as Florence had with the speakeasy where he used to go hunting for his seventeen-year-old sister. But he was a cop and he'd been a musician. He knew the smell of hipsters' tea.

The men were dressed like farmers, in denim and clod boots. Each held his rifle in different position. The one who looked youngest, though his forehead was leathery and his beard featured a patch of gray, stepped directly to Florence's window. He leaned in close enough to inspect her lower half, and used the opportunity. Then he raised dilated eyes to Tom's level. His moves were slow and jerky as a silent film smooch scene. Between the time his mouth opened and sound issued out, Tom cut in, "You boys growing muggle?"

The man leaned back, motioned for the gaunt, yellow-skinned fellow wearing a flat-brimmed western hat to replace him at the passenger window. Then he strolled behind the Plymouth and around to the front of the Packard while appraising the vehicle with a nod of admiration. Next he shuffled around the fender to the driver's window. Loud enough so Tom could hear, he said, "Broke down?"

The little man not only ran the play the way Tom had called it, he didn't look up at the visitor or open his window. Such obedient behavior started Tom wondering about him. Maybe he'd decided he'd rather see Florence survive. Or maybe he was so confident that the Hickeys would soon get ambushed, and he'd get rescued, he'd just as well relax and savor the luxurious ride.

The third man, who stood beside the flatbed, plump and grinning like the Cheshire cat in Elizabeth's book, had shouldered his rifle and now held it zeroed on Tom. When the bearded fellow arrived at Tom's window, he leaned an elbow on the ledge. "No matter what we up to, what's it to you?"

Tom gave the man a slight but knowing smile. "You boys from what, Texas?"

"I am saying again, what's it to you?"

"You acquainted with the Hearsts?"

The fellow made a wry chuckle. "Ain't nobody going to get any answers long as they keep on making up questions."

"Sure," Tom said. "Let's get acquainted." He turned to Florence. "Babe, fish in my top coat pocket, bring out the billfold?"

As he watched her tuck the knife under a pleat of her skirt, he slipped his right hand around toward his right hip, behind which he had stashed his .38. Then he turned back to the man at his window. "You boys been to Los Angeles?"

"Mighta. What's it to you?"

"What did you hear about L.A. cops?" He glanced at Florence and nodded. She held up Tom's police badge, first to the man at her side, then to the other.

The bearded fellow said, "Hear they mostly crooks."

"And mean sons-a-bitches," the yellow-skinned one added. By now his arm was leaning on Florence's window ledge, his head inside the car.

"Well," Tom said, "those are no unfounded rumors. So, where's that leave us?" With a nudge of his elbow, he cued Florence. Her left hand flew up, knocked off the hat and grabbed a clump of the yellow man's hair. Meanwhile, her right hand snatched up the knife, pushed the button, and set the blade poking his chin.

By now, Tom had his pistol in a similar place regarding the bearded fellow, who gulped then asked, "The girl a cop too?"

"The point is," Tom said, "you boys had best kill us, all three, or get yourselves on our good side."

Slow and cool as if this predicament were nothing new, the bearded man said, "S'pose we pick number two, how's it work?"

"Point us toward Mr. Hearst is all, and don't let us get wind that you ratted us out."

"Hell, that's nothing. That miserable Hearst want to snatch our livelihood. Kill him, you care to. Fletcher," he said to the yellow man, "I say we make friends with these folks. Objections?"

Fletcher wagged his head as well as could be done without Florence's knife dealing him lacerations.

The bearded fellow lifted an arm and pointed. "Up ahead, no more than a mile or so, you go left on the gravel road. It don't have a real name, but the swells call it Riverside Drive."

Chapter Seventy-six

As the Plymouth growled and struggled forward, Florence said, "Tommy, how do you suppose Mr. Hearst is out to snatch those men's livelihood?"

"One of his campaigns, outlaw marijuana and its cousin, hemp. Some companies use hemp to make paper. And Hearst not only publishes, he owns the trees that make the paper the news goes out on. And the paper he doesn't use, he sells. So he outlaws the competition."

Florence knew about the Hearst government-by-media strategy. Still Tom spelled it out, as a reminder to them both. "The trick is, you convince the people to make the laws, wage the wars, and build the roads and all that make your fortune, until you're so high and mighty you can tell them what else they ought and ought not to do."

He reached out the window and gave a signal with his arm. Then he braked and came to a stop, with only a tap from the Packard's front bumper. "No sense us sitting in the grandstand," he said, "while the little fellow back there gets box seats."

They traded cars. A mile later, the trail intersected a gravel road wide enough for a Rolls and a Bentley to pass without a scratch.

The road its residents called Riverside Drive was a boulevard of dreams compared to the rutted dirt they had left behind. Now, even over the crackle of tires, they could listen close and hear the McCloud's splash and tumble. When the cedar woods thinned or gave way to meadows, they saw the black slate and granite cliffs on the far side of the river gorge.

A few miles along, Florence spotted a high block wall. Tom signaled. Both cars braked. The Hickeys climbed out and looked all around. After some reflection, Tom asked, "Did you see the cutaway off to our right?" He pointed back up the road.

Florence shook her head and shrugged an apology.

Though a U-turn with two hitched cars was no simple trick, Tom and the little man succeeded with only one shift each into reverse. A half mile back, they sighted and followed the trail, which led through a tunnel of overhanging spruce and cedar to a riverside clearing, a building site all graded in preparation for the next grand tycoon's hideaway.

Tom unchained the Plymouth from the Packard. Once he'd packed the chain into the trunk and fetched out of his suitcase the Browning .32 caliber semi-automatic he'd been assigned to use on Donny Katoulis, he summoned the little man out of the Plymouth.

He led them toward the river. When he glanced over his shoulder, he noted that Florence lagged more than arm's length behind the little man. No doubt to prevent his using the cuffed hands to catch her in a choke-hold.

Nature or someone had deposited, only inches back from the riverbank ledge, a downed log the length of a small couch. The Hickeys each sat on an end and gave the little man the middle. The river was cobalt blue and foamy, neither a tranquil stream nor a rapid. The craggy granite wall on the far side was about thirty yards across from the mossy bank at the top of which they sat.

Tom faced the little man. "Okay, partner. Last chance to come clean."

"Drop dead."

Tom nodded to his sister, since he'd noticed the little man's glancing at Florence and assuming a curious smile, like Elizabeth at the zoo whenever she saw a new and colorful bird or cat, anything delightful.

Florence said, "I sure don't get why it would matter, you telling us who to thank for your presence here."

"Got a smoke?" the little man asked.

"Sorry, I don't. And Tom only smokes his pipe, now and then."

"The guy who put you onto us," Tom said. "Didn't he pay you enough to buy your own smokes?"

The little man rolled his eyes and shifted his gaze back to Florence. "Say, what's it matter who gives the orders, or who pays? They're all in it together."

"Who's they?" Tom asked, though he knew quite well.

The little man flashed him a look of intense disdain. "You know enough, buddy boy." Once again, he turned to Florence. "How about you telling me what's your beef with Mr. Hearst?"

She waited for an okay from her brother.

"Our daddy," she said. "See, he wrote an article Mr. Hearst didn't care to have published. Maybe he tried to pay our daddy off, or maybe he knew our daddy stuck to his principles. People called him a Wobbly. Anyway, Mr. Hearst turned the problem over to one of his gunslingers." She fixed sorrowful eyes on the little man. For a moment, while his lips stroked each other, he appeared on the edge of giving in.

Then he said, "Tough break," and turned toward the river.

Tom checked his Bulova. "Time's wasting."

Back at the cars, Florence kept the Luger at ready while Tom ordered the little man down beside the Packard's passenger door. He unlocked the cuffs, looped one of them through a slot in the running board, and secured the man's wrists again. Then Tom and Florence went to the Packard trunk. He picked out a couple of Florence's scarves. The kelly-green one, he wrapped twice around the little man's head as a blindfold.

Florence grabbed up two blankets and closed the trunk. She rolled the blankets and placed them as a pillow and cushion for the little man.

Tom got under the Packard hood and removed the cable from the coil to the distributor. He wrapped a rag around it, and stashed it in the shoulder strap purse Florence carried.

He led Florence to the Plymouth. They slid inside, Florence behind the wheel, at her brother's request. He asked her to roll up the window, so the little man couldn't overhear.

"Here's my strategy, babe. You take this heap and find Wyntoon. Stash the car pretty close but hidden in the woods as best you can. Then make your way outside the Wyntoon property, to the riverbank on the upstream boundary." He handed her the brown scarf. "Tie this around something so I can spot it from across the river."

"You're going across? Just you?"

"I figure one of us on each side is smartest, and I'm a better swimmer."

"Who says?"

"I used to be, anyway."

"We were kids. You were older."

"Anyway, I'm not wearing skirts, and once we get inside, you've got to look your best, or we lose a powerful weapon. For my part, the uglier, more beat up and mangy I look, the better.

"Here's how it goes," Tom said with authority, "We meet at the marker, where you put the scarf, as close as you can get to the upriver Wyntoon boundary. We try for five p.m. Maybe we'll go in right then, maybe we'll hold off a while. Either way, we don't want to finish our business and make our getaway until after dark."

"I'm a little scared, Tommy. Are you?"

Tom leaned and kissed her cheek. "Sure. Be careful."

"You too, big brother."

He slipped the Bulova off his wrist and handed it to his sister, then climbed out and didn't look back. At the riverbank, he sat, shoved off and slid down the mossy bank, which plunged him waist deep into an icy place where he couldn't get a foothold in the slippery mud. He pulled off his coat, dug into the left front pocket for the Browning and flung the pistol. It barely cleared the crest of the granite wall. He wrapped and tied the coat by the sleeves around his shoulder. Then he drew the Colt from his shoulder holster and flung it as hard as a downfield pass.

When he dove into the current and his feet left the ground, he got swept downstream. As far back as he could remember, he'd been a strong swimmer, having learned in the ocean off Santa Monica, taught by Charlie Hickey. Still, in the McCloud, he felt as though caught in a riptide. One he couldn't ride out, as lifeguards advised victims of a rip. No lifeguard would come to his rescue.

Chapter Seventy-seven

About fifty yards downstream, Tom grabbed onto a crack in the granite wall. The crack, which ran from below the waterline to the crest of the cliff, about twenty yards up, gave him the hand and footholds he needed.

Atop the cliff, he sprawled on his back and rested until his breathing came slower and steady. Then he stood and tramped along the cliff edge, avoiding the spongy mulch beneath pines and cedars, and the barbs and sharp branches of manzanita.

When he spotted the little man across the river, he ducked for cover in the woods. The man remained cuffed to the Packard but had shed the green blindfold, the point of which was to keep him ignorant of the Hickeys' moves.

Tom crept low between the pines and through brush and felled, rotting branches until he retrieved his weapons. With the Colt holstered, the Browning tucked under his belt, and his coat tied around his shoulders, he retraced his path downstream, favoring the granite cliffside over the woods. Soon the first of the mansions across the river appeared.

The block wall Florence had spotted enclosed manicured grounds, a patchwork of smallish lawns, numerous topiary hedges, and a brick Tudor house with ornamental woodwork framing a half dozen gables. Shuttered windows and a circular drive devoid of cars convinced him to move on.

Loggers hadn't yet invaded Tom's side of the river. The forest was old cedar and ponderosa pine, tall as skyscrapers and so aromatic Tom allowed himself some moments to daydream of a tall, icy, glass of retsina.

The only clearings were charred stumps and blackened mulch, reminders that lightning could spark fires and the rain that followed could subdue them. Tom hustled across the clearings but otherwise kept in the shadows of the forest.

Every few hundred yards another riverside estate appeared. Among them were a brick colonial, long and low as a prison, and a gray castle Tom might have suspected belonged to Hearst except its spires and turrets were out of proportion. Not the work of Wyntoon's architect, the inimitable Julia Morgan.

A sudden wave of fatigue threatened to rout the strength and compulsion that had driven him this far. He reached for the nearest big pine and let himself collapse. He sat backed against the trunk with his legs stretched out, but couldn't begin to rest. Deep though vague worries about his sister were already haunting him when he heard the crack of a rifle shot.

Chapter Seventy-eight

Florence was squatting, peering between the slats of an iron bar fence, when she heard what sounded like footsteps behind her. She spun slowly and found herself gaping at the hairy mug of a bear.

The creature was all black except the gray-brown snout upon which a gelatinous substance shined. On all fours it stood about Florence's height, once she had slowly risen. It stopped in what looked to her like a strategic place, just as far from her as one of its front paws could reach. Each claw looked the size of a woman's finger.

"Pretty bear," she said, and felt foolish, as if she'd thought the creature both knew English and could recognize obsequious flattery.

She muttered a prayer, considered making a dash or attempting to bound up and over the fence, and remembered that bears are plenty fast. She had seen one in action last summer when Tom treated his three girls to her most memorable vacation, except one long ago when she ran off with a bootlegger to Rosarito Beach in Mexico, and that wasn't truly a vacation.

Tom had taken her, Elizabeth, and Madeline for a weekend at the Awahnee Hotel in Yosemite. If she was about to die, she decided, rather than fight the inevitable, she would attempt to meet eternity while recalling the glorious sight of the firefalls off Half Dome.

The bear's mouth twitched. She heard a huff and a clack of teeth, and then the bear lumbered a U-turn and went loping toward the river.

Florence dropped to her knees and muttered thanks. Then a silly thought came. She imagined her boss preaching about how God rescued Sister Florence from a bear. She smiled, but only for a moment. Then reason intruded and she realized that if she encountered a bear on the populated side of the river, over on the other side Tom might get mauled, maybe eaten, by a pack of them.

She started for the river but stopped when she heard, "You let Patsy out, did you?"

The voice was gruff, the fellow tall and broad, holding a rifle at his side. A bodyguard, she thought, though he wore a khaki shirt spotted with evidence of gardening. His upper face was ruddy, the lower part pallid and blotched as though he had recently shaved a beard.

Florence approached him, then stood with hips slightly cocked, as gals from the Hearst social and Hollywood set likely would. With a smile that matched the pose, she said, "Good afternoon, sir. Is Patsy your bear?"

The man only studied her up and down.

"I assure you, letting her out of wherever she's supposed to be wasn't my doing."

She cocked her hips a few more degrees and cooed, "I wonder, might you direct me to Wyntoon?"

The fellow shot a glance over his shoulder and through the fence. "I ain't about to tell you where it is, but I'll tell you this, Mr. Hearst don't want no visitors." He lifted his rifle. "This here's private land. Get a move." The gun barrel twitched in the direction of the road.

As he marched her to Riverside Drive, she kept her neck loose and glanced back often, each time attempting conversation. When she asked, "No entourage this trip? Just W.R. and Marion?" he clearly nodded before he caught himself and censured her with a grimace and hooded brow.

On the gravel road, Florence walked full stride, hoping the fellow would believe he had spooked and chased her off. Although she couldn't grasp how a Hearst employee could fail to be on guard against the armed and dangerous Hickey gang, she hoped he believed she was simply a celebrity-chaser staying at one of the other mansions.

Once the road curved enough to put a thicket of trees between them, she entered the forest. She had found a suitable log and sat on the smoothest section, when the crack of a shot sent her bolting to her feet and behind a tree.

After a minute she went looking for a more secluded log and soon found one. She prayed that Tom hadn't taken a bullet. As an afterthought she prayed that Tom hadn't shot Patsy the Bear.

She hid out until Tom's Bulova read 4:45. Then she crossed the road, cut through the woods to the riverbank, and turned downstream toward Wyntoon.

Chapter Seventy-nine

Across the meadow from the iron bar fence, Florence lifted her skirt and slid halfway down the riverbank, which wasn't nearly so steep or mossy as upriver. She looped the brown scarf around her neck and waited for her brother on a narrow ledge.

A jalopy sputtered and clunked into the meadow. Florence stood, climbed a few steps, and peeked over the edge of the gorge. The car had parked. A Model A roadster. A slight, blondish man was climbing out. He went around to the passenger side, opened it and pulled out a fly rod, a small tackle box, and a net.

He walked a path that led upriver and became a zigzag descent into the gorge at least a hundred yards away and around a slight bend from the ledge she occupied. If she stayed quiet, Florence believed, the fisherman wouldn't notice her.

A few minutes later, Tom appeared. He came out of the woods like a Hollywood ghost in his taupe summer suit. His right arm whipped through the air. A gun flew across the gorge and passed high overhead. Another gun followed. Then he jumped and careened feet-first into the river.

He didn't surface for almost a minute. Then his head appeared and shook like a bathing dog's. He swam in a breaststroke to shore then climbed toward the ledge where his sister knelt with an outreached hand. She helped him onto the ledge. Even then, while he lay on his side catching his breath and bearings, she kept her grip on his wrist.

"I found the place," she said. "Beyond the fence across the meadow. And they're here, I think."

He pushed with an elbow and rose to his knees, then used his hands to propel himself upright. "You're the champ, Sis."

She said, "Every time you throw a gun, I duck. You know, in case it fires when it lands."

"Not likely. Are we ready to run our play?"

"Yep. And let's make a dash across the meadow. Hearst's got a big fellow on the prowl."

They scrambled up the bank, hustled to retrieve Tom's guns, and double-timed into the forest on the upriver side of the meadow, the far side from Wyntoon. They squatted on around back of a big pine. Tom was about to ask who belonged to the Ford, when Florence said, "The old car out there belongs to a fisherman. He's down at the river around the bend from where you crossed. I don't think he saw me. But you made a heck of a splash."

"Sorry." He pointed beyond the meadow. "Hearst's over there?"

"I'll bet he is. And he's got a bear. "

"A bear?"

"Yep. Maybe a whole tribe of them, I hear he likes big critters running around. I met one called Patsy. Scared the panties off me, almost. Did you meet any bears over there? Or wolves, or cats like pumas?"

"Not a one. Lots of birds, and a snake or two, was all. Patsy?"

"Yep. I turn around, there she is. Big as you, maybe bigger. And either she's a sissy, or else she saw the fellow coming and figured he didn't approve of a bear eating a girl. Anyway, he showed up and shooed me off the property, but not before I tricked him into spilling the beans. That's Hearst's place all right, or I'm buying dinner."

"Sure you're ready?"

"I think so."

"Luger still in your purse?"

"Still there. Funny thing, when Patsy came around, I forgot I was packing a gun."

"Some cop you are."

"I'm no cop. I'm a private dick, sort of. Let's go."

They crept across the meadow through maze of wildflowers, an Eden for hummingbirds, woodpeckers, and bees. When they reached the iron bar fence, they squatted and peered between slats at an emerald lawn ringed by tulips and peonies, the centerpiece of a circular drive in front of a smallish, three-story castle. Half stone, half timber, Bavarian style.

Tom led the way along the fence, which extended past the edge of the bank and several feet into the air, where the gorge had suffered erosion. Enough so that Tom and then Florence squeezed and squirmed underneath.

The woods between them and the castle were thicker than in the meadow, with pines whose girth could easily hide them, and whose height left the woods in cool shade but for stripes of warmth and light. As they hustled from tree to tree, Florence's right shoe caught in the wedge of a fallen branch. She toppled forward, and lay for a spell gnashing her teeth to keep from yelping in pain.

Tom helped her up, but when he offered his arm, she shook him off and limped ahead, toward a barn and a trio of barn-shaped sheds. When they reached the outbuildings, they used the sheds for cover, and arrived undetected around the back of the barn, looking into a Bavarian village.

On either side of the first castle was another castle. The three were placed in symmetry around the central green and the circular driveway. The steep roofs of each featured numerous gables, chimneys, and bay windows accented by timbers and arranged into an enchanting harmony, so they offered both complement and counterpoint to the rhythm of the river's rumble and the swishing of the breeze through the treetops. No doubt the work of Julia Morgan.

The only car on the driveway that surrounded the green was a light blue convertible, which Tom recognized as a BMW, as was appropriate in a Bavarian village. No Bentley.

He led his sister from tree to tree back to the edge of the gorge. Along the rear of each castle, a wide deck overlooked the river. Florence asked, "How do we know which building they're in, Tommy?"

"Look and listen."

"Maybe the middle," she said. "The car is closest to the middle one. But Paco said they were driving a Bentley."

"Maybe Paco doesn't know cars so well," Tom said.

Florence took the initiative. She darted across the clearing to the first castle and crept along the wall, limping and ducking beneath the windows, which were rather high on account of tall footings. Tom followed, a few steps behind.

She reached the far corner and peered around. Her head jerked back, but too late. The caretaker yelled, "Hey you." Then his big boots came tromping their way.

Florence rushed out to meet the fellow in a dirt and flagstone clearing between a castle and the barn. On her way, she called, "Hi there, sir. Remember me?"

All the while, with one eye on the caretaker, she gazed across the green beyond him and held her face in an expectant pose, to clue the fellow that any second another celebrity-chaser might come rushing to tackle him from behind.

The man was neither a genius nor an experienced tough guy. He not only followed Florence's gaze but turned full around, his back to the Hickeys.

Tom dashed past his sister and threw a high tackle, concluding with a headlock. He gagged the fellow with the inside of his elbow and jammed the barrel of his .38 into the base of the man's skull.

While he led and dragged the caretaker sideways toward the barn, Florence ran ahead into the barn, and returned to meet her brother just inside. She carried a rope and some rags that she proceeded to knot together and fashion into a suitable gag with which to replace Tom's elbow.

Florence fitted the man with the gag, wrapping it several times around his wooly head. Then she pulled the knife out of her skirt's hip pocket, lifted it to nose level and pushed the button. The caretaker flinched.

"Whoa," Tom said. "Don't make those fast moves. This gat damn near went boom." He offered a sinister cackle and moved the gun into his sister's free hand. "Shoot if you feel like, Betty."

The caretaker's bugged eyes stayed on the gun. Tom cinched the man's wrists together, and did the same to his feet, then set him down with his back against the post of a vacant stall and lashed him to it.

Once he considered the fellow secured, Tom knelt in front of him and gave his best leering impression of a bloodthirsty desperado. "See here, pal, we ain't alone. Betty and me, we're scouts. The rest of the boys ought to be pulling out of Redding about now. Thing you had best know is, suppose you were to get loose and go running to fetch the law, all the good it's gonna do is get your boss a head full of bullets and set you on the run. Only a loco would cross the Weaver gang. No sir," Tom concluded, "you had best lie back and take the day off."

Chapter Eighty

Tom made a stop at the barn workbench for a certain tool. Then he joined his sister in the shadow of the barn doorway and peered all around, expecting to spot at least a sniper or two.

Unless the trap that awaited them was inside the house.

For all Tom knew, Hearst and his lady might have detoured to Berlin for the Olympics and left behind a couple of understudies. He imagined a strange couple greeting them and bursting into laughter while cops or other gunmen materialized out of every shadow and hallway.

"You okay, Tommy?"

"Just second-guessing. You?"

"For Daddy," she said.

Tom stood a while longer, countering trepidation by assessing the castles, their inset murals of fine ladies dancing, the smallish, many-paned windows that weren't only decorative but also could dissuade prowlers. And on either side of the center castle doorway a grand cedar stood posted like a sentry, as if any sign of intrusion would bring it to animated life and action.

As they crossed the green toward the center castle doorway, Florence stopped and held up a finger. "Listen."

From inside came a man's muted shouting followed by a high and strident reply. Tom and his sister looked at each other and shrugged then hustled the last twenty yards to the center castle entryway.

The door was thick cedar, the knob a pewter rectangle, art deco, which most often partnered with the virtually pick-proof Yale pin-tumbler lock. "Ready?" Tom asked.

Florence's breast heaved and she nodded. Then her brother stabbed the forked end of the crowbar he had snatched from the barn into the slit between the door and jamb. He firmed his grip on the bar and pried, gently at first, then less so. Before the lock would give, the jamb cracked, the crowbar slipped out of its hold, and Tom toppled backward.

Florence caught the crowbar, which otherwise would've clanged on the concrete. She gave a hand, helped him up and passed the bar to him then leaned a shoulder on the door and nudged. "You got it, Tommy." She opened the door a crack. She and Tom peered inside.

Across a spacious parlor paneled in natural fir and adorned with classical busts, a Persian carpet, and faux El Greco paintings, a dark-skinned gal wearing an apron stood as though petrified. Florence reached her first, clutched a wrist and waved the shiv in front of her enlarged and watery eyes.

While his sister led the maid out of the parlor and down a hallway to their right, Tom stood still and listened.

"Who is this coarse person?" a woman demanded. "One has to come to Hollywood to meet such common people."

A man replied in a wavery tenor, "Aw baloney. Say, you punks trying to crash into Hollywood?"

With his .38 raised above his shoulder, Tom walked straight toward the voices. He passed through a small den furnished with two stuffed chairs, two lamps and hundreds of books on built-in pine shelves. The doorway across the den opened into a theater. A dozen or so cushioned armchairs sat in three rows facing a screen upon which Marion Davies, a pretty boy, and an old gentleman occupied a cafeteria table.

The star and her man, the tycoon himself, stood between the screen and the double French doors that opened onto the riverside deck. They were side-by-side, backed against the wall, looking to Tom as if they had considered making a getaway but stopped and stayed on account of simple curiosity. Neither of them looked particularly frightened, which made Tom expect to be set upon by a platoon any second. After some seconds passed, he wondered if the wealthy and sheltered lose their belief in the reality of death and other dangers.

He sidestepped to the projector. With one eye on his captives, he found the off switch and flicked it. The room dimmed. So when Florence ran in, at first she only noticed her brother. "I stuck her in a bedroom closet and shoved the bed against it. She'll stay put. What..." She gasped, having at last seen who Tom had cornered.

Then she tossed the couple a little wave. "Oh, hello there."

Chapter Eighty-one

If Marion Davies, Florence, and Millicent Hickey, all in their prime, had posed side-by-side, an observer might've called for a moment to inspect before deciding which was who. All three were stunners. All three had waves in their vanilla blond hair. All were just short of five and a half feet, and slender yet lusciously curved.

Tom would have distinguished by their expressions. Florence the bright and innocent, Miss Davies the curious and gay, Milly Hickey, the surly and proud.

Hearst was a tall fellow, un-stooped by age, though he had behind him twice as many years as his mistress. His gray blue eyes dominated, steady and probing, as if he had knowledge Tom didn't and was calculating in accord with that knowledge.

With a glance at Florence, Tom said, "Babe, get that item out of your purse, and show the lady out to the front room. Stay near the door but keep away from windows. Any visitors, she can shoo them off. She gets tricky or the visitors won't go, yell 'Tom' real loud. Tom, not Tommy. I'll get the message and kill him right now."

Florence dug in her purse for the Luger. She gripped it in both hands and kept it raised but aimed to the side of her would-be target. She used it to motion Miss Davies away from her man. The look the actress turned on Hearst might've wowed any director who had requested a portrait of courage. Then she let go of his arm and passed by Florence on her way to the den. At the doorway, she looked over her shoulder and showed Tom a face both gentle and sorrowful, as if she had gotten betrayed by a dear friend.

"W.R.," she said, "please don't let your blood boil. In case you don't remember Tom, he's no villain. You ran the story, remember, how he risked everything to solve the Echo Park lynching? I'm sure as can be he's nothing like his mother." On the last word, her voice rose a pitch, making her appraisal into a question.

Once the women were gone, Tom shifted two theater chairs face-to-face, ushered Hearst into one then seated himself in the other. He studied the tycoon's gray eyes, and let him have the first words.

"Haven't we met?" Hearst asked, in a voice and manner so soft and genteel, he hardly seemed American.

Tom wondered if the man had failed to hear a word of his mistress' introduction. "On the bluffs at Santa Monica. Nineteen twenty-five. I asked why your *Examiner* failed to report the murder of Frank Gaines."

Hearst glanced downward and pursed his lips, as though attempting to recover a memory. He began tapping his fingers on his knee. "Afraid I don't recall."

"Let's go back a few years earlier. Maybe you remember killing my father?"

The man looked up with an expression at least as perplexed as fearful.

"You killed Charlie Hickey. I'm his boy. And I didn't come all this way to get denials or excuses. I know the whole story, what happened, how it happened, and why." Tom raised the pistol, sighted on the tycoon's nose. "Look, I'm not here to chat, only to get a few answers, then kill you. Unless I have a change of heart, which is damned unlikely. How could I while I'm looking at the vermin that had his stooge shoot my father in the back?"

A shadow appeared and darkened Hearst's eyes to steel gray.

Chapter Eighty-two

"Ambrose Bierce," Tom said. "You sent him to Mexico to use his formidable wit to make certain no gang of peons turned an acre of your precious Babicora into a socialist *ejido*."

Hearst opened his mouth.

"Stop," Tom commanded. "You made Bierce for one of your stooges, only he was the wrong player, nobody's mouthpiece. Meaning he was disposable, at least in the big game with stakes that made winning worth a whole lot more than the life of one old man whose best stories were probably behind him. It was war, a time when lots of people have to die. It was politics, manifest destiny. The United States taming and civilizing the hemisphere. One more chance to impose your will, like when you led the patriots into Cuba.

"Besides, this one had gotten personal. Bierce turns on you, not only does Villa occupy Babicora for keeps, but the account Bierce might take to Pulitzer would clue the old buzzard about you playing both sides in the Mexican revolution. Which means you're done with politics. I mean, back then you were in the prime of your public life, the height of your powers. With a war brewing in Europe and all, how would the world survive and progress if folks can't trust and follow your guidance?"

Again Hearst opened his little mouth. This time a hitch of Tom's pistol convinced him to shut it.

"See, I know you've made your fortune out of bending the truth, when you weren't outright lying. A master of persuasion, a genius in the art of government-by-media. See, I know my limitations and at least some of my tragic flaws. I'm like Hamlet only not so eloquent, but the same sort of character, so if I let you talk, maybe I'll go to thinking too much."

"One question?" Hearst got out before Tom could wag the pistol.

"Nothing doing."

Tom crooked his elbow, rested the elbow on his knee, the gun angled up and aimed at the center of the tycoon's chest. "So, time flew, the wars concluded, nine or ten million dead in Europe, another million or two in Mexico, and along came Charlie Hickey, this nobody with writer ambitions.

"Charlie wants to resurrect a story that's long gone and forgotten. You figure that, in a world littered with bones and graves, how much can one more dead fellow matter if silencing him will spare a latter-day Napoleon like yourself, a mighty promoter of peace and progress, from having to battle against scandalous accusations, from all the world calling you a murderer?"

After that windy sentence, Tom allowed himself a breather, then a minute to decide whether he should bring up the mysterious death of Thomas Ince, the actor and movie mogul whom headlines reported was shot to death on board the *Oneida*, Hearst's battleship-sized yacht. He decided no.

His silence must've emboldened the tycoon. "Mightn't I ask one question? Speak one sentence."

"Which will it be?"

"A question, followed by a single declarative sentence."

"The question."

"Do you intend to kill Marion?"

"Crafty fellow, aren't you?" Tom said. "You figure, what man could bump off such an innocent beauty, unless she had personally done him wrong. And in killing you, I'd have to kill her, or leave a deadly witness.

"The thing is, maybe Florence already killed her. My sister's the daughter of a monster, as you may recall, and she's way too smart and female to fall for Miss Davies' sweet tootsie act."

Hearst attempted to square his sloped shoulders and sat up as tall as an old fellow could.

"Now the one sentence you want to declare," Tom said.

"I have never ordered a killing."

Tom shrugged.

Chapter Eighty-three

For ten years, Tom had investigated crimes, made arrests and delivered the villains to jailers. From there, lawyers took over and eventually presented their findings to a judge and jury, who ruled then passed along the guilty to those who executed punishment.

Until now, Tom hadn't imagined carrying the weight of all those occupations together. Never before had he felt such deep respect for the workings of the law.

"Sis," he called out. "I need you. And her."

Marion Davies came rushing down the hall and entered the room with eyes flashing, as if fearful lest Tom might've silently slain her man. He stood and motioned her into his chair facing Hearst.

While she appeared to curtsy onto the chair, brushing back her skirt, Florence entered. Tom pointed to the French door that led to the riverside deck. She nodded, opened the door and stepped out.

"Miss Davies," Tom said. "You and the big shot can talk, but don't either of you move. All that's going to separate us is glass, which isn't likely to stop a bullet."

She appraised him with a mind-reader's earnest gaze.

Tom followed his sister outside and closed the glass-paned door.

"What'd you tell her?"

Florence had leaned her back against a post, her face toward the river. "Just the basics. Mr. Bierce was going to smear Pancho

Villa, get him so mad at Hearst, he'd probably take over Babicora. So Hearst ordered Mr. Bierce dead. Charlie came along later and got to snooping, spilled the ugly truth to the wrong guy. Hearst got wind of it, ordered Charlie dead."

"And she says?"

"She says, 'But W.R. wouldn't kill a fly.' Tells me a story about in France they ran over a goose, so he buys the farmer lady a new goose and delivers it in a car, and gives her the car to boot. I'll say this, Tommy. I'd bet the bank that if Mr. Hearst orders somebody dead, he doesn't come home and report to her. She thinks he's a gentle soul, honest to God."

"Suppose he never once gave an order to kill, or even an okay? I mean, it's easier, cleaner, lighter on the conscience, if you simply hire the right boys to look out for your interests."

Florence nodded assuredly. "You want to know what I figure?"

"Sure do."

"Well, it could be Mr. Hearst didn't even hear about our daddy. And maybe he never even on purpose hired a gunman. Tommy, that man is so lousy rich and powerful, some folks mistake him for God and would gladly kill just to be able to walk around thinking they saved God some grief."

Tom glanced at the river then back at the couple beyond the glass. Hearst's hand rested on Marion's knee. Her hand covered his.

"Sis," Tom said, "didn't I used to be smarter than you?"

"Yeah, I always thought so, except when you were bossing me around."

"What happened?"

"Huh?"

"I mean, how is it that now you're smarter than me?"

She turned her gaze from the river to Tom and stared long enough to detect any sarcasm. "Well, if I'm the smart one it's because I think more than you do."

"I think a lot," he said.

"Sure you do, but mostly about how to get some rascal off the streets, or how to please Madeline, or how to bring up a wild kid like me, and now Elizabeth, to be somebody good and true."

Tom sighed. "And while I'm brooding on all that, what are you thinking about?"

"Oh, pretty much of everything."

Chapter Eighty-four

He instructed his sister to take Miss Davies back to the parlor and explain to her, as she had explained to him, that no matter if Hearst had or hadn't given orders, he had spent a lifetime playing God. So if somebody mistakes him for God and acts accordingly, say bumps off innocent folks to safeguard respect for his holy name, it's the tycoon's own damned fault.

"Think you can get that through her head?"

"Sure, Tommy. She's no Gracie Allen. She's plenty sharp. But while I'm out there, what are you going to do?"

"Keep them guessing at least until dark, or shoot him."

"Until dark. You think we're being watched, don't you? Could be a whole posse out there in the woods, couldn't it, getting ready to move?"

"Could be," Tom said.

"Tommy, if you shoot him, what about Marion?"

Killing Hearst would most likely be the end of Tom, he had known all along. What became of Marion Davies would depend upon whether he decided he could trust her to go to bat for his sister, assure a verdict of innocent. But if he needed to choose between the woman and Florence, Davies was a goner.

He said, "We'll see when the time comes."

"Okay." For the first time all day, she looked and sounded severely distressed. "You think Mr. Hearst will break down and take the blame, maybe beg for mercy?"

Tom shrugged. "Sometimes all you need to break a guy is keep him worried long enough. And some do just fine until the sun sets, and then the fear grabs them."

Florence opened the door and motioned for Davies to stand. The lady complied. When Florence pointed toward the hall that would lead them toward the front room, Miss Davies cast a final hopeful look at Hearst then led the way into the hall.

Tom remained standing while his mind harbored visions. In one of them the front door flew open and a shot cracked. His sister folded and collapsed, knocking over a pedestal and a crystal vase of crimson columbine.

Even after the visions passed, he waited a minute and listened for the slightest alarm before taking his seat.

A hint of defiance had possessed Hearst's expression and posture. Tom looked away, attempting to think, and let his gaze roam wherever it pleased, at the projector, the shelves crammed with film canisters, the painting of villagers that could be a Rembrandt. He avoided looking for long at the love seat. The quilted flower pattern reminded him of Milly and fed him several grim memories. Then he turned to business.

Having captured the suspect and played the prosecutor's role, now his tasks were those of judge and jury.

Aside from the distractions of keeping one eye on the tycoon and an ear out for any sign of danger, he sat in silent deliberation for two hours. He only paused twice. Once for a trip to the deck during which he sprinkled a rosebush while watching Hearst through the French door and holding the gun at ready. Again to accompany the tycoon to the deck and oversee while Hearst took his turn sprinkling the begonias.

During his meditations, he imagined Florence telling the lady why her man deserved whatever he got, why any plea for mercy would only sound ridiculous after all the folks Hearst had sentenced to death by sending them to war against Spain for his own political ends. And the Jews, Catholics, Gypsies, Communists, and Wobblies all over Germany whom the mighty Hearst could have saved with a determined stroke of his pen, but hadn't.

He imagined Florence advising Miss Davies that Hearst's estates, San Simeon, Wyntoon, Babicora, were nothing but monuments to avarice and phony pride. He saw her telling the lady that if the tycoon had a morsel of humanity he would've sold out piece-by-piece and fed the destitute, like Florence's boss Sister Aimee was doing in these dark times.

He turned and met Hearst's eyes. A tiny blue droplet gleamed in the corner of one.

Tom stood, and called out for his sister.

She and Miss Davies came together, side-by-side down the hall. As they entered the room, Tom thought no matter how many treasures Hearst collected or mansions he built, none would match the beauty of his mistress. Even up close, she was almost as lovely as Florence.

Tom gave his sister a meager smile. "Nothing suspicious out front?"

"Nope."

"Babe, do you really believe in God?"

Miss Davies knitted her brow, folded her hands in front, and awaited the answer.

Florence said, "Sure."

"But why?" the lady asked. "How do you know God's real?"

"Oh, I don't," Florence said. "I don't know anything. I just believe, is all."

"I get it," Miss Davies said, while the men held their peace. Tom sent the women back to their post.

Until the shadows on the river and deck clued him that the sun had dipped below the forest, he studied the man whom many were convinced held President's Roosevelt's reins. Who could surely, if he so willed, turn his nation hard against the Nazis. Who might very well wield more power than anyone alive.

Tom entertained visions of Hearst on his knees, with the barrel of the pistol assigned to kill Donny Katoulis filling his small mouth, while tears big as eggs spilled over his cheeks and whimpers issued from him.

But for now, Hearst sat virtually still, free from nerve twitches or tremors. Maybe he had grown resolved to his fate. Or felt assured of an impending rescue. Or he made Tom for a coward ruled by fear or timid conscience, who lacked a martial will.

If the latter, the man was sorely mistaken.

That he could kill, in cold blood or battle, Tom knew with utter certainty. As in all ventures, the easy part was action. The tough part was deciding.

Chapter Eighty-five

Dusk rushed in, dimming the room and deleting the blue tint from Hearst's gray eyes. A raven came to perch on a deck rail. Its bold leer seemed to fix on the tycoon. And while Hearst and the bird appeared intent on staring each other down, Tom noticed a shudder of the man's slight shoulders.

The sight inspired Tom with a notion. He believed Hearst had just realized, maybe for the first time, that all his grandeur, wealth, and power meant nothing, that he was nothing, that everything he treasured and stood for could be gone in instant, that William Randolph Hearst was no more than a vapor.

As the raven flew off, Tom reached his verdict.

The only way to make decisions, he had learned over the years, was to gather evidence and speculations, to reason as well as you were capable. And when an answer comes out of the air like a quarterback's pass, grab and run with it.

He shouted "Sis, I need you."

When the women entered, he thought they both looked strangely pale and unhinged, like angels gone mad.

"Miss Davies." Tom pointed with his free hand to the love seat. She jumped in that direction as if he had turned the gun on her. Once she was seated, he motioned for Hearst to join her. The tycoon rose, stiffly as though climbing out of a coffin.

Florence came and stood by her brother. "Yes, Tommy?"

"I'll give the verdict," he said, "but it's not final unless you concur."

She patted his shoulder. "I'll concur."

Tom let the pistol hang at his side, while his gaze shifted back and forth from the tycoon to the lady.

"Guilty," he said, and raised the pistol.

Florence closed her eyes and then covered them with her hand.

"Only," Tom said, "I'm going to stay the execution. Let's say a year to the day. All the while, you'll be under surveillance, and using your power to take down the Nazis. Get it?" Hearst stared as if the concept had failed to register. But the lady nodded vigorously.

"Otherwise," Tom said, "you'd best send your killers to take care of me. Get it?" Tom snapped.

The tycoon gave the slightest nod and muttered, "Yes."

"Excuse me?" Tom jerked the pistol.

"Yes, sir."

Tom turned to his sister, who took his free arm, while he holstered the assassin's gun. "Lead the way, babe," he said.

Before they reached the hall, Florence stopped and turned to the lady. "You've got a maid in a closet and a caretaker tied up in the barn. Thanks for the lemonade."

Outside, as they passed the statue Tom guessed was Diana the Huntress, he asked, "Does he believe me?"

"Well, I don't think a fellow could get so big without reading people. Tommy, you know, we're okay, you and me. I mean, we're no saints, but we're not devils either."

"Still …" Tom gave her a look she remembered from her wild days, the one that told her he meant every word he said.

"Sure, I know," she said. "You might have to come back and kill him. And if the day comes, promise you'll take me along, will you?"

Chapter Eighty-six

They went out back to the deck, down the steps, and along the riverbank, retraced their path past the barn, through the woods, under the river gorge end of the iron bar fence. They cut diagonally across the meadow to Riverside Drive, listening and peering all around.

Florence led the way up the road and around a stand of thick juniper behind which she had stashed the Plymouth.

She gasped, "My God, this is where I left it. Honest." She bent and grabbed her knees, caught her breath then straightened up and twirled around, searching the woods. "Am I going crazy?"

"Maybe the little man got loose and found it."

"How'd he get loose?"

"Somebody found him."

"Whoever hired him, maybe?"

"Could be."

"If they took the Packard," Florence said, "we're in a jam."

Since dusk was giving way to dark, Tom decided cutting through the forest would be treacherous. They backtracked to the road, crossed it and stayed close to the nearest trees. They walked full stride for at least a mile, then found the trail Florence had marked by placing a stone on a yellow sock fairly hidden by some leaves.

They jogged up the trail and into the meadow. By now, dark was complete. The moon and most all the stars were hidden behind the surrounding colossal trees. Tom's flashlight was in the Packard glove compartment, but they didn't see the Packard. And only after an ardent search did they find another car.

The fisherman's Model A was parked about where they had left the Packard.

They crossed the meadow to the gorge, and peered upriver and down for the fisherman. After some minutes, they gave up and returned to the jalopy. Tom opened the driver's side door in hopes he would find the fisherman inside napping. He found nobody. But on the driver's seat lay a car key, and a note on the back of a handbill. The note, in cursive large enough for Florence to decipher in the dark, read, "I am a PI. DA hired me. Sincerely, K.P."

"The fisherman sprung the little man," Tom said.

"The fisherman works for the DA too?"

"More likely fishing was lousy down there, so he tried upriver and happened upon our captive."

"And as a reward for cutting him loose and helping him find his Plymouth, the little man gave him the Packard."

"I wonder how they found the Plymouth."

Florence said, "He's a private dick, like me. We're a mighty resourceful bunch."

Tom sat on the Model A running board and pounded it with his fist. His sister sat beside him and chuckled. "Imagine, we go to the cops and say that while we were holding hostages and threatening to murder them this fellow swiped our stolen car, and *we want* justice."

Tom wasn't ready for mirth. But he quit pounding. Then Florence hopped up. "Come on, Tommy. We stick around here, they'll soon have us surrounded."

"Who's they?"

"Beats me. But they're somebody, aren't they?"

"Must be."

While Tom worked the crank, which required a half dozen mighty tugs, Florence searched the interior and found no evidence about the owner of the Ford except a Bible with a tract marking a page in the book of Acts.

As Tom pulled the jalopy onto the road, she squinted to read in the meager starlight. "How about this, Tommy? The guy's reading a Foursquare giveaway Sister Aimee wrote. Wait till he gets nabbed and finds out the Packard belongs to Sister. God, he just might run out and hang himself, like Judas. God, I hope he doesn't. I mean, if the police call Sister, she might just say, 'Oh, officer, I gave that old car to the dear man.' She loves to get money, but even more she loves to give it away."

At the crossroads, Tom decided to follow the pavement. According to a sign, it would lead them to Redding. Though the road was narrow, it was easier to drive than the wagon trail they had followed out of McCloud. But easier driving proved to be hardly any blessing, as it allowed Tom to dwell upon the task that remained. The fate of Bud Gallagher.

Every thought of Bud shot more poison into his belly and brain. Bud was Charlie's best friend. The guy who, more than anyone except Leo, had ushered Tom through the years when he was only a boy yet the guardian of a wild kid sister.

To distract from the misery such thoughts inspired, Tom said, "So tell me, Sis, what exactly made you fall for Sister Aimee? I mean, knowing what you do about her swindling the public with the kidnapping affair and all?"

"Why," she said, "I never fell for Sister. We just like each other plenty. Besides, she's no more crooked than I am, Tommy. And around her and the Temple I usually feel pretty close to God. See, God is who I fell for. Not Sister."

She leaned out the window, looked up toward a patch of whirling stars, then returned to sitting straight and facing him, wearing the look of a girl about to weep. "Tommy, you want to know why I fell for God?"

"Sure."

"It's all your fault."

"Huh?" He pulled to the side of the road, shifted into neutral and faced her. "How so?"

"See," Florence said, blinking away the pools of light in the corners of her eyes, "when you really know love, when you find yourself being truly loved, you can't help thanking God."

A tiny sob issued out of her. Then she scooted closer. Tom sat speechless, wondering if his heart might explode.

Florence rode with her head on her brother's shoulder. As distant headlights approached, she said, "The thing is, when you truly thank God, you sort of feel him smile. Then you fall for him. That's all."

Only minutes after Tom pulled back onto the road, he said, "Damn, is this a mirage coming at us, or an L.A. police cruiser?"

Chapter Eighty-seven

"Damn," Tom repeated. "It sure is. One of those armor-plated Chryslers."

He tapped the brakes and pulled to the shoulder. If the narrowest trail that might've led to a cabin had appeared, he would've taken it. But the road was solidly fenced by tall pine. "Duck," he said. "That blond mop of yours might as well be a flare."

He pulled his hat low and hoped the Plymouth would blaze by with a toot of the horn to thank him for giving it right of way. But as it neared, the cruiser slowed and its spotlight blinded Tom so that he couldn't be sure the backseat passenger on the driver's side was Larry Loftus.

Still he let off the brake, yanked the throttle, and cursed the fellow who had left this tinker toy in trade for the twelve-cylinder Packard. When the siren blared and echoed, and Florence yelped, "Faster, Tommy. Here they come," Tom pulled the Browning from under his coat and passed it to his sister.

"I'll shoot the tires." She leaned toward the window.

"No you don't." He grabbed her arm and tugged her closer to him. "You just hold onto the monster. Let me think."

"Think fast," she said.

Tom felt like an ogre. He should've left her in the care of Miss Davies, whom Tom believed had too much of a heart to allow her man to bring charges against anybody except the ringleader, whom he would no doubt be delighted to see gunned down.

Maybe Tom had needed his sister, and she needed for her own sake to help him pursue their father's killer. But Larry Loftus and Two Gun Davis were no business of hers. He said, "When I slow and pull to the right, you open the door. Wait till I say go, then dive and roll and get lost in the forest."

"The hell I will."

"Babe—"

"Stop it, Tommy. Mind your driving. I've got a mansion waiting for me, remember."

"Huh?"

"In Heaven."

"Yeah, well I don't, so I'm not letting you go there. Not yet, anyway."

Tom knew that short of lunging for the passenger door and pushing her out, he was stuck with her. By now the Chrysler had roared up behind them, so close he could probably have braked, gotten rear-ended, and possibly escaped while the cops recovered from the collision. But he noticed the spacing of second growth timber on the left, and made a rash call. "Hold on," he shouted, and jerked the wheels.

The Model A squirted between two sugar pines, losing only fenders, mirrors, and running boards. Then it cut right and, tires spewing up bark and mulch, cut right once more, then wobbled and righted itself on the pavement, pointed toward Redding.

The Chrysler didn't fare as well. As Tom and Florence chugged away, she hollered, "They got stuck between those two trees. Thank God."

"Don't I get any credit?" Tom asked.

"Maybe a little." She hopped upward. With her knees on the seat, she planted an earnest kiss atop her brother's head. "Tommy," she said, "Is this a balding spot?"

"Mind your manners," he said.

After a mile or so, during which Tom grew ever more convinced they wouldn't encounter a soul until the outskirts of Redding, they rounded a bend and spotted lights, which issued from an establishment that proved to be a cross between a market and a roadhouse.

The building was near the center of a meadow. With the ground summer dry, the entire clearing could have served as a parking lot. Two Fords and a battered Dodge pickup sat in front. Tom pulled around back and sidled up close to the building.

When he heard his sister's strategy, he agreed, as he'd thought the same. He would hide at the edge of the forest while Florence entered the establishment and purchased or otherwise cajoled a lift into Redding. If she didn't return in five minutes, Tom would follow her in.

She rounded the building. He heard the door shut as she entered. And in no time, a minute or two, she returned, chaperoned by three men. The youngest of them, who owned and had volunteered one of the Fords, looked about seventy-five. He breathed in whistles through a bulbous nose. His name was Fletcher.

On the road, he talked like someone starved for companions. He gave them a wealth of news about local government, from an insider's view, as he had served on some commission the purpose of which neither Tom nor Florence quite grasped. They were busy attending to every light that blinked behind them and to the forest hoots and screeches that sounded too much like laughter.

Then, Fletcher fell silent.

Maybe, Tom thought, the old man heard some danger. Or he'd observed and caught the meaning of their watchfulness. Or he noticed the lump Tom's shoulder holster made. Or he glimpsed the Browning or the Luger in Florence's purse when she opened it to offer the men caramels she'd picked up at Wyntoon.

"Say," Fletcher said, as he reached toward the floorboard, "you two ain't Bonnie and Clyde, are you?"

Chapter Eighty-eight

Florence grabbed the old man's elbow. When she saw he was only scratching, she patted him on the knee. "Bonnie and Clyde got shot down a year or so back."

"Sure they did," Fletcher said. "I read the news, don't I? Don't believe a tenth of it, though."

A half hour later, he dropped them at the first motor court in Redding. They entered the office and watched out the window until his car vanished up the road.

Then Tom begged pardon of the sleepy blonde desk clerk and led his sister outside. They followed the road to the Sacramento River and turned south along a riverside path. Soon they came to a pleasant cluster of cottages called the Turtle Bay Inn, whose signage boasted of a telephone in every room.

Tom's most fervent wish was to hear the sweet voice of Elizabeth, and Madeline's voice, unless it came tainted by anger. But the intrusion of common sense convinced him to give the operator Leo's number.

Violet Weiss answered. "Tom, we've been sitting by the phone. Are you safe?"

Before he could answer, Leo must have snatched the phone away. "Did you meet up with Loftus?"

"Briefly," Tom said, "if he was riding in the backseat of a cruiser. What do you hear?"

"About an hour ago, Loftus was calling the dispatcher begging for a tow truck. Florence is okay?"

"Sure. You know Florence. A fellow who gave us a lift made her for Bonnie Parker."

Leo sighed with relief then made a sipping noise. "You want to come home?"

"That's a harebrained question."

"What kind of shape is Hearst in?"

Tom used some moments to ponder. "Older and wiser, I hope."

"That case," Leo made another sipping noise, "first thing tomorrow, call in your resignation. From there on, leave it to Kent Parrot."

"What about the cops, Loftus and the others? They come on duty, or on their own?"

"Not a one of them could wipe his…" He must have gotten an elbow or punch from Violet. "…behind on his own. Sure, Loftus volunteered, but the chief sent them. You bump off Hearst, Davis is in the clear, like so: your homicide is way out of his jurisdiction, and anyway he's done his part, sending the three stooges. If you take them down, the city loses nothing and saves a couple pensions. Now, when can we expect you?"

"I'll let you know soon as check the train schedule."

"Train? You're driving a stolen Packard."

While Tom gave him the thieving, tract-reading fisherman and car chase story, Florence couldn't help but titter now and then. Threatening to murder the ruler of the world, spending hours with a movie legend, and escaping from the police had left her slightly giddy.

Chapter Eighty-nine

Between calls, the operator informed Tom and the desk clerk that $9.57 would be charged to his bill. He checked his billfold, and asked Florence to dig into her purse and decide if they needed to rob the savings and loan.

Then he called Madeline, first at the Atwater. The hotel operator asked for a minute then returned and read him a note that directed any callers to a number he knew quite well.

When she picked up, she didn't even say hello, but demanded, "Tell me it's all over."

She meant the whole Charlie Hickey story. He looked at Florence, who either had heard the question or just understood. She gave him a nod of triumph. He reached for his sister's hand and, though he felt lousy for speaking a half-truth, he said to his wife, "Yeah, babe, that it is."

Now was not the time to mention Terence Poole and Bud Gallagher.

Leo had reached her first and let her know that he and Violet would arrive at the Hobart Place cottage in minutes to fetch and take her and Elizabeth on an all-night drive.

When Madeline gave the phone to Elizabeth, the girl said, "Daddy," at least a dozen times, in a squeal that faded into a whimper.

All Tom could manage, with his swollen heart and throat blocked by joy, was, "Hurry, baby, please hurry."

Tom allowed a few minutes to step outside, fill his pipe and smoke most of a bowl. Then he returned to the phone. "One more call," he promised Florence.

"Bud?"

He shook his head. "Bud can wait."

An L.A. operator gave him a number for Leslie White, and connected him person to person.

White didn't bother with hello, only "Been wondering when I'd be hearing from Tom Hickey."

"About a little man wears brown, drives a Plymouth coupe?"

"Kenneth Pringle. Works for the DA now and then."

"And I'm guessing you've still got your nose in the DA's office."

"Not my nose. An ear."

"Let's not quibble, Les. I'm sleepy."

"Kill anybody?"

"Not yet."

"Good thing. I was betting on you to keep your head. Did you give the old reprobate the scare of his life?"

"Did my best," Tom said. "Now tell me how we got away with it."

"Connections, Tom. The system, like always. You got on Davis' bad side again, about a month ago. Search me why this time."

"I make a habit of it, just for laughs."

"Ah. So Davis rings up my former boss, says get me some lowdown on Tom Hickey, will you? The boss turns it over to a chum of mine, a current DA investigator, who then gives me a jingle. I tell him I know the right op to put on the detail. A straightshooter, out from the Texas panhandle.

"I tell him the boy works cheap, and I'll not only vouch for him, I'll keep in touch, both ways, save him the trouble. Kenny phones in about once a day. Say, who were the tough guys caught you off guard in Tucson?"

"You wouldn't believe me."

"Try me."

"Keep talking," Tom said.

"Right. Last night, Kenny calls, tells me you're in McCloud. I get the picture, and forward the report, only I get it skewed a bit. The way I tell it, Kenny followed you and Flo into a diner in Mount Shasta City. The Black Bear. Fine grub, whopping portions. You need to try the place one of these days.

"The way I tell it, Kenny overhears you talking about all the fun you two mean to have in Portland before you ship out on a freighter bound for Russia, where all good Wobblies end up, if they live long enough.

"Davis' boys go blazing past the McCloud turnoff. They're up in Oregon, way past Medford when they get word truth is you're in McCloud. Who it was ratted on you being in McCloud, beats me."

"Robbie."

"Any Robbie I know?"

"You'd like him. Thanks, Les. I owe you. Florence too."

"Forget it. All I did was get the story wrong. Say, while I've got you on the line, warn your sis, the wife kicks me out, my first stop is her place."

Chapter Ninety

The next evening, after an all-day drive and a short nap, Tom joined his sister on the concrete patio behind the Hobart Place cottage. He occupied the Adirondack chair next to hers.

Florence closed the Gideon Bible she'd been reading by the overhead bulb and laid it on her lap. "Tommy, when they catch the bum that made off with Sister's Packard, let's all go back up north and fetch the car ourselves. We could take a whole day to swim in one of those pretty rivers. I wish we had a river in L.A."

"We do."

"I mean one that still has water in it."

"Yeah," Tom said absently. He was trying to decide whether to call Bud Gallagher now or tomorrow. He wondered whether anything he could do would add or subtract to the misery Bud must have suffered over the past thirty years. For all Tom knew, the disease that had turned the big man to a skeleton was nothing more than guilt. Still, Tom wasn't likely to pardon the guy whose crime and lying heart cost him and Florence their father.

Mind-reading, Florence asked in a gloomy way, "What about Bud?"

"We could send him Benny Katoulis' gun."

"Do you think he'd get the message?"

"Sure he would."

She bent and wrapped her arms around her knees. "And he'd do it, wouldn't he? Kill himself?"

"Yep."

Her eyes closed and remained closed so long, Tom began to wonder if she meant to sleep on the question. But she sat up and said, "Let's don't kill Bud."

"Do you know why they have jury trials?" Tom asked.

"To give the guy a fair shake," she speculated, "and to guard against crooked judges taking bribes."

"Right you are," Tom said, "but also, mostly, I suspect, so no one of us has to pass the judgment and carry that weight around all alone. I mean, cops have got it easy. All we do is deliver the suspects. If I can go the rest of my life without passing judgment on anybody, I'll be damned glad."

From the way Florence glanced at the Bible on her lap, Tom knew she could point him to corroborating wisdom.

But she had the sense to let it rest.

Chapter Ninety-one

Leo drove Tom to fetch his car in the lot beside Ralph Clifton's meat market. On the way, while Tom gave his version of Terence Poole's death and Charlie Hickey's flight from the law, Leo groaned frequently, in self-reproach or shame.

Florence and Elizabeth rode the streetcar to Echo Park while Tom drove his wife to San Pedro. She caught the *Pilgrim* to Catalina, which would give her time to doll herself up before her singing date.

From San Pedro, Tom drove north to Santa Monica and east on rush-hour Wilshire Boulevard, turned right on Citrus Avenue and parked at the curb in front of Bud Gallagher's bungalow. Then he packed and lit his pipe and sat in the car until the bowl burned empty.

What Tom felt toward his and Charlie's old pal wasn't quite anger, or disgust, or disillusion, but all of those and something more. The deepest feeling was loss. Now that he knew his father was dead, and why, and that Leo had lied to him for years, and that Bud was a murderer, it seemed as if a portion of his heart had gone sour. As if he'd been called to quarterback a big game in which he had no desire to play.

He was still in the car when Bud came hobbling up the sidewalk and turned on the gravel path to his front door.

Tom climbed out of his Chevy and called, "Hey."

Bud stopped cold but didn't turn around. The bag he was carrying dropped to the gravel. Several books spilled out. He left them and proceeded to the front door, which he unlocked and shoved open. He entered and held the door for Tom.

As Tom passed him, Bud said, "You're going to arrest me, let me get a bracer first."

"Sit down," Tom said.

"Sure." Bud went to the closest chair, a rocker beneath a still life with marigolds, which Tom knew Bud's late wife had painted.

For a moment, Tom admired the painting and wondered if Bud loved his wife more before or after he killed on her account.

"I'm no cop," Tom said. "Not since a couple hours ago."

"Fired."

"As good as."

"Just as well," Bud said. "You're not cut out to take orders. How about a bracer?"

Tom shook his head and leaned against the wall across the small room from Bud and the marigolds. "You ever have dreams about Terence Poole?"

"Sure do. But the thing is, Tom, I didn't kill him."

Tom felt his eyes flame, while his hands fisted and he strode toward the old man.

"Whoa," Bud said and held up a withering hand, as if it could shield him. "Charlie didn't kill him. See, I could tell you who did, but I'm not about to."

Tom stopped, stood staring, then backed until again he leaned against the wall. "So, you're going to tell me Charlie lit out, left me and Florence behind with mad Milly, to save the neck of some other guy who's a murderer?"

"Here's what I'm going to tell you. Some men are strong, like Charlie. And you. And Florence. Then, some of us aren't so strong. And the strong ones, if their hearts are full of good—like yours, and Florence's, and Charlie's—-are always going to take care of the weak ones."

"What the hell are you talking about?"

"It's all you're going to get out of me. If you're smart, you'll figure it out. If not, you won't. One way or the other, I'm done." Bud creaked to his feet and hobbled toward the kitchen.

Chapter Ninety-two

Close to midnight, hours after Elizabeth fell asleep on Florence's sofa, Tom and his sister sat on the wicker chairs with cups of tea. They had finished most of a pot while reviewing Bud's words and puzzling aloud over the message he'd challenged Tom to discover.

Florence had urged her brother to recollect every butcher, salesman, and janitor from his own years at Alamo Meat, since the knife that killed Terence Poole had come from that place. Tom had long since exhausted his memories when Florence said, "Tommy, did Bud have a son, or not?"

"No. Why?"

"Well, back when you were trying to tame me, you came home all sad and wanted to talk it out. And you told me you went to Bud for advice, because some butcher had said Bud had a son, name of Frankie, who worked cutting meat for a spell and that he was a wild one, dropped out of school way too soon. So you asked Bud had he learned any wisdom that could help you with me, and Bud told you he didn't have any son. And you said he gave you a hurt look, like maybe not having kids was a subject that pained him."

"It's coming back," Tom said. "So?"

"Could be Frankie Gallagher killed Terence Poole."

Florence came and knelt in front of her brother. She gripped both his hands and held them firmly. "And he ran off, like Charlie did."

Tom loosed his right hand, leaned to the edge of his chair, reached to the sofa where Elizabeth lay, and petted her silky hair.

Chapter Ninety-three

Nearly two hours passed while Florence used her key to enter the Bible school young ladies' quarters and convince a plain, earnest and precociously innocent student named Lucy to sneak out, come to Florence's place and babysit Elizabeth.

By the time his sister knocked on Bud Gallagher's door, Tom's fury had gotten so roused, he would've rather kicked the door down.

But lights were burning and right away they heard footsteps on the hardwood floor. The door creaked open, with Bud holding on. "Good work, Tom," he said, then turned and reeled from the door to a wall and from there to another wall. When he pushed off that one, he staggered and collapsed on the sofa.

Tom said, "Your Frankie killed Terence Poole."

Bud stared with bloodshot eyes, and a face otherwise blank and pale. "Sure he did. Frankie got wise that Poole was having his way with Frankie's Melinda and painting the town with her to boot. A couple weeks passed, then Frankie went and stabbed Poole to death. And then he panicked and snatched up the gun Poole waved at him, the one that might've got him a self-defense charge if Poole weren't the son of a big shot.

"Then Frankie ran off, and took Melinda along. She blamed Poole for the whole affair and Frankie bought her story. A knockout like Melinda could wrap a guy around her finger." Bud glanced at Florence, then closed his eyes and wagged his head.

"They landed in Boise, out in Idaho, and they had a couple kids before the floozy ran off and took the kids with her. After that, Frankie gave up, took to liquor, which doesn't help a whole lot, as I can vouch." He reached for a tumbler on the sofa's end table and found it empty.

"Last year, Frankie plugged himself, right through the eye socket. With Terence Poole's gun."

Tom choked down a shout, glanced at Florence and willed his voice to come softly. "Why didn't you come clean, Bud?"

The old man gazed at Tom as if he'd been asked the most ignorant question imaginable. "You just don't rat on your own flesh and blood, Tom."

"Even after he's dead?"

"Even then. Besides, I figured if anybody could dig out the truth, it'd be you."

Tom's fist had knotted so hard, the nails dug into his palms. Every part of his mind and every instinct wanted to scream his outrage and beat the old man into pulp and splinters, for two dozen years of secrets and lies, and for Charlie's sake.

Florence looked as savage as her brother. She had hold of her wavy hair. Her lips had curled into a demon's snarl. She was bent and leaning forward as though any second she would plunge and perform everything Tom ached to do.

When she took the three steps to Bud's sofa, Tom felt certain she would break the man's face into shards.

But Florence, as usual, amazed him. She bent and planted a lingering kiss on Bud Gallagher's brow, in the middle just above his eyes.

When she turned, all the anger had fled. "C'mon," she said. "We've got lives to live. Good ones, Tommy."

To receive a free catalog of Poisoned Pen Press titles, please contact us in one of the following ways:

Phone: 1-800-421-3976
Facsimile: 1-480-949-1707
Email: info@poisonedpenpress.com
Website: www.poisonedpenpress.com

Poisoned Pen Press
6962 E. First Ave. Ste 103
Scottsdale, AZ 85251